Praise for
Forever an Ex

"Murray spices up her story line with plenty of juicy scandals . . .
Readers seeking an inspirational tale with broad themes of trust,
betrayal, and forgiveness will do well by choosing Murray's latest
effort."

—*Library Journal*

Praise for
Fortune & Fame

"The scandalous characters unite again in *Fortune & Fame*, Murray
and Billingsley's third and best collaboration. This time brazen
Jasmine and Rachel, who has zero shame, have been cast on *First
Ladies*, a reality TV show that builds one's brand and threatens to
break another's marriage. Sorry, buttered popcorn is not included."

—*Essence*

"Priceless trash talk marks this story about betrayal, greed, and stepping on anyone in your way. A great choice for folks who spend
Sunday mornings in the front pew."

—*Library Journal*

Praise for
Never Say Never

"Readers, be on the lookout for Victoria Christopher Murray's
Never Say Never. You'll definitely need to have a buddy-reader in
place for the lengthy discussion that is bound to occur."

—*USA Today*

Stand Your Ground

VICTORIA CHRISTOPHER MURRAY

TOUCHSTONE

New York London Toronto Sydney New Delhi

Touchstone
An Imprint of Simon & Schuster, Inc.
1230 Avenue of the Americas
New York, NY 10020

First Touchstone trade paperback edition June 2015

TOUCHSTONE and colophon are registered trademarks of Simon & Schuster, Inc.

For information about special discounts for bulk purchases, please contact Simon & Schuster Special Sales at 1-866-506-1949 or business@simonandschuster.com.

The Simon & Schuster Speakers Bureau can bring authors to your live event. For more information or to book an event contact the Simon & Schuster Speakers Bureau at 1-866-248-3049 or visit our website at www.simonspeakers.com.

Interior design by Akasha Archer

Manufactured in the United States of America

10 9 8 7 6 5 4 3 2 1

Library of Congress Cataloging-in-Publication Data
Murray, Victoria Christopher.
 Stand your ground / by Victoria Christopher Murray.—First Touchstone trade paperback edition.
   pages ; cm
 1. Trials (Murder)—Fiction. I. Title.
PS3563.U795S73 2015
813'.54—dc23
                    2015003165

ISBN 978-1-4767-9299-6
ISBN 978-1-4767-9300-9 (ebook)

Why I Wrote
Stand Your Ground

Not again were words that kept reverberating through my mind on February 15, 2014. We were just about six months from George Zimmerman's acquittal of Trayvon Martin's murder, and as I watched the verdict come down in the first trial of Michael Dunn (the man who murdered Jordan Davis) I felt like this country was taking giant leaps backward.

It had happened again. While Michael Dunn had been found guilty of attempted murder, the jury couldn't reach a verdict on the murder charge for Jordan Davis's death.

Of course my social media timelines blew up. People were upset and rightfully so . . . though, I didn't understand the specific reactions. People were attacking the men and women of the jury, and then there were those who were once again calling for America to boycott one of its own states. "Nobody go to Florida!" became the social media mantra.

That confused me—I didn't understand how people could get upset with Americans who had not only stepped up to fulfill their jury duty, but who were following the law. And it was even more confusing that people wanted to boycott Florida when two dozen other states had some version of the same law. So, what . . . were people going to boycott every state? Were they going to boycott the states where they lived?

I couldn't make sense out of what I thought was nonsense. I couldn't understand why people were attacking juries and attacking states, and not going after the real culprit. Why not make this a political rallying cry? Why not register thousands of people to vote? Why not go after the law?

Yes, people are behind the law, but not the people who would suffer under a boycott. And not the people who fulfilled their civic duty by serving on the jury.

It was that night and those reactions that started the seed of this novel growing inside of me. I so wanted to get people to understand that the law was the problem. I wanted people to understand the law better, I wanted people to know that Stand Your Ground is not a defense in itself, it is part of self-defense. And though I had never been through anything like this myself, I wanted people to really think about the families in these situations. Maybe all of that would get us to finally stand *our* ground . . . stand up and do something. Do something that would matter, do something that would count.

And while this idea began to brew inside of me, one of my friends on Facebook said, "Victoria, you should write a book about this." Others agreed, saying they believed that I could teach something. That was when I knew that I did have a platform to reach thousands of people about this—I could do it through entertainment; I could do it through a book.

It was my editor who challenged me to add layers to this story and to show both sides of this tragedy. It was my publisher who gave me the title.

And so it was on and I was ready.

But then I wasn't as ready as I thought. When I sat down and thought about these women in *Stand Your Ground*—the mother of the victim and the wife of the shooter—it became such a difficult book to write. Of course, the emotions that I had to write for the mother were clear and obvious. What I didn't expect was to feel for the wife of the shooter. These were two women who were suffering—in different ways, but still, both suffered. And as I lived with both of them in my head for all of those months, I suffered with them.

Another thing that surprised me a bit about writing this book was the language. I believe in always being true to my characters, but to this point, profanity hasn't had any place in my novels. It's not as though there is much in *Stand Your Ground*, but I'm sure you can imagine that the N word—a word I abhor—comes up a time or two.

But if I wanted to write the truth—which I always try to do—if I wanted to speak to the two opposing sides of Stand Your Ground, I had to speak their language, especially the language they would use in this particular situation.

So, I went with my characters. And I took this journey. Never before could I say that a book I've written has changed me. But writing this one did. It wasn't writing this book alone that changed me—it was that I was halfway through when Eric Garner was choked to death in New York and then Michael Brown was executed in the streets of Ferguson. I wrote this novel while those incidents and their aftermath played as background music in my mind.

And I changed.

I wrote and I changed. I wrote and I became an Angry Black Woman.

My prayer, though, is that I will channel that anger in the right way. I was able to work some of that anger out in the pages of this book. Now, I hope that I'll be able to work that anger out in a way that will help to change America—for the better.

And that begins with repealing Stand Your Ground.

We must know the facts. We must never forget . . .

PART ONE

Janice Johnson

I WISH . . .
I COULD
HAVE BEEN THERE . . .
TO SAVE HIM

MAY 12, 2014

Chapter 1

There is nothing like being in love with a naked man.

Now, I'm not saying that I didn't love my husband when he was fully clothed. But right now, right here, all I could do was perch myself up on my elbow and enjoy as my husband strutted around our bedroom as if he were looking for something. He wasn't looking for a doggone thing; Tyrone was just giving me a show.

And what a show it was, 'cause there is nothing like a naked, carved, then chiseled to perfection, chocolate man.

I sighed and my heart swelled with even more love than I ever thought possible. I didn't know it could be like this. Didn't know it could be like this after sixteen years of marriage. Didn't know it could be like this after the betrayal of infidelity.

"What are you staring at?" Tyrone's voice broke through my thoughts. He flexed his pecs and inside, I moaned. "What? What are you looking at?" he asked again.

Really? He was standing there, full frontal, and he was asking me what I was looking at? Did he want me to describe the human statue of excellence that he was to me?

I answered my husband. "Nothing. I'm not looking at anything."

He busted out laughing, then leaned over and kissed my forehead.

I tugged at his arm, trying to pull him down on top of me so that I could do more nasty things to him. If our life were a book, it would've been titled *Love and Sex*. It had started with the marriage counselor that my best friend, Syreeta, had referred us to after "the cheating incident."

"Stay in the bed," the counselor had advised. "You have to connect again with one another sexually. Once you get the trust back in bed, because that's where it was broken, you'll be able to get the trust back in every other aspect of your life."

That had just sounded like some man talking at the time. And trust me, it had been hard on both of us. But after a couple of months, we needed therapy to get us *out* of bed. It was like we couldn't stop. And the counselor had been right. We connected again, in bed first, and everything else followed.

But even though my husband was always down for second and third sexual helpings, this time he pulled back and I frowned.

"Don't worry," he said. "I'll be right back." Turning away, he grabbed his bathrobe from the chaise. "I'm going to check on Marquis. Make sure his homework is done and he's getting ready to turn in."

I bounced back in the bed and sighed. "Tyrone . . ."

"Don't start, Janice."

"It's barely nine o'clock and you're sending him to bed? He's seventeen! Come on, now. When are you going to let up on him?"

The expression of pure pleasure that had been on my husband's face just a minute before faded fast. "Let up on him?" Tyrone grumbled. "We're raising a black boy in a white world. I will never let up. I will never go easy. We've got just one chance to get this right."

"I get that," I said, having heard this lecture so many times. But if he was going to give me his speech, then he was going to once again listen to mine.

"It's been a month since he was suspended. And he's done everything that we've asked him to do. All he does is go to school and then come home. He's back on track."

"See, that's my point right there," Tyrone said, jabbing his finger in the air. "He's *back* on track. He should never have been derailed in the first place and I want to make sure that he never gets derailed again."

"But what else do you want from him? We've got to let him know that there is redemption after repentance. We've got to teach him that he can do something wrong, but then he can make up for it by doing something right."

"He's a black boy. In this country, he won't get a makeup opportunity. In this country, he won't be given a second chance, and our son has to learn that lesson now."

"That may be how it is in this country," I said. "But we've got to let him know that it's not like that in this house. At home, he has to know that we trust him again."

Tyrone shook his head.

"It was one joint, Tyrone," I said for what had to be the millionth time since our son had received that three-day school suspension a month ago. "Don't make it out to be any bigger than that." When Tyrone opened his mouth to lecture me more, I added, "Don't forget you smoked when you were in high school."

"Yeah, but now that I know better, I've done better. And I wasn't at Winchester Academy when I smoked. I wasn't at some highfalutin school where the people there were expecting and waiting for me to fail."

I sighed as Tyrone went on and on about how our son's mistake was much worse since he was at Winchester—one of the top college-prep academies in the country. It had been my idea to send Marquis there since I recognized his brilliance from when he was in my womb. Seriously, though, our son was smart and I wanted my only child to have the best opportunities, to give him a future that I could've never imagined for myself when I was growing up motherless, fatherless, oftentimes feeling homeless as I was shuffled from one foster home to the next.

"You know I'm right, Janice." Tyrone broke through my thoughts. "Those white folks don't want him there, and he goes around acting a fool."

"He was acting like a seventeen-year-old . . ." I held up my hand before Tyrone could pounce on my words. "And yes, he was wrong," I continued. "But he's learned his lesson and all I want you to see is that Marquis is a good kid. A really good kid who's going to do great things in life."

"I know he has that potential. But if he's going to be great, he has to understand that he can't get caught up. He has to do everything right."

"Everything right? Really?" It took all that was inside of me not to shake my head and roll my eyes at this man. Sometimes Tyrone spoke as if he were the only parent with dreams for our son, but I wanted the same, perhaps even more, for Marquis. While Tyrone focused on his academics, accepting nothing less than straight A's, I focused on the fullness of the life that I prayed Marquis would have. I wanted him to be well educated, but happy, with a wife and plenty of children who called me Grandma. I wanted to see him grow up doing the things he loved, playing the saxophone and piano, writing poetry, and participating in amateur golf tournaments.

But none of that extracurricular stuff mattered to Tyrone. He was a strict disciplinarian who walked a straight military line. I understood structure and parental control; it was just that sometimes, Tyrone was so strict, even I felt stifled.

"I *am* letting up a little bit," Tyrone said as if he heard my thoughts. "I let him go out tonight, didn't I?"

I couldn't help it; I laughed. "You let him go to the library!"

Tyrone grinned with me. "I let him go to the library . . . with Heather," he said, referring to our son's girlfriend.

While those words made Tyrone smile, the thought made me want to shout, and I wasn't talking about shouting hallelujah! This discussion was going fine—why did Tyrone even have to bring up Marquis's girlfriend? His *white* girlfriend. She was the only thing that made me regret busting my butt, working those extra shifts at the post office so that we could send Marquis to Winchester.

"I guess you don't have nothin' to say now, huh?" Tyrone chuckled.

My husband was torturing me and he knew it. He knew how I felt about Marquis bringing that girl home when there were all these beautiful black girls that he knew from growing up in church, and even a few at Winchester. Every day, I brought up a new name to him, but Marquis could not be moved. I have no idea where I went wrong, but sometime after Marquis became a teenager, he suddenly and only had eyes for girls who looked like Snow White.

It sickened me, though his son's preference for girls with blond hair and blue eyes didn't seem to bother Tyrone. I didn't get that. My husband was always talking about white people this and white people that and how he lived *in* this country, but he was not *of* this country. Well, why didn't he have an issue with his son dating a white girl?

"Okay, I won't tell him that he has to turn in," Tyrone said, saving me from myself. Because thoughts of Heather were getting me riled up. Now that Tyrone had mentioned Heather, I was beginning to think maybe we should keep Marquis on lockdown (and away from that white girl) until he left for college in the fall.

"Thank you," I said to Tyrone.

"But I'm still gonna talk to him. Make sure that his head is on straight since I did let him go out earlier. And I'm going to talk to him about the suspension . . ."

This time I did roll my eyes.

"Make sure he understands the seriousness of it."

"He does."

"Make sure he knows it could've messed with his scholarship to UPenn."

"He knows."

"Make sure he understands why he won't be valedictorian now, even though he earned it."

"He understands."

"Well, if you can guarantee that he knows all of that, then he's off lockdown." Tyrone shook his head. "You're a softy, you know." He kissed me again as he tied his robe. "Our son better thank you, 'cause if you weren't so cute . . ."

I laughed, but then stopped suddenly when the doorbell rang and a hard knock followed.

Tyrone and I frowned together. It was just a little after nine now, and I couldn't imagine who would be coming by our home. Marquis and his friends knew that they couldn't hang out on school nights, even when Marquis wasn't on lockdown.

No more than a couple of seconds passed before the visitor on the other side of our front door rang the bell again and then another knock.

"Who can that be?" I asked, pushing myself up from the bed.

Tyrone held up his hand. "You stay here. I'll get it."

But before my husband could make it to the top of the staircase, I had wrapped myself inside my robe and stepped into the hallway. Marquis's bedroom door was closed, which was the only reason why I was sure he hadn't bounced down the stairs to get to the door before his father.

By the time I made my way to the top of the stairs, Tyrone was at the bottom and opening the door.

"Mr. Johnson?"

The door was open wide enough for me to see the two policemen, one black, one white, standing shoulder to shoulder, looking like soldiers.

"Yes," my husband said, his voice two octaves deeper now, the way it always dropped when he stood in front of men wearing uniforms.

"May we come in?" the black one asked.

Those words made me descend the stairs even though I wasn't properly dressed for company. Not that two policemen showing up in the middle of the night could ever be called welcome visitors.

"What's this about?" My husband asked the question for both of us.

The policemen stepped inside, though Tyrone hadn't extended an invitation. Both men glanced up at me as I stood on the second stair, gripping the lapels of my bathrobe to make sure it didn't open and trying to come up with a single reason why two officers would be in our home.

"Ma'am." It seemed that the black officer had been assigned to do all the talking as the white one just nodded at me.

"What's this about?" Tyrone asked again.

They still stood shoulder to shoulder, at attention, as if this were a formal visitation. "Would you mind if we went in there?" The black officer twisted slightly, nodding toward our living room. "I'd like for us to sit down."

If the officer had been speaking to me, I would've said yes just because it seemed like the right thing to do.

But Tyrone said, "That's not necessary; just tell me what this is about," because that was right to him. My husband had been raised on the hard streets of Philly, where a policeman, no matter his color, was never an invited guest.

The officers exchanged glances before the black one said, "Marquis Johnson, is that your son?"

Tyrone's eyes narrowed while mine widened.

"What's this about?" It felt like that was the fiftieth time my husband asked that question, and now I needed to hear the answer, too.

"There's been a shooting . . ."

"Oh, my God," I gasped, and covered my mouth. "Did something happen to one of our son's friends?"

The officers looked at each other again before the black one continued, "No. It's your son, Marquis. He's been shot."

"What?" Tyrone and I said together.

"That's impossible," Tyrone continued. "Marquis is upstairs. He's in his room." And then he yelled out, "Marquis, come down here."

I didn't let even a second pass before I dashed up the stairs, taking them two at a time, moving like I hadn't in years. Not that I had any doubt. Of course Marquis was in his bedroom. He'd come home while Tyrone and I . . . had been spending some personal time together. I mean, he hadn't come into our bedroom, but he never did when we had the door closed.

Tonight, he'd been home by eight, nine at the latest. I was sure of that.

Since Marquis had become a teenager, I never entered his room without knocking. But tonight, I busted in. And then I stood there . . . in the dark. I stood there staring at the blackness, though there was enough light from the hallway for me to see that Marquis wasn't sitting at his desk, he wasn't lying on his bed, he wasn't here.

"Marquis," I called out anyway, then rushed back into the hall and headed to the bathroom. "Marquis!" Just like with his bedroom, I busted into the bathroom and stared at the empty space.

It was only then that I felt my heart pounding, though I'm sure the assault on my chest began the moment the policeman had told that lie that my son had been shot.

"Marquis," I called out as I jerked back the shower curtain that revealed an empty tub.

"Marquis," I shouted as I now searched our guest bedroom. No one, nothing there.

I returned to his bedroom, turned on his light, then swung open the door to his closet before I crouched down and searched under his bed. "Marquis," I screamed as I went into my bedroom, wondering why my son was playing this game of hide-and-seek, something we hadn't done since he was four. When he finally came out of hiding, he was going to have to deal with me!

I rushed back into the hallway and bumped right into Tyrone.

"He's not up here," I said to my husband as he grasped my arms. "He's downstairs somewhere. Did you check the kitchen?

Wait, I know," I continued, without letting my husband speak. "He's in the family room. I know you said he couldn't watch the TV in there, but you were about to take him off lockdown anyway and you know that Marquis—"

"Janice." Tyrone shook me a little.

I looked up into Tyrone's eyes, which were glassy with tears.

"What?" I frowned. "You don't believe those policemen, do you?"

He nodded at the same time that I shook my head.

"No, they're lying."

"They're not lying," Tyrone said softly. "They showed me a picture, just to make sure."

Now I whipped my head from side to side because I didn't want to hear anything else from Tyrone. I couldn't believe that he would accept the word of two men in blue. Wasn't he the one who always said that you couldn't trust the police?

Well, if he wasn't going to look for our son, I was. "Marquis!" I screamed.

Tyrone still nodded, and now a single tear dripped from his eye. "Janice, listen to me."

For a moment, I tried to remember the last time my husband had cried. And I couldn't think of a single time.

"Janice." He repeated my name.

"No!"

"Marquis is gone."

"No!"

"He was shot over on Avon Street."

"No!"

"He's dead."

"Why would you believe them?" I cried. "Why don't you believe me?"

My husband looked at me as if I was talking foolishness. And I looked at him and begged with every fiber of my being for him to tell me that he was wrong. Or for him to wake me from this night-mare. Either scenario would work for me.

But Tyrone did neither of those things. He just held me and stared into my eyes. And as I stared into his, I saw the truth.

Not many words that Tyrone had shared had made it to the understanding part of my brain. But four words did: Marquis. Gone. Shot. Dead.

"Marquis is gone?" I whispered.

Tyrone nodded.

"Someone shot my son?"

He nodded again.

"And now he's dead?"

This time, Tyrone didn't nod. He just pulled me close, so close that I could feel the hammering of his heart. But though there were few times when I didn't want to be held by my husband, I didn't want him to hold me now. I didn't want him to comfort me. Because if what Tyrone and these policemen were saying was true, then I didn't want to be in my husband's arms.

If everything they said about my son was the truth, then all I wanted was to be dead, too.

Chapter 2

*D*eath.

I couldn't get that word out of my head.

Death.

Even though I kept trying to.

Death.

I had to stop thinking about it because if I didn't, the whole world would have to end.

"Okay, Mr. and Mrs. Johnson," the officer said as he opened the door, "if you can have a seat in here, I'll be right back."

"Please, I need to know about my son," I said. They had already kept us waiting in the front of the police station. Had us sitting there like we were in the reception area of a doctor's office or something. And now they were herding us back to some room, just to leave us to wait some more?

But our waiting didn't seem to be any kind of concern to the officer. He looked at me with eyes that didn't seem happy about having to explain himself again. "I need to get the detective and we'll be back."

"But when will I see my son?" I asked right before he closed the door.

Turning around, I moved farther into the room and imagined this had to be how it felt to be confined in a prison cell. This room was that small . . . and that cold. A rectangular table consumed most of the space, which was lit only by a single bulb hanging loosely from the ceiling. There was a window, a small one, but no light came from the outside. There was only darkness.

Edging toward the table, I took in the glass on the opposite wall and I wondered if the police were behind that mirror, like on TV, watching me. Though I wasn't sure what they expected to see . . . I was just a mother about to die from grief.

I wanted to stand, but there was this blackened cloud that hung over me, making me weary. So I sat on the wooden chair that felt harder than it probably was. But I sat on the edge, ready to jump with joy when the police came back and told me this had all been a mistake.

It wasn't until Tyrone took my hand and squeezed it that I even remembered he was with me, and if I'd had the strength, I would've thanked him. He hadn't left my side since we'd heard this news—what? One, two, three hours ago? He'd done just about everything he could, except breathe for me since. From dressing me (to make sure that I didn't walk out of the house naked), to holding me steady on my wobbly legs, it was because of Tyrone that my heart was still beating. He didn't know it, but he'd kept me away from the medicine cabinet that housed all kinds of old prescriptions that I never threw away, but couldn't stop thinking about from the moment he'd convinced me that what the police had said about Marquis was true.

"What are the police doing?" I asked Tyrone. But I didn't let enough time pass for him to answer. "Why do they have us locked in here? And why won't they let me see Marquis?"

He held my hand tighter as if that gesture was part of the answer. "They want to talk to us first. Get some answers."

"What kind of answers can I give them? I'm the one with all the questions."

"I know," my husband said. "But let's be patient."

That was when I knew for sure that the world had turned on its axis. My husband was calling for patience? With the police? For the first time I realized that he was in shock, too.

Tyrone kept on: "They have to talk to us now because if they let us see Marquis first . . ."

He didn't have to finish. Talk first because after seeing Marquis, not only would I no longer be able to speak, I doubted if I'd even be able to breathe.

I moved to stand, but before I could get out of my seat, the door opened and in marched the white officer who'd come to our home and with him this time was a different black man. This one wasn't wearing a uniform.

It was the one I hadn't seen before who said, "Mr. and Mrs. Johnson, I'm Detective Ferguson; I'm really sorry for your loss."

"Thank you," Tyrone said, though I didn't say a word. For me, for my heart, it wasn't official yet that I'd lost anything.

"We just want to ask you a few questions."

"I understand," Tyrone said. "But the thing is, my wife and I have questions, too." My husband continued in a soft voice that I'd never heard come out of him before. "What happened to our son? All we know is that he was shot dead."

The men exchanged a glance before the one named Ferguson nodded to the other. The other officer said, "Yes, but I think if we get some questions answered, we'll be able to fill in a lot of the blanks. Just a few questions."

Tyrone nodded his cooperation; I didn't move a single muscle.

The officer asked, "Do you have any idea why your son was over on Avon in Haverford?"

Tyrone said, "He was probably heading home after dropping his girlfriend off. She lives somewhere over in that area . . . I think."

The officers looked at each other before the one who'd been doing all the speaking asked, "Girlfriend?"

Tyrone nodded. "Wait, was she with him? Is she all right?"

The officer asked, "What's her name?"

"Heather . . ." And then Tyrone stopped.

He liked Marquis's girlfriend so much, but he didn't even know her last name. I answered, "Nelson. Heather Nelson," because I didn't like her. So I knew everything about her.

"And Heather lives in that neighborhood?"

"Yes, but is she all right? Was she with Marquis?" my husband asked again.

"She's fine. She was with him. We only asked because we wanted to make sure that we were talking about the same young lady."

"Oh, my God," I pressed my hand against my chest. "She was with him when this happened? Then I need to talk to her."

"We've talked to her, ma'am, and that's why we needed to talk to you. Your son, is he a member of a gang?"

"What?"

"No!" Tyrone said at the same time. And then, the way my husband's shoulders rose up, I could see that the patience he'd told me to have wasn't a part of him anymore. "And why would you ask us that?" he asked, his voice once again strong, once again two octaves deeper. "You need to answer that question and a whole lot more for me. What happened to my son?"

They had mistaken my grieving-and-in-shock husband for a

passive black man. But the way he sat now, leaning forward with his palms flat on the table, and his eyes giving them a stare that could have sharpened stone, the policeman decided to answer.

"The reason we're questioning you is because we don't know exactly what happened and we're trying to put it all together."

"Well then, tell me the part that you do know," my husband said as if he was the one in charge now.

There was a brief moment of silence as the men glanced at me, then back at my husband. "It seems your son was in the car with his . . . girlfriend . . . and they were approached by someone," the one who'd been doing all the talking said.

"A gang member?" Tyrone asked, then before the police could answer, he added, "I don't care what that other boy told you, my son was not in a gang."

Another glance exchanged, and then, "Well, that's why we're asking you these questions."

"So do you have the shooter in custody? Do you have the boy who murdered my son?"

"We're still trying to gather the information," he said, his voice as steady as a weatherman's.

"So are you going to tell me the name of the punk who killed my boy?"

"We don't want to tell you something and then later find out we were wrong."

"Well, right now you're not telling me anything!" Tyrone's volume rose.

The officer kept his voice level as he said, "We're telling you what we know and we're trying to gather everything so that we can give you a full account."

"How are you gathering information from us when we weren't there?" I asked.

"You know things about your son—"

"Like whether or not he was in a gang?" Tyrone spat.

The officer nodded, as if he were now the one with patience. "We had to ask that."

"Because that's the first thing you think of when you see two black boys, right?" my husband said, his tone accusing them. "Well, I don't know about the other boy, but our son wasn't in a gang."

The officer glanced at the detective, but the white officer was the one who kept speaking. "We had to ask, just like we have to ask did your son carry a firearm."

Tyrone slammed his fists on the table, startling me and making both officers jump, though only the white one raised his arm as if he were reaching for his gun.

Just as quickly, I placed my hand on Tyrone's arm, feeling the bulge of his biceps. My husband was ready to punch these men out. But since I'd just lost one-half of the reason why my heart beat every day, I had to do everything that I could to keep the other half with me.

So I kept my hand on him, and just like I always did, I calmed him down by my touch alone.

"Mr. Johnson." Those were the first words Detective Ferguson spoke since his greeting, and he called my husband's name in a tone that sounded like he was giving him a warning. "We want to find out what happened as much as you do."

A couple of long moments and hard stares passed between the two black men before Tyrone finally sat back and held up his hands. "We'll answer your questions, and then you answer ours."

The detective gave a slow nod. "Fair enough." He paused, glanced at the white officer, then leaned over. "Okay, so did your son have any guns?" Ferguson asked, taking over the interrogation.

"No."

"Not that you know of?" the other officer said.

With a glare, my husband repeated, "No."

Then, "What about anything else that he had in his car?" Ferguson asked.

"What do you mean?"

"Any kind of weapon?"

"Look, my son wasn't like that. Let me answer your next ten questions for you. My son wasn't violent; he was probably eight the last time he had a fight. He wasn't in a gang, he didn't sell drugs, he didn't carry any weapons of any kind."

"What about a baseball bat? Did he carry a bat?" Detective Ferguson asked.

I squeezed Tyrone's arm, but this time it was more for me than for him. Because this time, I wanted to stand up and punch somebody.

Tyrone said, "No, he didn't *carry a bat.*"

"Not that you know of," the other officer said again.

Detective Ferguson must've known that was all my husband was going to be able to take. "Okay, so let me tell you what we know," the detective offered. "Your son and Heather were sitting in his car . . . just talking, maybe. And this is where it gets murky. It seems that your son and the man who approached the car exchanged some words, but the man walked away. Apparently, that was when your son got out the car and there was some kind of confrontation that turned into an altercation." Then the detective stopped as if that were enough of an explanation.

"So how did my son end up dead?" Tyrone asked.

"That's what we're trying to figure out."

"So some guy just shot my son?" I said. "For no reason?"

"Your son got out of the car, ma'am," the white officer said as if that were reason enough.

"And now there's a death sentence for getting out of your car? That's why he was murdered?" I cried.

"As we explained"—Detective Ferguson was back to talking—"we don't have the full picture yet."

"I just want to know one thing," Tyrone said. He glanced at the men as if he were telling them that they'd better have the right answers. "The boy who killed my son . . . Has he been arrested?"

"Not yet . . ."

"Why not?" I screamed, feeling my tears on their way.

"Because we're still working on this," Ferguson said.

The other added, "He's claiming self-defense. And if it was self-defense, then . . ."

I frowned. "Self-defense? But I know my son. He didn't attack anybody."

"He got out of the car and there was a confrontation, ma'am. And if anyone feels as if his life is in danger, he doesn't have to retreat. He can stay and protect himself."

My frown deepened as I thought back to the times when I'd heard words like that, similar ones on the news, with all of the recent killings of young black men. But that was down south. In Florida. That kind of thing couldn't happen here. Not in the North. In Pennsylvania. And it certainly was never used when one black man shot another.

"You're making it sound like . . . like this . . . like he's saying he was standing his ground or something," I said.

The officers nodded together and one said, "Pennsylvania is a stand-your-ground state, ma'am."

"But . . . I thought that was just in Florida?" I was doing all the talking now.

"No, it's not."

I wanted to burst into tears right then. I didn't know much about self-defense and stand your ground, except that everyone who used it in court seemed to get away with murder. Did this mean that the boy who shot my son was going to walk, too? And that's just what I asked the officer.

He shrugged. "We're going to do our best to find out what happened and to make sure justice is served . . . either way."

I sat there, stunned. The way these men were talking—this was just some black-on-black crime to them. They weren't giving any indication that they would put much effort into this case.

There was nothing else for me to say, but that was all right because I knew Tyrone would take over now. And this time, I wasn't even going to try to hold him back. I didn't care if he started flipping tables or punching walls. Tyrone would demand justice, and by the time my husband finished, these officers would run out of here and arrest whoever had taken the light out of our lives.

I watched and I waited. Then Tyrone finally opened his mouth, but the only thing he said was, "When can I see my son?"

Chapter 3

There was nothing but silence in the car, though actually that wasn't completely true. There was Tyrone's silence and my tears. The police had dragged us down to the station, kept us there for hours, asked us questions that had nothing to do with Marquis, and in the end, they still didn't let me see my son!

"The body is with the medical examiner," the detective had said to Tyrone when my husband asked.

The body? That was no way to describe Marquis.

"So?" Tyrone had said. "We still want to see our son."

The detective had shaken his head. "That's not possible. Your son will be released to you when the medical examiner completes his report."

He'd already reduced my son to just a body, and then he spoke like my son was the property of the state. All I'd wanted to do was stand up and demand that they bring my son to me. But then I saw Tyrone rise up in his seat, and before he turned that prison cell/ interrogation room out, I rested my hand on his shoulder, doing my best to hold back his rage.

My touch settled him. Or maybe it was my tears that made Tyrone turn his attention to me. Either way, instead of grabbing one or both of the detectives, all my husband did was take my hand and lead me out of there. Neither one of us looked back, nor did we utter a word.

But now that we were in the car, I was so close to telling Tyrone to turn back. Maybe we could plead with the police, convince them somehow that we had to see Marquis.

Or maybe I was just stalling because I didn't want to face my house without my son.

"I don't want to go home," I said.

Tyrone kept his eyes on the road, the muscle in his temple throbbing. After a moment, he asked, "Where do you want to go?"

I wanted to tell him that I would go anywhere except where we lived in West Philly. But when I opened my mouth, "I want to see Heather" came out.

He shook his head and I explained, "I want to know what happened."

It didn't take more than a moment before he said, "I don't think that's a good idea."

"But she was the last one to see Marquis alive. I want to know, I have to know what happened."

He gave it more thought, but still said, "No. We need to go home. We need to make . . ."

I completed his incomplete thought. He wanted us to start making plans for the rest of our lives without our son. But I couldn't do that. Not yet . . . not until I found a way to understand this. Not until I saw my son myself and got my brain to convince my heart what I still didn't want to believe.

And Heather could help.

"Don't you want to talk to her?" I asked.

"No."

"Don't you want to know?"

"I know everything that I need to know."

Well, I needed to know more. I needed to know what happened between yesterday when Marquis kissed me before he dashed out of the house and this moment when I had to live with the truth that I would never again feel my son's touch against my cheek.

I didn't say that to Tyrone, though, because in the best of circumstances, I couldn't change his mind. So I just let him drive as the sun began its slow ascent, bringing the light and hope of a new day.

But there would never be light, there would never be hope in my life again.

Tyrone rolled our car to a stop in our driveway, but even when he turned off the ignition, neither of us moved. And even though I didn't turn to look at my husband, I knew that he was taking in the same view that I was.

Our home.

The second floor.

The window to Marquis's room.

Tyrone blew out a long breath, then slid out of the car. As always, he came around, opened my door, and held my hand as I got out. And then, with slow steps that were as heavy as my heart, I followed him.

I watched every move that Tyrone made, how he put the key in the lock, turned it, pushed the door open, then stepped into our home. He looked back at me and then frowned as I just stood outside. I wanted to follow him in, I really did.

But I couldn't.

"Come on, Jan," Tyrone whispered. He held out his hand, knowing that I needed a little extra help. And I wanted to take his hand, I really did.

But I didn't.

Instead, I turned and ran.

"Janice!"

I jumped into the car, grabbed my keys from my purse, and revved up the engine. By now, I expected Tyrone to be by my side. But he was still standing in the doorway. With tears in his eyes that matched mine.

I put the car in reverse, but I didn't pull out until Tyrone did what he always did before I drove away. He pressed the tips of his fingers to his lips, then blew me a kiss.

I wanted to give him a smile, but the corners of my lips were permanently fixed downward. So I just nodded, backed out, and drove away.

I never liked Heather Nelson. I mean, she was only a teenager and probably okay as a person, I guess. I didn't really know her like that. Even though she and Marquis had been dating for a year, I spent as little time as I could with the two of them.

That was my way of protesting, of letting my son know that I didn't approve. But now, Lord Jesus, what I would do to get back those moments. To just have a little bit more time with Marquis, even if Heather was with him.

I was parked in front of the imposing two-story brick home, but I still hadn't turned off the ignition. Instead, I sat and listened to Marquis's voice in my head.

"Mama, there's someone I want you to meet."

By his tone, his excitement, I knew he wasn't talking about introducing me to some guy. As I stood at that stove preparing dinner,

I couldn't help but smile. My little boy was growing up and that tickled me.

I had already made the promise to myself that I wasn't going to be one of those women who didn't like any girl her son brought home. No, I was going to be accepting so that Marquis would always know that he could come to me about anything.

But then he walked into the kitchen, and when I looked up from the pan of onions I'd been sautéing, I had to use Herculean strength to stiffen my face and hide my shock. Or maybe it wasn't shock, maybe it was horror that I felt.

"Mama, this is Heather. Heather, this is my mom, the best mother in the world."

I said hello, and nothing else to the blond, blue-eyed, thin-lipped, no-butt girl. After all, what else could I say in front of her since I only had one question for Marquis: What the hell?

Since those were the only words I could think of, I kept them to myself and just smiled. I didn't say another word until Heather left.

Then I went in. "Really, Marquis, a white girl?"

"Mama, I never knew you didn't like white people."

"I didn't say that. I'm saying that I don't like you dating a white girl."

"Why you gotta be prejudiced?"

"And why can't you like one of those pretty black girls in your school?"

"'Cause none of them are like Heather. None of them will do the things for me that she'll do."

I was too afraid to ask him what that meant.

Then Marquis went on to tell me, "Mama, I can't help my heart."

"Boy, you're sixteen. You don't have a heart yet."

He had laughed; I didn't, because there was nothing funny
about facts. After that meeting, my only hope had been that my
son would be like every other teenage boy and drop his new girl
after two weeks.

But that had been a year ago, and even though I'd made a dozen
attempts to set him up with a girl I approved of and could be proud
of, Heather Nelson was still the love of his young life.

So my hope had switched to college. I prayed that when he
enrolled at the University of Pennsylvania and when Heather was
three hundred miles away at MIT (yes, I had looked up the distance between the two schools), their relationship would fizzle.

Those had been yesterday's worries.

Pushing myself out of the car, I looked up at the grand house
that was like so many of the other houses in Haverford. I'd never
been here, but from the moment I met Heather, I'd made it my
business to know everything about her, including where she lived.
Because I was *that* mother—involved in every part of my son's life.

That mother. Now that my only child was dead, was I still
a mother? Or was I a motherless child who was now a childless
mother?

My heart contracted, forcing a moan through my lips, but I
didn't let it stay there. I wouldn't be able to talk to Heather if I were
sprawled out, bawling in the middle of the street.

So I sucked it up, then trudged up the long driveway until I
stood in front of the door that looked like it had been made for a
giant. I pressed the bell; the chime echoed through the door. Made
me want to raise my hand and press the bell again just to hear the
first few notes of the Mozart sonata, the piece that Marquis had
played at his piano recital last year. But if I rang the bell and heard

it again, Heather and her family would open their door and find me on this step buckled over in grief. So I stood there and tried not to cry. And then the door opened.

I wasn't sure what I expected. It wasn't like I had the strength of mind to think this encounter all the way through. But I didn't expect to be looking into the eyes of Agnes Nelson.

Her eyes were bright blue, and matched the silk blouse that she wore along with her tan pants. But not at all welcoming. Not that I expected the roll-out-of-any-color-of-carpet, but it wasn't like she didn't know me. We'd met at various programs at our children's school and we'd always been cordial, though we'd never shared a genuine smile.

Agnes Nelson didn't care for me, not that it was personal. I was just the mother of the black boy that her daughter was dating. So our disdain and the reason for it was mutual.

But even if our children had never met, Agnes and I would never have been friends. How could we be when we were from worlds that were so far apart we could've been living in different galaxies?

She'd been born and raised right here in Haverford, one the most affluent neighborhoods in Philadelphia. I was from the heart of Philly. Her allowance as a child had probably rivaled what I earned now as an adult. And don't even start me on our politics. I'd read that she'd hosted a Mitt Romney fund-raiser at her home. Of course, I was on the other side.

"Mrs. Johnson," she said softly. She spoke to me through a sliver of a crack in her door. As if she didn't want me to see or even think about coming inside.

"Please call me Janice."

She nodded and then waited for me to say more.

She had to know why I was here, so I waited. But when she said no more, I continued: "Is Heather home?"

And then for the first time, I thought about time and space. What day was this? What time? Was this a school day? Had Heather already left for school?

Again Agnes nodded. "Heather's home, but she's resting," she said, not opening the door even a few more inches.

"I need to talk to her—about last night."

"I'm really sorry," she said, finally acknowledging my sorrow, "but I don't want her involved."

I frowned. "But she was there. She has to tell me—"

"She already spoke to the police," Agnes said. "They brought her home and they were here for hours. She didn't get to bed until very, very late."

"Please," I said. "She was the last person"—I swallowed—"to see my son alive."

If this woman had liked me, this would've been the moment when she opened her door and her heart and let me in.

But Agnes didn't make any kind of move like that. "I don't think it's a good idea for Heather to talk to anyone," she said. "The police—"

Then, from behind her, I heard, "Mom, let her in."

Still, more than a couple of seconds passed before Agnes stepped away from the door. And in her place, there was Heather. She looked normal enough, in a white T-shirt and rolled-up-to-her-knees gray sweatpants. But her eyes told me part of the story. I could hardly see the blue of her eyes for all the red that was there. She opened the door wider and the moment I moved beyond the threshold, she pulled me into her arms, holding me tight.

"I'm so sorry, Mrs. Johnson," she sobbed into my shoulder. "I'm so sorry."

I closed my eyes and held on to her, feeling every tremble of her body. To this moment, I didn't think anyone's grief could match mine. Not even Tyrone's. Because I was the mother.

But as I held Heather, I learned in her embrace that my sorrow was shared.

Finally pulling back, I asked Heather, "Can we talk?"

"Of course."

She led me into the living room, which had three walls of glass and looked as if it could hold the entire first floor of Tyrone's and my home. But I didn't have time to marvel at the extravagance of a lifestyle that I had never known. Instead, I sat on the brocade sofa and reached for Heather's hand when she sat beside me.

Tears were still rolling down her cheeks when she said, "I can't believe this. I just can't believe that he's gone."

"What happened?"

"Heather, maybe you shouldn't . . ."

That quickly, I had forgotten about Agnes. Looking over my shoulder, I saw her standing there, under the arch that led to the living room, her arms folded, like a gatekeeper.

"Mom, it's okay."

"But your father and I . . . We don't think you should get involved."

"I *am* involved," Heather said. And then, as if she were dismissing her mother, she turned back to me. "I don't even know what happened," she began as she shook her head. "Marquis and I were sitting in the car, just talking. We weren't doing anything. And then the man came up and tapped on the window. He asked if I was okay. And even though I said I was, he kept asking us questions.

And then Marquis told the man to mind his business and get away from his car.

"Then the man told Marquis to get out of the car and say that to his face. I tried to stop Marquis, but he jumped out anyway. And then it was like just two seconds later and . . ." She lowered her head and her tears dripped onto our entwined hands.

I waited a moment, knowing she needed time. But I had to know, so I encouraged her with my question again. "What happened?"

"I don't know," she sobbed, looking up at me. "I was trying to see out of the back window of the Jeep, but it was dark and all I saw was the man. I didn't even see Marquis because he was on the side of the car. And then I heard the shot. I was too scared to move. I didn't know if the man was going to shoot me, too. So I just crouched down on the floor and called 911."

I squeezed her hand. "I'm really glad that you're okay."

She nodded.

"So he just shot Marquis?"

"Yes. Marquis didn't even do anything," she cried. "The man just shot him as he came around the car."

I still held on to Heather's hand, but now it was because I thought I was going to pass out. Hearing the way someone had just shot my son in cold blood. He'd shot him . . . why? Did a gang member really just walk up to my son's car and shoot him? And in Haverford?

But then, right behind all of those questions, I had a thought. Because of the way Heather referred to who killed my son.

The man.

The man, she'd said over and over.

She never talked as if he were a peer. "So you didn't know *the man* at all?"

"No! I'd never seen him before."

I wanted to come right out and ask, but instead I phrased the question in the politically correct way. "What . . . what did *the man* look like?"

"Heather!" Her mother said her name as if she were giving her a command and marched right over to the sofa. She stood over us and took Heather's hand away from mine. To me, she said, "I hope you'll understand, Mrs. Johnson, but I think that's enough. This has been traumatic for Heather and I'm sorry about what happened to Marcus, but now I have to look out for my daughter."

"My son's name is Marquis," I said, hoping that my words didn't sound like the growl that I felt rise within me.

She gave me a dismissive nod and said no more.

I glanced at Heather, hoping that once again she would defy her mother. But even though I pleaded with my eyes, her lips were pressed together as if they'd been zipped and locked.

I wanted to sit there until I heard the answer to the most important question. But from the way Agnes stood, I knew she would not be moved—and she wouldn't let her daughter be moved either.

So I pushed myself up only because I had no choice, then turned away from the two women. Neither of them made any moves; I guessed I had to find my own way out.

Then, right as I put my hand on the doorknob, Heather called out, "Mrs. Johnson."

I paused.

She took a few steps toward me. "The man who shot Marquis . . ." More steps brought her closer until her mother put her hand on her shoulder. But Heather slipped from her grasp and came to me. Looking straight into my eyes, she finished, "He was white." She paused, then put her sentences together. "The man who shot Marquis was white."

I took in her words, took in their meaning. I whispered, "Thank you," then left their home.

But once I stepped outside, I couldn't move. So I leaned against the door that had been made for a giant and let the reality settle inside of me.

My son had been shot by a white man. And the reason for his death was inside those words. My son was murdered simply because he was black.

I'd wanted to know why; I'd wanted to understand. Now I did.

And the blackened cloud that I'd been carrying since the police had come to my home last night weighed heavier and became darker, darker than midnight.

Chapter 4

It was only God's grace that got me home. That was the only way I could explain driving for twenty minutes crying blinding tears and still making it here.

By the time I rolled our car into our driveway, I was exhausted. Grief was a heavy burden to carry.

And now there was a new albatross that had brought a different kind of pain.

A white man.

It just hadn't occurred to me. Even when we were at the police station and they were asking all of those questions, I thought some kid had rolled up on my son. Maybe it was because the detectives talked about gangs and drugs, maybe that's why I'd made that assumption.

I was empty of tears and drained of strength, so I had to take a moment before I had enough inside of me to push open the door and swing my legs out of the car. I was still steps away from our front door when it opened and Tyrone came out to greet me. He pulled me into our home and into his arms.

"You were gone for so long," he said, pressing me to his chest. "I was going to go out and look for you, but then I remembered, you had the car." When he released me, he chuckled just a bit, though it was so strange—to hear a chuckle and see a tear.

"I'm sorry, babe," I said. "I just had to go."

"Where?"

"To . . ." Before I could tell him my news, from the corner of my eye, I saw Delores, Tyrone's mother, rushing toward me.

"Oh, my God, Jan!" She grabbed me in a hug that felt like she never planned to let me go.

There had never been a time when she'd held me this tight. Not that I had any doubt that Delores loved me. After all, if it hadn't been for her, I had no idea where I'd be now. Seriously.

Delores Johnson had found me living on the streets when I was fifteen; I'd just run away from what had to be my tenth, eleventh, or twelfth foster home; I couldn't remember.

Whatever the number, the Saturday Delores found me, she'd been out with her church, witnessing to the downtrodden and forgotten. They were in Love Park, which had been my home for about three weeks.

Of course, people thought living on the streets was dangerous, but to me, the outside was safer than the inside. I'd had to fight off grown men who always wanted to put their hands on me, and I'd won those battles, giving more than one a busted lip or a blackened eye.

There were always repercussions, of course: I was beaten, not fed, locked in rooms and closets —I was never raped, though.

But I got older, and it got harder. So I left. I left my foster home, left the system, and met Delores, that third Saturday in October in 1996.

She told me about my Savior in heaven and then she saved me on earth.

"The streets ain't no place for a pretty young girl like you. You need to be at Harmony Hearts Home."

"What's that?"

"My church has a home for people who need a place to stay. If there's a room, I'm gonna get you in there."

She gave me her number on the back of a napkin, but I never called her. That home she'd described was just like the places I'd lived. But a couple of weeks later, she came back to the park and convinced me to at least give it a try.

My plan was to stay there for one night. But the home turned out to be decent, and I stayed way longer than the thirty days everyone was given. With Delores's guidance, I became one of the teen counselors encouraging girls like me to leave the streets behind. I lived and worked there until I graduated from high school.

"How are you, baby?" Delores asked, pulling me from the memories of my dire past into the torment of this present.

She didn't wait for me to answer, just took my hand and led me down the hall toward the family room. It wasn't until I followed her that I noticed her attire—black pants, a long-sleeved black blouse. Where was the orange or yellow or red caftan that she almost always wore?

Then I remembered.

Inside the family room, the first thing I did was grab the remote and turn down the television's volume.

"Why's the TV up so loud?" I asked my husband, who'd followed us.

He shrugged. "I didn't even notice." And then he ran his hands over his bald head. At any other time, that would've got me thinking about the things I loved to do with that man . . . and his head.

But now the only thing that move did was remind me of Marquis.

"Daddy, can I shave my head?"

"No, son."

"But why, Daddy? I wanna be like you."

I closed my eyes and remembered the pure joy that was on Tyrone's face when Marquis had said those words.

"Well, maybe one day, son, but right now you're only six . . ."

A sob tried to escape from my throat, but I pressed my hand across my mouth and pushed it back.

Delores and Tyrone sat together on the sofa, leaving me with only one alternative—the recliner. The recliner that Marquis had bought for his father (with my money) last Father's Day, but the recliner where Marquis had sat more times than his father and me combined.

I didn't want to sit there now.

But I did.

Because I was too weary to stand.

We three sat with the chatter from the television slicing through our silence. We stared at the TV as Tyrone flipped from one channel to the next.

"I keep thinking," Tyrone said as he clicked the remote again, "that one of these news stations"—he clicked again—"is gonna have something"—another click—"about my son."

"It's probably just too soon," Delores said. "There'll be something on there later today. I just know it. But what we've got to do now"—she turned and looked at me—"is start planning the funeral. Do you have a pen and paper, Jan? I can take notes."

I wasn't going to begin planning anything—not until I saw Marquis. All I was going to do now was inhale and exhale; that would have to be enough.

It had to be the look on my face that made her add, "Now, Jan, I know this is hard. But we have to do this."

"No."

"Yes," she said as if my word and my feelings didn't count. "You may not be ready, but we have to do it. Remember, blessed are those who mourn, for they will be comforted—" And then, suddenly, she crumbled. Collapsed right there on the couch.

If I'd been mean, I would've said something like: *See, it's too soon for any of us.* But I said nothing as I watched Tyrone shift on the sofa so that he was closer to his mother.

"Mama" was all he said as he wrapped his arms around her.

She sobbed into his chest and I wanted to cry, too. But at this moment, there was no one to hold me, so I kept my tears to myself.

I just sat and waited, knowing her crying spell would pass. Just like mine. I let a couple of minutes go by before I said, "There's nothing that we can plan. We can't bury Marquis because the police still have his body."

"What?" she said, sitting up. "Why?" She sniffed.

"Because the police have to finish the investigation," Tyrone said.

His words reminded me: "There's part of the investigation they didn't tell us." I told Tyrone and Delores about my visit to Heather.

"She said that she and Marquis were just sitting in the car talking when the man came up to them. She said Marquis got out of the car and the man shot him. She was too scared to get out herself."

"That poor baby," Delores cried, pressing her hand to her chest.

Grief works in mysterious ways. Because Delores liked Heather about as much as I did. For the same reason. This was the first time she'd ever said anything close to kind about the girl.

"So, just like that?" Tyrone said, confusion all over his face. "Some punk kid shoots my son?"

I took a deep breath and then exhaled the most important part: "And . . . he was white. That's what Heather said. He. Was. White. A white man."

Tyrone sat as if my last words had frozen him, but I wasn't surprised. Grief had stifled his brain, too. Just like me, he had never considered that the murderer wasn't a punk black kid.

My husband leaped off the sofa. "Wait! What? White?"

I nodded.

Tyrone stomped back and forth in front of the television. "I thought the police said it was a gang member. I mean, yeah, white boys are in gangs, but . . ." He paused and looked at me. "White?"

"Oh, Lord, Jesus! This is just like all them other cases," Delores cried out. "We've got to call Al Sharpton."

I stopped myself from rolling my eyes and saying, *Really?*

"Well, I know who I'm gonna call," Tyrone said, looking at me. "You still got that card the detective gave you?"

I paused for a moment, having forgotten that Detective Ferguson had rushed behind us and tucked his card into my hand right before we walked out of the station. I shifted through all the stuff in my purse, found the card that had slipped to the bottom, and handed it to Tyrone.

It didn't take him two seconds to dial the number. "I need to speak to Detective Ferguson," he said with authority. "This is Tyrone Johnson; my son was murdered last night by a white man and I need to speak to Ferguson."

Now I was the one who sat frozen. Frozen and grateful that we weren't at the police station because with the way my husband was shaking, it wouldn't have been good for him or for the detectives.

"Yes, this is Tyrone Johnson. I spoke to you about my son, Marquis Johnson." Tyrone didn't even pause before he said, "And I want to know if you arrested the white man who murdered him."

A pause.

"What do you mean you don't want me to say 'murdered'?" Tyrone's voice rose but I didn't try to stop him the way I did last night. This time, I let his rage, rage. Maybe that would get the police to respond.

Tyrone said, "A white man murdered my son and both of us know why." A pause. "No, you can't tell me that my son confronted him. And even if he did, my son was unarmed." Another pause. "Well, how long is all of this gonna take?" More silent seconds.

Then my husband asked the question of all questions. "All right, then, what's the man's name?"

I wish I'd been thinking and had gotten the cordless from the kitchen when Tyrone first made this call. But I couldn't move now; I couldn't miss any part of this conversation.

"Oh, yeah, right. You have to protect him, but who was protecting my son?"

The muscles in Tyrone's jaw were moving back and forth, in and out, up and down, and I stood. And it was a good thing because when Tyrone said, "Look, you better have that man arrested or I will not be responsible—" I grabbed his shoulder, stopping him from finishing.

Yes, my husband had every right to say what he was going to say. But I knew how things worked in America. His words wouldn't be taken as those of a grieving father in search of justice. He'd be considered a terrorist and the police might even rush over here and arrest him.

My touch made Tyrone calm, and instead of telling the

detective how he would go on his own murderous spree, he only said, "That man needs to be arrested and I need to know when you finally do it." Then he slammed the phone down without giving Detective Ferguson a chance to respond.

"What did he say?" Delores asked.

I looked at her with big eyes. Couldn't she tell? I didn't want Tyrone repeating that, reliving that, taking his rage from zero to sixty all over again.

But I guess the question seemed natural to Tyrone. "They haven't arrested him because they haven't completed their investigation. And right now it's not considered a homicide."

"Well, if it wasn't a homicide, what was it? A suicide? Did my grandson get out of that car and shoot himself?" Delores asked. "Is that what the police are gonna say?"

I wanted to tell Delores to keep quiet! Couldn't she see the steam rising from the top of Tyrone's head?

His rage was now approaching one hundred when he said, "And they don't want to release the man's name for *his* protection."

"That's it," Delores said, jumping up. She waved her finger in the air. "Call Al Sharpton. I'm not kidding."

"Well, I know who I *am* going to call." Tyrone looked at me and said, "My brother."

I didn't let a moment pass before I said, "No."

"What else am I supposed to do, Janice? That cracker murdered my son and I want justice."

"I do, too, but I don't want it that way. It's been less than twenty-four hours, Tyrone. Let's see what the police will do."

"Really? You want to wait for them? You know they're not going to do the right thing."

"But that doesn't mean we have to do the wrong thing." I could see that my words weren't convincing him. I added, "This time, the police might do right by us."

He grimaced. "We're black, Janice. The police will never do right by us or anyone who looks like us. We have to take care of and look out for our own. That's what my brother is all about."

I wanted to say that his brother wasn't about anything except trouble, but all I said was, "I don't want Marquis remembered that way."

Tyrone stood silent, though by the look that he gave me—he could have heated all of Pennsylvania with the fire that burned in his eyes. It was just because of what he'd learned, but still, his glare made me want to step back. Made me want to reconsider and maybe tell him to go ahead. Call his brother. Let him organize bike rides and rallies and rioting. Let his brother, Raj, do what he always did. Cause havoc.

But I stood my ground. Because what I said was true. I didn't want our son to be remembered for anything besides the wonderful young man that he was. I didn't want Marquis to be part of a movement that led to looting and lunacy; I just wanted to hold on to his memory.

"I'm just praying . . ."

Tyrone let out a half chuckle, half growl at my words.

But that didn't stop me from continuing: ". . . that it will be different for us. I'm praying that this time, the murderer will be arrested and justice . . ."

Tyrone laughed. He just leaned his head back and laughed out loud. But there was no joy in the sound. After a while, he stopped. "All right." That was all he said before he stomped out of the room, leaving me alone with my grief, now peppered with fear. Because if Tyrone got his brother and his brother's friends involved, this would be a mess.

I stood wondering if I should go after Tyrone because right now I didn't want to be without him. And surely, he needed me.

But sixteen years of marriage made me know that this was one of those moments when Tyrone needed to be alone.

"Janice."

I'd forgotten about Delores. When I faced her, she said, "You know Tyrone is going to call Raj, right? He's probably upstairs calling him right now."

I shook my head. "No, he'll wait."

"No, he won't. First of all, he has to call his brother to tell him that Marquis was killed. And once Raj and the Brown Guardians find out about this, they're going to make sure justice is done . . . one way or another," she said as if she were all right with that.

I sighed. It was the one way or another that I knew to be true.

"You married into the Johnson family, baby," Delores said as if I needed that reminder. "And I told you a long time ago, that with the Johnson men, you've just got to let the men do what the men have to do."

She wasn't telling me anything that I didn't already know. And what I already knew scared the hell out of me.

Chapter 5

Last night, I had closed my eyes for one reason—I wanted to see Marquis. If I couldn't see him while I was awake, surely I would see him in my dreams. I was absolutely sure that when I laid my head down, he would come to me. I knew that he needed to see me as much as I needed to see him.

I almost couldn't wait to get to bed. That's why even though we had a house full of people, I'd come to my bedroom and closed the door on what felt like madness in the middle of my mourning.

I'd lain down, but I didn't undress. I just closed my eyes and rushed into unconsciousness.

But my dreams were empty. Filled with only darkness.

And now it was morning.

At least, it felt like morning. I hadn't opened my eyes, not wanting to face this day—this first full day of the rest of my life without him.

Rolling over, I reached across the bed for Tyrone. His arms were just what I needed; his embrace would get me through.

But then I opened my eyes slowly. My husband's side of the bed was empty, just like my dreams. I pushed myself up and leaned against the headboard. Had I slept alone all night?

Maybe he had come to bed and awakened before me. I didn't know. We didn't get to say much to each other last night. Not with our house filled with so many people.

For hours, all I did was answer the door, and then balance heavy aluminum pans packed with fried chicken and ham, collard greens and string beans, macaroni and cheese and dirty rice. And then, of course, there was cake after cake and pie after pie. How had these people come up with these home-cooked dishes so fast? Did they have food stashed in their refrigerators, saved for a time such as this?

Our home bulged with more people than the walls had ever seen. Just about everyone was there for my mother-in-law, though Tyrone had called his shop and a few of the mechanics who worked for him came by right away.

I hadn't called a soul, not that there were many for me to reach out to beyond my coworkers. I never bonded well with others. Maybe that was because I was already fifteen when I met the first person who ever cared about me—Delores. And I was sixteen when I was loved for the first time in my life—Tyrone.

Growing up without knowing my mother or my father made me feel like I'd hit the lottery when I had a husband and a son. Add to that mix my best friend, and those three blessings had been enough for me.

But though I wished Syreeta was here, I hadn't called her yet. Since she was living in Germany teaching English as a second language to high school students, I wanted to wait until I could say more than "Hi, Syreeta; Marquis, your godson, is dead."

So I'd spent the time surrounded by all of those people, and never had I felt so alone.

That's why I kept moving. Between the living room and the

dining room and the family room, dishing out food, serving up drinks to people I hardly knew.

More than once, someone said to me, "Janice, you need to sit down. Let us serve you."

But I just smiled. And kept moving. And kept breathing.

And kept wondering, why were all of these people in my home and when were they going to leave?

Not that I didn't appreciate their kindness, and not that I knew the proper etiquette for grieving a child, but I had a feeling that it should have been just me and Tyrone. Together. In private.

What I wanted didn't matter, though. Our home swelled with folks and the sound of sad chatter, a mournful noise that hovered like lead above us.

But then the mourning turned militant. In every room, the conversation was the same:

"He was shot . . . by a white man!"

"What? Why?"

"You know why. Because he was black."

All kinds of exclamations and expletives followed that. And then more expletives than exclamations came when they were told that the murderer had not been arrested.

Tyrone moved from room to room, repeating his mantra: "They've been hunting our boys and now they've killed my son!"

Men jumped up, women shouted—it felt like a rallying cry to me. There were so many stories that had started out this way— black boys whose murders had turned into movements.

I didn't want to be part of anything like that. I didn't want to be the mother living out her grief in front of the country. I didn't want my son to be remembered for how he died; I wanted the world to know how he lived. And I didn't want my son's death to be used as any kind of excuse for any kind of violence.

But that talk kept on, becoming more belligerent.

Someone yelled out, "Where are the Brown Guardians?"

Someone else said, "They'll know what to do!"

Another voice: "You know they were responsible for that six-car pileup on the interstate that killed that cop."

"Yeahs" rang out, sounding like cheers and that was when I knew there was no place for me in my own home. Not that I hadn't heard about that accident four months ago.

Nicholas Watson, a young cop who'd shot a black boy in an altercation inside a convenience store, but who had never been arrested, had been killed nine months later in what the police eventually called a freak accident.

But Marquis had told me that word on the street was that the accident had been the work of the Brown Guardians. The Brown Guardians, who considered themselves a neighborhood protection group, but who were nothing more than a vigilante motorcycle gang to me.

There was no way I wanted to hear the Brown Guardians mentioned in the same sentence as Marquis.

So I'd exited to our bedroom. And lain on the bed. And waited for Marquis. Who never came to me.

Now I wondered again if Tyrone had come to bed. Or had he been up all night caught up in the emotions of what happened to our son?

I rolled out of bed, stretched, then thought about freshening up. At least, I should change out of my dress, brush my teeth, splash water across my face. But I kinda felt that if I did any of that, I'd be moving on.

So instead, I walked into the hallway, then stopped. Right outside of Marquis's room.

The door was closed and I didn't remember closing it. But I knew I couldn't open it, so I turned toward the steps.

Sounds of life rose from below. Downstairs, I stood at the kitchen's opening, watching Delores at the sink. Just like me, she was dressed in the same clothes she'd worn yesterday and I wondered if she'd even gone home. She piled plates on top of plates, pots on top of pans, all left over from last night, I supposed.

I opened my mouth to tell her that we had a dishwasher, but then I stopped. Delores knew that.

My eyes roamed through the room and I could see Marquis in every crevice, in every corner. I paused when my glance settled on the bar stool at the counter where I'd sat . . . When was that? Two days ago?

"I can't believe you ruined Mother's Day for me," Marquis said.

I stuffed my mouth with a forkful of blueberry pancakes. "How did I do that?"

"I was supposed to cook you breakfast, and serve you in bed."

"Yeah, but you did that last year, and remember how that turned out?" I laughed, reminding my son of the runny scrambled eggs and the crispy bacon that was way on the other side of burned.

I was too hungry this morning, so I wasn't about to leave my nutrition to Marquis, no matter how admirable his intention.

"It just doesn't seem right that you had to cook your own breakfast on Mother's Day."

"That's okay," I said. "I'm just happy to have a good meal and to share it with you."

He grinned. "Happy Mother's Day, Mama," he said, before he kissed my cheek. "And may we share many more."

With the tips of my fingers, I caressed the spot where Marquis had kissed me, and I could almost feel his lips. I sobbed, or maybe I just gasped. I did something that took my breath away at the thought that I'd never celebrate another Mother's Day.

"Oh!" Delores turned and rushed toward me, wiping her hands on the apron she wore. My apron. *World's Best Mom* was embroidered on the black cloth in red.

Pulling me into her arms, she said, "I was just about to check on you. Are you okay?"

How was I supposed to answer that? "I'm good," I said, because words hadn't yet been created that would describe how I felt.

Delores shook her head at my lie. She said, "Well, sit down and I'll fix you breakfast."

I glanced once again at the bar stool where I'd sat Sunday morning. "I'm not hungry."

She said, "But you have to eat. People will be here soon, and you won't even think about eating then."

More people? This soon? Too soon!

My eyes moved to the digital numbers on the microwave. It was barely nine.

I asked, "Have you seen Tyrone?"

She nodded as she returned to the sink. "He slept in the family room with me."

"He slept in there?" I asked, sounding like I didn't believe her, though I did. It was just hard to believe because once we got back together, Tyrone and I always slept together. Always.

Delores glanced over her shoulder at me. "Yeah, by the time everyone left, it was so late he didn't want to disturb you. And he didn't want me to be by myself. I'm just so upset by this, you know?"

She said that as if I might not understand how upset she was.

"I slept on the sofa and he slept on the recliner," Delores continued. "He was still asleep when I came in here." She looked up. "What about you? Did you sleep okay?"

It was another one of those questions that I would never be able to answer. So all I did was turn around, and over my shoulder I said, "I'm going to talk to Tyrone."

Tyrone was in the family room, but he wasn't asleep. He was on the edge of the recliner with his elbows resting on his knees, his head in his hands, and his pain hanging heavy in the air. When his shoulders began to quake, I ran to him.

Crouching down, I held him, resting his head against mine.

"They killed Marquis," he sobbed.

"I know," I whispered, and cried with my husband.

"They killed my boy."

"I know." I held him, never planning to let him go.

"I wasn't there to protect him."

That was when I leaned back a little. "You have been the best protector, the best provider, the best father."

"But I told him that he could go out last night."

"He went to the library, Tyrone! A trip to the library shouldn't be fatal." When more sobs raked through him, I said, "This is not your fault; this is *not* your fault."

For a long while, he said nothing. Just looked into my eyes, then pulled me onto the recliner with him. There wasn't enough room in that narrow chair for the two of us, but we made it work. I wanted to be this close, skin close. Really, from this moment forward, I hoped that Tyrone and I would never be more than a few inches apart.

I whispered, "Did you get any sleep?"

"No," he said. "What about you?"

I wanted to tell him that I'd slept deeply. Probably the deepest sleep I'd had in a while. But then I'd have to explain how in my sleep I'd searched for Marquis. So I just answered with a shrug before I went on to my next question. "How late did people stay?"

"Probably till about one, two. I don't know, it was pretty late, but time doesn't seem to matter right about now."

I knew what he meant. I didn't care about time—except that I wanted time to stop. Completely. Or even better, I wanted time to go back. Back to the moment when Marquis had come into our bedroom early yesterday evening and kissed me good-bye.

"I'm heading to the library."

"I know you're glad to get out of the house for something besides school."

"Yeah." He grinned. *"Dad missed his calling. He shouldn't be fixing anybody's car. He needs to open a prison."*

I laughed, but I was serious when I told him, "Just don't do anything to get locked up again."

"I won't, Mama," he said before he kissed me. *"You don't have to worry about that. I won't smoke another joint for as long as I live."*

And then he waved good-bye. And then he was gone.

Forever.

Tyrone broke into my memory. "I wish . . ." He stopped and pulled me even closer.

And I wished, too.

So for minutes, Tyrone and I just lay there together, wishing. Our hearts synchronized, the two feeling as if they were beating as one. And though I longed for Marquis, for the first time since my son died, I had a little piece of peace.

Then, "You know what I forgot to ask you two?"

His mother barged into the family room, her voice sounding like a scream as it invaded our silence. She stood over us as if she didn't notice that her son and I were sharing a private moment.

She said, "Your pastor. Pastor Brown. Have you called him?"

I held Tyrone for just a moment longer before I pulled away. Tyrone was going to have to explain this one.

He let a couple of seconds go by before he said, "No, Mom. We don't go to his church, any church, anymore. I told you that."

And then he sprang up as if he had new energy.

"But why?" Delores asked.

Tyrone didn't respond or turn around. He just stomped out of the room. So Delores turned to me. "What was that about?"

I pressed my lips together, pissed that she had interrupted us and pissed that she'd taken me and Tyrone to that place.

But the fact that Tyrone had just run out of the room, the fact that I sat as if my lips were sewn together, didn't seem to be enough for Delores.

She pushed her fists into her waist. "Do you want to tell me what's going on?"

And then the doorbell rang.

I rushed to the door, swung it open, then did everything I could not to slam it shut in the face of the only person on earth who I could say that I came close to hating.

There stood Raj. Tyrone's brother.

Chapter 6

We stood there, Raj and I, just staring at each other. From his expression, I could tell that he was as surprised to see me as I was to see him, though I had no idea where his surprise came from. Did he forget that I still lived here?

"Jan." He said my name and then paused.

I looked him up and down. At least he'd come dressed properly. In just a long-sleeved black T-shirt and jeans. I couldn't remember the last time I saw him without one of the brown leather jackets favored by the Guardians.

"Jan," he said again. "I'm so . . ." I turned around and walked away, thinking that he was lucky that I hadn't slammed the door in his face.

"Who was at . . ." Delores paused as she peeked outside, and then answered her own question.

I was halfway up the stairs when I heard her say, "Come in, son." I imagined that she pulled him into her arms and hugged him because of her next words. "I'm so glad you came."

That was all I heard as I stomped down the hall and into our bedroom. As I stepped inside, Tyrone came out of our walk-in closet, dressed only in his briefs. But I'd just lost my son and I'd just seen Raj, so not even my nearly naked husband caused me to pause. "Your brother's here," I said, forgetting all about how just a few minutes before we were lying together. So close.

I plopped down onto the bed, picked up my cell phone from the nightstand, and scrolled through. I wasn't looking for anything or anybody; I just needed for my hands to be busy. Or else I might punch the wall or something.

"Janice, you knew he was coming."

"Did you call him?" I asked; my accusation was all in my tone.

"Yeah, I did." He gave me attitude back. "Because he's my brother. He's Marquis's uncle. And he has to be here for that reason."

I nodded, but when I looked up, my warning was in my eyes. "I don't want any trouble, Tyrone."

He pinched his lips together as if my words made him angry. "What kind of trouble are you talking about?"

I paused. What I wanted to say was *the kind of trouble that your brother causes whenever he's around.* But I said nothing.

Tyrone heard my thoughts in my silence and shook his head. "He's changed, Janice. You know that."

There was a long pause before he added, "And if anyone should understand people changing, it should be you."

I froze. By the time I looked up, Tyrone had marched to the bathroom and slammed the door behind him. Even when I heard the sound of the shower, I just sat there, thinking about the low blow that he had just thrown.

I couldn't believe I was sitting here, with a dead son, and arguing with my husband about his brother. I couldn't let Raj come between me and Tyrone. Especially not now. And especially not again.

So I sat on the bed waiting and thinking of the right words to fix it with Tyrone.

His shower was too short; I wasn't ready. When he came out of the bathroom and gave me a quick glance, I said nothing. Just sat, still trying to get the words together.

Behind me, Tyrone moved around, getting dressed. I knew him so well, I didn't have to see him slipping the T-shirt over his head or sliding his arms through his shirt. I waited until I heard the zipper of his pants to stand, face him, and say the words that had taken me all that time to come up with.

"I'm sorry."

He said nothing, looking at me as if he were measuring my sincerity. I guess I passed because finally he nodded, then beckoned me to come to him.

"I don't want to fight," I said as he held me. "I need you more than I ever have."

"And I need you, too, baby." He leaned back, and with his hands on my shoulders, he said, "But you've got to know that Raj is going to be here with me, for me. And for you."

I tried to nod, but I couldn't get any part of my body to respond to that.

When I didn't say anything, Tyrone kept on. "He's not like that anymore. He's not violent, he's not vindictive." And then he added as if he were proud, "The Brown Guardians helped to change him."

What in the world do you think the Brown Guardians are about? They were all about violence; they were completely vindictive. I bit my tongue—literally—praying that would keep me quiet.

"Okay?" Tyrone said.

Somewhere from deep inside of me, I found the strength to nod.

He smiled. Kissed my forehead and said, "I'm going downstairs. You coming?"

"I want to get out of these clothes first." I was so glad I had that excuse.

He kissed me again before he left me alone. And I returned to the bed. And sat. And wondered how was I supposed to get through this . . . with Raj Johnson in my house.

And now that he was here, the Brown Guardians weren't going to be far behind. I had to stop it, but how? No one seemed able to stop them, not even the police; though I'd heard long ago that the Guardians and the police were flip sides of the same bad penny.

It hurt my heart, though, that I seemed to be the lone black person in Philly who saw the true colors of the Brown Guardians. They were heroes to so many, men who turned a wrong into a right. No one saw what I knew—that they were nothing more than motorcycle thugs, outlaws at best, terrorists for real.

And my brother-in-law was one of them.

But my son? He wouldn't have chosen to ride with them when he was alive; I wasn't going to allow them to recruit him now that he was dead.

Marquis Johnson was not going to be a cause for the Brown Guardians. No matter what I had to do.

I had made the transition—I changed my clothes. The dress that I'd worn to the police station then slept in last night was in the middle of the floor, right where I had stepped out of it. I grabbed it, rolled it up, and then stuffed it into the small trash can by our bedroom door.

Reaching for my cell, I scrolled down to the number that I'd locked into my phone yesterday, then clicked to make the call.

When a female answered, I said, "May I speak to Detective

Ferguson, please?" She asked my name, and I told her and added, "I'm Marquis Johnson's mother."

I figured by now everyone down there had heard about the black boy who'd been murdered by the white man. And I must've been right because just like Tyrone had been yesterday, I was patched straight through to Detective Ferguson.

"Mrs. Johnson." He called my name in a tone that sounded like we were friends. Nothing like the professional drone he'd used with us in the middle of Monday night. I hoped that was a good sign.

"Thank you for taking my call."

"No problem; you just caught me. How may I help you?"

"I was wondering; do you have any more news about my son?" Then I paused because I needed new oxygen for my next words. "We'd like to . . . there are arrangements . . . I want to . . . prepare for . . ."

It didn't matter that I couldn't complete a coherent sentence; Detective Ferguson seemed to understand me. "No, Mrs. Johnson. I'm sorry I didn't make it clear to you yesterday; it's going to take a couple of days."

Had that only been yesterday?

He said, "We have to do an autopsy, and a toxicology report."

"A toxicology report? Why? We told you our son wasn't on drugs."

"It's routine, Mrs. Johnson," the detective explained.

For the second time today, I was mad. Routine? There was nothing routine about the murder of my son.

"Mr. Ferguson," I began, trying to come up with a comeback. "Do you have any children?"

There was a pause before he said, "No, ma'am."

"Maybe that's why you can't understand how offensive your words are and this whole process is."

"I'm really sorry. I'm just doing my job."

"And I'm just being a mother. I have to see my son. You don't know . . . what it's like." I held back my cries. "I've lost him, and now I can't even see him. Do you know how hard this is for me?"

"I can only imagine."

"Is there any way for you to arrange it? For me to at least see him?"

He didn't even try to hide his sigh. "No, ma'am." He paused and added, "We can release his car to you," as if that were a consolation prize. As if I would ever drive the Jeep I shared with my son again. When I didn't bother to respond, Detective Ferguson finished with, "I give you my word, we're doing the best we can."

Without a good-bye, I hung up because that was the best that I could do. Sitting on the edge of the bed, I stared at the phone and wondered if I should call back. And this time beg. Beg until I got him to understand that I was dying to see my dead son.

But I decided to leave that alone for now, and instead, I stepped into the hallway, hoping that my brother-in-law was already gone.

For a second, I stood at the top of the stairs, but heard nothing. It wasn't until I was halfway down that I heard Tyrone, Raj, and Delores in the family room.

So instead of turning to the right, I veered to the left. I'd hide out in the kitchen for a bit, and then go back to my bedroom if Raj wasn't gone by then.

The moment I stepped into the kitchen, my stomach rumbled as if it were trying to tell me something. In my head, I calculated when was the last time I'd eaten. The days were running together, except it hadn't been that many days at all. Today was just Wednesday. Only about thirty-six hours since the beginning of my despair.

I wasn't hungry in my head, but I needed to handle my body. So I dumped a single slice of bread into the toaster, then poured a glass of orange juice. Waiting, I leaned back against the counter, sipping, thinking, mourning.

At the same moment that the toast popped up, a voice behind me said, "Hey." Both sounds made me jump a couple of inches into the air.

"I'm sorry. I didn't mean to scare you."

Turning around, I faced Raj. If I didn't have such contempt for this man, he might actually be a little attractive in that Boris Kodjoe perfection kind of way. Though that wasn't my kind of man at all. I needed ruggedness, an obvious bad-boy attitude. Raj didn't have that on the outside like Tyrone. What he had was worse; he had evil on the inside.

"You don't scare me."

He nodded. "You didn't give me a chance earlier, Jan, but I really wanted to tell you how sorry I am about Marquis."

Though there was little that I believed or trusted about Raj, I did know that he loved his nephew. Back in the day when he was my beloved brother-in-law, he was our go-to babysitter. Anytime Tyrone and I needed help with Marquis, Raj was there. But we were a long ways away from those days.

"Thank you," I said, and then, turned my attention back to the toaster. If I could've thought of a way to be even ruder, I would have done it.

"How's Syreeta?"

It had to be grief because I couldn't remember ever being so angry this many times in one day.

I swung around, and with all the pain in my voice that came from losing my son, I said, "She's good, Raj. Now that her face has stayed out of the way of your fists."

It wasn't enough for me that I could almost see the heat rising beneath his skin. No, since he was bold enough to come to my home, since he was bold enough to confront me, since he was bold enough to ask about my best friend, I had to go in. "And don't ask me for her number so that you can track her down and beat her again."

"I would never do that."

"Yeah, right."

"I already know she's in Germany."

That made me pause and get mad at Tyrone all over again. My husband and I had a deal; he was never supposed to tell his brother anything about Syreeta.

"Look," Raj began, holding up his hands as if he were surrendering to me. "I didn't mean any harm by asking about Syreeta. I just wanted to know how she was."

"I already told you. She's away from your fists."

He pressed his lips together like he was holding back words. Then he had the nerve to say, "Please tell her I asked about her."

"I'm not telling her a thing about you. If she's lucky, she'll die without ever hearing your name again."

That got to him, I could tell. But it got to me, too. I didn't want to talk about death right now—not even with Raj.

But it was just that I really didn't like this man. He and I had fought a battle that he almost won. It had started because of my girlfriend Syreeta. I couldn't even remember how many years ago it was when I introduced the two, but only months after the introduction, they'd become live-in lovers. That had lasted for years.

Until their lovefest turned into some kind of boxing match that only Raj could win.

I would never forget that first call.

"Jan, please, come and get me," Syreeta cried.

"Ree! Where are you?"

"At home. Raj got mad, and he hit me."

"Oh, my God," I said, not able to believe it.

"He beat me up," she continued.

"I'll be right there."

I still had a couple of hours to go before I was supposed to get off from work, but I told my supervisor that I had a family emergency and she let me clock out. I raced to Raj's apartment, and when I got there, I was shocked to see that my best friend had lied. Raj hadn't beaten her up. He'd kicked her ass like she was a man.

There had never been a time when I shook as much as I did when I helped Syreeta toss a couple of things into an overnight bag. I got her out of there, but then the next decision was where she would go. She didn't want to come home with me, and I agreed, thinking that my home would be the first place Tyrone's brother would look. Not that I ever thought Raj would go up against his brother; still, I didn't want to take that chance. So we checked her into a Ramada Inn.

When I was sure she was okay, I left her at the hotel and went home to find out from my husband what the hell was wrong with his brother.

Tyrone was just as shocked as I was, though, and he kept asking me, "Are you sure?" *as if I couldn't trust my eyes.*

"I'm sure. And she needs to have your brother arrested."

Tyrone had called his brother, not reaching him until the next morning, when Raj told Tyrone that he was at the hotel, picking up Syreeta.

"We just had a little lovers' situation," Raj had convinced Tyrone.

I was shocked, until I spoke to Syreeta.

"He said he's sorry, and he won't do it again."

"Syreeta, you know that's not true."

"He means it. And I believe in giving everyone a second chance. I love him. And I know it won't happen again."

I had prayed that night that Syreeta was right; it turned out that she was wrong.

But even as I remembered that time and how awful it was, gazing at Raj now, standing in front of me with an expression that looked like I'd cut him, I wished I hadn't talked about death.

It was just that every time I saw this man, I wanted to hurt him. He'd caused so much chaos—not only with what he'd done to Syreeta, but also by what he tried to do to me . . . and Tyrone.

"I'm sorry," Raj said. "About everything, Jan, I'm really sorry."

I didn't know what it was. Maybe it was the grief that had my heart so hard. But all that came out of me was, "You're right. You are sorry."

"You're not going to give me a break, are you?"

"No more than the breaks you gave to Syreeta. Let me see." I held up my fingers as if I were about to count them off. "You gave her a broken nose, a broken arm, a broken—"

"I'll leave now."

I lowered my arms. "Do that."

He took a couple of steps away from me and turned back. "I've changed."

"I think Charles Manson says that every time he's up for parole."

"Wow!" He shook his head. "Well, I've heard that you've changed, too. I guess that's something that you, me, and Charles have in common."

He turned around and walked out, leaving me alone with that zinger ringing in my ears.

Damn!

My son had just been murdered and now I had to deal with this? There was no way I would be able to handle it.

No way.

Chapter 7

I was in this never-ending state of inertia. The clock ticked, but time didn't move. My days became known by numbers and today was day three. The third full day of my life without Marquis.

But then I rolled over in my bed and felt the cool sheets. In my mind, I changed the number of this day. Now this became day two. The second morning that I woke up without Tyrone in the bed next to me.

I pushed myself up and once again wondered—where was my husband? Had another night passed when I'd slept alone? It wasn't until I was sitting all the way up that I noticed a piece of paper peeking out from beneath his pillow.

Babe: I'm at Raj's house. We're working on a few things. Mama's there with you. And I left the car. Call me the moment you wake up. Love you, babe. Need you. Call me.

"Love you, babe," I whispered as I folded the paper in half. "Need you, too."

My husband's concern showed all through the note. He cared so much that he didn't want me to be alone. But he didn't care enough to be the one here with me.

Reaching over to the nightstand, I picked up my cell phone.

I scrolled, then clicked, then asked, "May I speak to Detective Ferguson, please," when the phone on the other end was answered.

And like yesterday, I didn't have to wait.

"Ferguson."

"This is Janice Johnson. I was calling to see when I would be able to . . . see my son."

"Good morning, Mrs. Johnson," he began in that friendly tone again. I'd expected something else this morning; I'd expected to feel as if I was becoming a nuisance. "I can check on that and get back to you."

"Please do."

Like yesterday, I hung up without a good-bye or a thank-you. I didn't have room for niceties as long as my son was being held hostage.

The tap on the door made me look up, and when I said, "Come in," Delores stepped inside my bedroom.

"Good, you're awake." She was already dressed, today donning a black wrap dress. "I didn't want to knock too early."

"I was just getting up." I raised the paper that I still held. "Tyrone left me a note. He stayed with Raj?"

Delores nodded as she sat on the edge of our bed. "Nobody is getting a lot of sleep around here."

I didn't bother to tell her that she was wrong about that. Breathing was almost impossible and eating was almost unthinkable . . . but sleeping? I was doing that well.

She continued, "They knew you weren't comfortable with Raj and his friends being here. So, since they wanted to talk about . . . some things, they headed over to Raj's house."

My eyes narrowed.

Delores added, "Tyrone wanted me to stay with you and take you over to my place this morning."

I folded my arms across my chest. "I hope Raj isn't trying to talk Tyrone into doing something stupid."

Delores popped off the bed, pursed her lips, and looked down at me as if I'd just insulted her because I'd insulted her son.

"You know that the Guardians are nothing more than vigilantes," I kept on, not caring about how Delores felt. "And if they do something, that's only going to make this situation worse."

"I don't know how anything can be worse than this, Jan," Delores said, resting one hand on her hip. "How can anything be worse than Marquis being dead?"

It must've been the way I glared at her that made her say, "Look, I just think that everyone's nerves and feelings and emotions are fragile right now and—"

"That's not it at all. Even if this weren't about Marquis, I wouldn't want to be involved with killers."

"They're not killers!" But then, when I stared her down, she backed down. "Well, sometimes violence is what you need. Sometimes violence is the only language that white folks understand."

I couldn't believe this churchgoing, Bible-reading, scripture-quoting woman was saying this.

"Really?" I said. "What about the violence that hurts and even kills innocent people? Six people died in that car accident when the Guardians killed Watson."

"That is sad," she began. But then Delores had the nerve to shrug. "There are casualties in combat. Lots of good people die in war."

And that right there was the problem. Because smart people, people whom I respected, were buying the Guardians' propaganda, and then trying to sell it to others.

I glared at her, wanting her to take those words back. But she glared right back at me until she said, "I need to get to my house before people start coming by."

"Coming by?"

She nodded. "You know, people want to keep us company, they want to make sure we're okay."

"So they're not coming *over here* today?" I said. For the first time since Monday night, there was a little glee in my voice.

"No, we can all tell that it's a bit too much for you," Delores said. "With the way you keep going to bed early. It's a little insulting when the hostess leaves."

Hostess? This wasn't a party, though last night, it sounded like one.

Our home had filled up with even more people than the day before. People sat around pontificating about how everybody, everywhere, was against every black person. The gathering had turned into a hatefest that had nothing to do with Marquis.

"We really need to get going," Delores said. "Someone from your job called a little while ago and I gave them my address. They were on their way, so let's get a move on."

If I didn't want to sit with all of those people in my house, why would I go to her house and do it?

"Uh . . . there are some things I want to take care of here, so . . . you go on and I'll come later."

Delores looked at me with a *stop lying* expression. "Tyrone doesn't want you to be alone."

"I won't be alone."

She tilted her head in question.

I said, "I mean, I'm not going to stay here. I'm going to go out." I had two seconds to come up with a good lie. That was why only a bad one came out of my mouth. "I need to go shopping. Get some groceries."

Delores looked at me. "If you want to stay here by yourself, that's all you need to say." She shook her head as if I'd annoyed her. "I'm gonna call Tyrone. He's not gonna be happy." She pivoted and marched out of my room.

I stayed in place, sitting on my bed, and since Delores had left my bedroom door open, I sat until I heard the front door open then close. Only then did I push myself up and out of the bed.

But once I stood, the silence hit me.

I'd heard this silence before. Times when I'd found ways to get Tyrone and Marquis out of the house. Back then, I craved the peace that came from this quiet.

But this didn't feel like peace. The silence was so scary, so eerie, that I wanted to run after Delores and tell her to wait, that it would only take me three minutes to get dressed.

But I didn't do that. Instead, I walked from my bedroom, into the hall, then a few more feet, and I faced my greatest fear.

Standing in front of Marquis's closed bedroom door, I built up courage, and when I had enough, I rested my hand on his door, turned the knob, then pushed it open.

I inhaled, thinking just how normal it all looked. First, there were the miniblinds that were drawn as they always were.

"Marquis, open up those blinds. Open up those windows."

"Mama, what's wrong? I like it like this."

"Your bedroom is like a cave. You're not supposed to spend your life in the dark."

"Who says?"

"God! It's in the Bible. Look it up."

I heard Marquis's laughter as I stood in the hallway, and my glance roamed through his room, from his bed, to his desk, to the golf clubs that were propped up in one corner and his saxophone that sat in the other.

And then there were the bookcases, the two that he'd built with Tyrone. A project to earn a Boy Scout badge when he was just ten. It was an ambitious task that Marquis was so proud of when he finished. Especially once he stuffed the shelves with dozens of his favorite books.

My son. The reader.

That was when I closed his bedroom door.

Maybe I would have been able to go inside if Tyrone were here with me.

But he was not. So this was a big enough baby step for today. Now there was something else that I had to do.

It hadn't taken long to shower and dress. It was easy to move fast when you couldn't wait to get out. So no more than twenty minutes after Delores left, I pulled out of the driveway, and with a couple of quick lefts and then right turns, I was on I-76. The morning rush hour was drawing to an end, so it only took a little over fifteen minutes to maneuver my way to University Avenue.

I edged my car into a "No Parking" zone right in front of the Spelman Building, then I turned off the ignition.

The Thursday-morning pedestrian flow was in full swing as folks rushed to be at their desks before nine a.m. But even though there were plenty of people, I hardly saw them. Instead, my eyes, my focus, were on the windows.

This was so silly, I knew that. But silly hadn't stopped me. I kept peering at the building and wondering if there were any way for me to find out which window framed the room that belonged to the medical examiner. And where exactly was the morgue? Was it on the first floor, the second floor, or in the basement?

Yeah, this was definitely silly, but as silly as it was, I felt close to Marquis. Closer than I'd felt since he walked out of our home on Monday.

I leaned back in the seat even though I was sure Philly's Finest would soon be cruising by, telling me to move or get a ticket. Maybe they would let me stay if I told them that I was here to be near my dead son.

Closing my eyes, I took my mind inside that building and imagined the halls. I roamed through the space, checking each room until I found Marquis.

And then I sat with my son and wondered how he felt. Was he cold? Or was he hot? Was he aware of all of this? Or any of this? Could he see me? Feel me?

Did he know how much I loved him?

Shaking my head, I opened my eyes. "This is ridiculous." I needed to start my car and get away from this place. But it was my head that wanted me to leave; my heart told me that it was all right—I could stay.

I picked up my cell and clicked on the number that was locked in my phone. The rings were long like they always were and then, "Girl, can you say perfect timing? I just walked outside of my classroom. What's up!" Syreeta sang.

Her voice was filled with all kinds of cheer; she had no idea that I was about to ruin her day, her week, her month, her life.

"Hey."

"Jan," she said. "What's wrong?"

We'd only been friends for eighteen years, since our sophomore year in high school. But we had a heart connection that felt like we'd been together since birth. And that connection meant that I knew her and she knew me.

"Where are you?" I asked.

"I'm at school, getting ready to go in the lounge. What's wrong?"

"I have something to tell you, but I want you to be by yourself."

"Okay, I'm going in there now." There were a few seconds of silence before Syreeta said, "What's wrong?"

I took a deep breath, though I didn't take my eyes away from the building, away from the windows.

"I have some bad news."

"Is this sitting-down bad news?"

Even though she couldn't see me, I shrugged. Did it really matter if she was standing or sitting? What was the best position to hear the worst news of your life?

"It doesn't matter and I'm not going to drag this out." I paused. Others had spoken these words to me, but this was the first time the words would pass through my lips. I pushed them out. "Marquis is dead."

It was her turn to pause. "Marquis who?" she said.

I waited because I knew her response was nothing more than shock. After a couple of seconds, she added, "Please, Jan. Please take that back."

"I want to. I can't."

"Oh, my God," she cried. "What happened?"

I began at the beginning, chronicling my nightmare. I took my best friend through every step of my horror—from the police coming to our door to this moment. "And I decided to call you because I think I'm going crazy."

"Of course you are. Oh, my God, Janice."

The sorrow in Syreeta's voice pumped up the potency of my pain, reminding me once again of just how much this hurt. A tear seeped out, blinding me just a bit, obstructing my view of the place where my son lay, and I blinked that blockage away.

"Are you sure he's dead?" Syreeta asked.

That wasn't a dumb question. Because how many times had I asked myself the same thing?

"Yes, honey. I'm so sorry."

"Don't comfort me; I've got to comfort you. Oh, my God. I've got to come home. When's the funeral? When are we . . ." She paused and sobbed, "Oh, God!"

I wanted to hang up and just let her cry alone. Just let her get it out so that when she called me back, we'd be able to talk. But there was still one more thing that I needed to tell her.

"I have some more news."

"What else could there be?" she cried. "Nothing will ever be as bad as this!"

"This is not that bad . . . or maybe it is. I don't know." I took a breath. "Raj asked about you."

Silence.

"And he knows you're in Germany."

More silence.

"I'm sorry, Ree. I think Tyrone told him. I asked him not to, but I'm sure it was because he's—"

"Tyrone didn't tell him," she whispered. "I did."

If anyone had peeked into my car at that moment, they would have called the EMTs. Because I'm sure with the way I sat there, with my eyes closed, my mouth open, and my face contorted, I had to look like I'd just had a heart attack.

"Jan! Are you there?" Syreeta shouted into the phone.

"Uh . . ."

"I know what you're gonna say, but I knew he was worried about me and I wanted him to know I was safe. So I called him, and I call him . . . sometimes. Not often, but . . ."

She stopped as if she had explained it enough. There was so much I wanted to say, so many lectures I wanted to give. But all I said was "I understand."

"Do you really?"

No, I thought. "Yes," I said.

She must've felt that now she had my permission because she went on to ask about him. But I was too grief-weary to say anything except, "I think he's stirring up trouble. Tyrone stayed at Raj's place last night and I think they're trying to organize something."

"Good! They should! The Guardians will find out who did this and they'll take care of it. I know you don't like Raj or the Guardians, but they got started for exactly these kinds of situations and you've got to let those men do what men do."

Her words were so similar to what Delores had said to me.

"I really want to be there with you," Syreeta said.

Suddenly, all I wanted was to be alone. Just me and Marquis. "Can you call me later?"

"Of course. What time?"

"Anytime. There's something I have to do now."

"Okay. And, Janice, I'm so sorry, and I love you."

"I know." Then I hung up. For a moment, I took my eyes away from the building and looked down at the phone. But I didn't want to spend time trying to figure out the nonsense of grown folks. This time was for me and Marquis.

So I put down my phone and stared at the building for a little bit longer. I did that mind-tour thing again, sat in a room with my son, and then I started the ignition.

I rolled the car away from the curb, and I headed . . . I didn't have anyplace where I needed to go. So I headed to the place where I didn't want to be.

I headed home.

Chapter 8

My despair worsened when I saw Raj's truck parked in the driveway. I edged my car next to the truck, then marched to the front and unlocked my door with an attitude.

But then, there stood my husband, at the bottom of the stairs with outstretched arms. And I ran into his embrace.

"I'm so glad you're home," I said as Tyrone held me the way I needed to be held.

"Mama said that you went to the supermarket; why would you do that with all of the food that we have here?"

"No . . . I just needed . . ." I backed away from him. "I just didn't want to go to her house. And I knew your mom wasn't going to let me stay here alone, so I made that up."

"I told her not to leave you."

"And she didn't want to." With a sigh I turned into the living room. I waited until Tyrone sat down on the sofa with me to say, "I've been suffocating with all of the people; I just needed some space."

He nodded and took my hand. "So where did you go?"

I thought about it for a moment, then said, "To the morgue."

His eyes stretched wide. "They let you see Marquis?"

"No, I didn't go inside. I just needed to be close to him." I gave Tyrone a sideward glance. "You know what I mean?"

He nodded, and I leaned over, resting my head on his shoulder. He sat back and held me. "Not being able to see him is killing . . ." I paused. This situation had definitely made me more aware of my words. "It's so hard not to be able to see him."

"I know." He squeezed me tighter.

It was amazing the way Tyrone changed the sounds of silence that were in the house now. I was still cloaked in the black shroud of sadness, but with Tyrone here, I kinda had the feeling that I'd be able to shake that off one day, maybe like twenty or fifty years from now.

Then Tyrone pushed me away and interrupted our peace.

"Where are you going?" I asked when he stood.

"I need to take a shower. I came home to change."

I blinked. "You're going in to work?"

He shook his head. "No, I've got to get back to Raj's."

My eyes narrowed as I slowly stood, too. "Why? What are you doing over there? Why do you have to be over there every day, every night?"

He paused and then said, "We're making plans."

"For what?"

"Just for some rallies and protests, Jan. We're making calls now. Trying to get some advice."

"Advice about what?"

"We need the police to release the name of the man who murdered Marquis. They were supposed to do it right away, and we're going to make sure that happens."

"Tyrone, I really don't want you involved—"

"How can you say that?" he asked, not letting me finish. "I'm already involved. It was my son who was murdered."

"And he was my son, too, but if you go down to the police station and start trouble—"

"First of all, this isn't about trouble. This is about getting the police to do the right thing."

"And you know that nowhere in this country can black people force the police to do anything."

"Well, we're gonna try."

"And that's what scares me. Because if you confront the police, they're not going to back away. They're going to beat you up, then lock you up. I can't, Tyrone. I can't be grieving for Marquis and worried about you."

"There's nothing for you to worry about."

"I would've believed that before Monday night."

"I can take care of myself."

I nodded. "And I believe that—except for when the police are involved. And I won't be able to live if something were to happen to you, too."

He paused and softened his tone, but not his words. "Well, I'm sorry, Jan. But this is all about justice for me." I shuddered when he added, "And I don't care what price I have to pay."

I rubbed my arms against the chill that his words ushered into the room.

He said, "Don't you want justice for Marquis?"

I stayed quiet for a moment, thinking. What was it that I wanted? Finally, "I do. I want justice for my son. But I want my son more than I want justice."

His eyes were thin slits when he asked, "What does that mean? What do you think the police will do?"

"I don't know. But don't you remember that case where a body disappeared from the examiner's office?" I didn't give him a chance to answer. "It's bad enough that we've lost Marquis. But if his body disappeared and I couldn't lay him to rest . . ." I shook my head. "I don't know what I would do."

"That's not going to happen."

"How can you say that? Look at what *has* happened. With what happened to Marquis, we now know that the improbable is possible."

He didn't even take a breath before he said, "Well, you know what? If they keep Marquis, if they don't return him to us, if they lose his body, it doesn't matter."

I pressed my hand against my mouth, shocked at his words. "How can you say that?" I cried.

"Janice, our son is already gone. None of that is going to bring him back, but if I can do something about *why* he's gone, then I've got to do it."

"But all I'm asking is that you wait. It's just been a few days. Why can't you wait and see what the police will do?"

"I already know what they're going to do. Hell, they're already doing it. They're protecting the man who murdered our son. So there's nothing inside of me, as a black man in this country, that will let me wait."

Tears sprang into my eyes as my mind filled with all kinds of visions of what was about to happen.

His voice was calmer when he said, "I understand how you feel, but you've got to understand me." He placed his hands on my shoulders and made me face him. "I'm a man. And they took my son. And now they have to do the right thing. Or . . ."

I waited for him to finish his sentence, but he just stood there as if he'd given me a complete thought. "Or?"

He shook his head and then turned away from me.

"Tyrone."

He kept moving, out of the living room, and then I heard his footsteps as he trotted up the steps.

"Tyrone!"

By the time I couldn't hear him anymore, tears had dampened my cheeks. Standing there, I put all kinds of finishes on Tyrone's sentence.

Or . . . we will find the man who did this.

Or . . . we'll turn this city upside down.

Or . . . someone will pay for our son's death.

Slowly, I lowered myself back onto the sofa. There was no way this was going to end well. But what was I supposed to do? How could I stop Tyrone from doing what he really believed he had to do?

I was so caught up in the fear that when my cell vibrated, I jumped. Looking down at the screen, I frowned.

Private.

I never answered private numbers in the past. But the past had changed my present. So with one hand I swiped away my tears, and with the other I accepted the call.

"Hello."

"Janice?"

It was his voice. And it rendered me silent.

"Janice?" He called my name again.

It was the way he said my name, the way he always said my name, that made my heart flutter. Still.

"Yes, this is Janice."

I said it as if he didn't know.

"This is Caleb."

He said it as if I didn't know.

"Hi." And then I stopped because I couldn't get my brain to tell me what to say next.

"I'm calling because . . . I just had to speak with you."

The last time I'd heard his voice, he'd called and said those same words. But the last time, three years ago, I'd hung up on him. And that was exactly what I should've done now.

But I didn't.

As if he knew that I couldn't speak, he said, "I heard about Marquis, and I'm so sorry."

I found my voice and a couple of words. "Thank you." Then after I let a few more seconds go by, I was able to add, "How did you hear?" I only asked that question to fill up the space of time. Though I hadn't been out much, the news had to be spreading, at least through the neighborhood. So it wasn't such a big surprise that it had reached the church. My church. The church Tyrone, Marquis, and I used to attend.

But then Caleb said, "I saw it on the news. It's on right now. And as soon as I saw it, I called you."

"What? It was on the news?"

I jumped up and sprinted from the living room, glancing up to the second-floor landing before I dashed to the back of the house and our family room.

"Yes," Caleb said as I searched for the remote. "You didn't know?"

I didn't even answer him as I clicked on the television. "What channel?"

"I saw it on NBC, but I'm sure . . ."

The rest of his words didn't make it to my ears. My mind could only process one thought at a time, and right now what filled the television screen was most important to me. I sank onto the couch.

There was a man and a woman in the front, dozens of men behind them. The woman held the mic in front of the man, who wore brown fatigues and a brown beret, just like the rest of the men.

The man in the front spoke. "That's all we want," my brother-in-law said. "Justice for our family. Justice for Marquis. We want to make sure that murderers stop getting a free pass to kill black boys because of this racist law called Stand Your Ground."

"I hope I didn't upset you." Caleb's voice came through.

"No." I pressed the phone to my ear, but I didn't say more as the reporter said, "So there you have it."

The woman, Clarissa Austin, was one of the main reporters in Philadelphia. She always handled the hard news, street news.

The camera had turned away from Raj and was now totally on her.

"This shooting happened three days ago, on Monday, the day after Mother's Day. And the family has been given no information, no details about the death of their son. We contacted the police commissioner, but were told they have no statement at this time. Back to you in the studio."

The camera switched to the news anchors at the desk of the local station, and the black man said, "So, Clarissa, the name of the shooter has not been released?"

The image switched back to the reporter on the street; she shook her head. "No, and that's all Marquis Johnson's family has been asking for, at least at this time. They want to know the name of the shooter, the circumstances of the shooting, and they want to know why, with another young, unarmed man being dead . . . why more hasn't been done to move along the investigation. But we're going to stay on this case."

I muted the television, though my eyes didn't leave the screen. It wasn't until I heard, "Are you there?" that I remembered Caleb.

"Yes," I said. "I'm sorry. I hadn't seen the news report."

"Well, then I'm glad I called. Again, I am so sorry, Jan. I can't imagine what you're going through. Marquis was such a special young man."

"It's been tough," I said. "And what's even harder is that we're just waiting."

"I know. Waiting for the police to do an investigation has got to be—"

"No, not that." And then it poured out of me. How I hadn't seen Marquis, how I wanted to see him so badly, how I'd spent the morning like a crazy mother hanging outside of the morgue.

I talked to Caleb the way I used to. Talked to him the way I did right before I ended up in his bed.

"I can't believe you're going through this, and I know it's scary. But you have to trust God. You've got to know that He's not going to give you more than you can handle."

It was one of those Christian clichés, but you know what? It was good enough for me. Because no one had given me anything else to hold on to.

"Is there anything that I can do?"

He was already doing what I needed—he was listening to me, he was understanding, he was with me on the phone, and I knew that if I asked him, he would be right here, sitting next to me on the sofa.

"No, but thank you for asking, thank you for calling."

"Well, there is one thing that I want to do. I really would love to pray with you. I mean, I know maybe we shouldn't be speaking to each other. But I feel in my spirit that we should. I feel like I should be there—"

"Janice!"

Startled, I sat up. Looked up. And there stood Tyrone.

How long had he been standing there?

"I'll call you back" was all I said before I clicked off the phone and stood.

I expected my heart to be ramming its way through my chest, but it wasn't. It didn't feel like it was beating at all.

Tyrone frowned. "What's wrong? Who was that on the phone?"

"Uh . . . uh . . ." I thought about all the lies I'd told before when I was involved with Caleb. I thought about how I'd promised Tyrone that I'd never lie again. "It was Wilma. You know, Wilma. From work. From the post office."

"Oh, is she going to come over?"

"Yeah," I said, then prayed that she wasn't already over at my mother-in-law's house.

He released a small breath like he was relieved. "That's good, because I really don't want you to be alone."

Then stay, I thought.

He said, "I really want you to come with me."

That was not going to happen, but I didn't tell him that right away. Instead, I said, "I saw the news. They were talking about Marquis . . . with Raj."

When he made no moves to grab the remote to replay what I'd just watched, I realized that he was not surprised. "Good! Great! We're making progress."

"They were talking to Raj," I said. "And the Guardians were there."

"You know the media is always interested in what the Brown Guardians are doing. That's why they were there, that's why they're involved."

"I wish you had told me." Then I wrapped my arms around myself. "I just hope that the police don't get pissed off."

"They need to worry about the fact that I'm beyond pissed off," Tyrone growled. I mean, he actually growled.

"Tyrone . . ."

The plea in my voice made him bring it all the way down.

"They're not going to do anything to Marquis," he said with certainty in his tone. "Now that the media is involved, they're going to play their cards straighter. We still can't trust them, but . . ." It must have been the way I shuddered that made Tyrone wrap me inside his arms. "We still can't trust them, but now we have a better chance of everything going our way."

I said nothing, just breathed and hoped and prayed.

"I just want you to understand," he said.

I nodded as if I understood, though we both knew that I didn't. But there was nothing more for me to say.

"I wish you would come with me," he said again.

I guess there *was* one final thing for me to say. "No."

Now he nodded like he understood, though we both knew that he didn't. He said, "What's going to happen when Wilma leaves? You'll be alone."

"Then stay. Stay so that I won't be by myself."

His eyes looked like the words he was about to say caused him pain. "I want to, but I can't."

I shrugged. "And I can't."

I could tell that I was breaking his heart, and I wondered if he knew how much he was breaking mine.

Tyrone leaned toward me, resting his lips on my forehead for a long, long moment. "I'll be back as soon as I can."

I nodded.

"But promise me . . . if you have to, need to, go over to Mama's." Tyrone kissed me good-bye, turned around, and walked out the door. I followed him to the front, then, from the window, watched him jump into Raj's truck and roll out of the driveway. But once he hit the street, he punched the accelerator, blasting off like he was on a mission.

Turning around, I sighed and returned to the family room. The news was still on, though there was no sign of the Guardians.

I sat for a couple of seconds, trying not to do what was on my mind. But still, I picked up my cell phone.

It was Wilma.

My lie still hung in the air—right next to the loneliness that Tyrone had left with me.

After only another moment of thought, I scrolled through the last calls, and saw it—*Private*.

I'd forgotten. Now how was I going to call Caleb back?

Was he calling from the cell that he had three years ago? Even if he was, I didn't have that number, having deleted it on the night that Tyrone and I reconciled. Maybe I could call him at the church.

But I shot that thought down. I didn't need to be talking to my ex-lover, my ex-pastor.

Especially not now.

Chapter 9

I was sipping coffee. Alone. Then I heard his car, probably Raj's truck, when it rolled into the driveway. In the past, whenever one of us heard the other coming home, we'd meet at the door. But this morning, I didn't even move. Just sat there sipping mocha. Because . . . the past had changed the present.

I listened for his movement, heard his footsteps on the walkway, his key in the door, the lock click, and then a few more moments and he stood next to me.

"Hey, babe." He spoke and then kissed my forehead, as if his staying out all night was normal, an acceptable thing. As if he didn't remember all that had happened when he stayed away like this before. Yes, the present was different from the past. But . . .

I wanted Tyrone to know I was pissed without saying it because it seemed so petty to be mad when we were dealing with all of this. But I couldn't help it. I *was* mad. Because Tyrone didn't want to spend his nights with me.

Now, of course, he could say that I didn't want to spend my days with him, but my position seemed much more sound than his.

"Did you sleep well?" he asked.

I took a long sip of coffee, the coward's way of not speaking.

But after I swallowed, I said, "I did." What good would it do to let him know that this was the first night that I hadn't closed my eyes? That I had lain stretched out on the sofa in the family room, staring at the recliner where Marquis should've been sitting. And that I had kept my eyes open, hoping and praying that Tyrone would come home to me, even if it had been just for an hour.

"We're not doing much sleeping," he told me as if I'd asked him. "But we're getting things done." He didn't even pause. Just kept on talking as if this were a normal morning. "I hope Wilma stayed with you for a while. You didn't answer my texts last night, so I just thought you were asleep after Wilma left."

"Wilma?"

"Yeah, Wilma. When she came over yesterday. I hope she stayed for a while," he said as he popped a K-Cup into the Keurig.

I was so mad that I wasn't even going to cover up that lie. I just nodded—that was going to have to be enough of an answer for him. And then, when he just nodded, I got even more pissed. That *was* enough for him. It was like my husband didn't even care about what I was going through, what I was going through alone.

When his coffee cup was full, he took a sip, then turned back to me. "I really hate that you were here by yourself last night."

Well, at least he did care. Kind of.

I put my cup down on the counter and willed myself to keep my voice steady. Even though I was angry, an argument was not what I wanted. "I just don't understand why you have to be out all night."

He sighed as if he were tired of explaining it to me, but then responded as if he were trying to be patient. "We're getting things done."

"You still need to rest."

"I can't."

"You have to."

"I can't," he said, his voice a bit louder, his patience dissipating. "I can't close my eyes. Because every time I come close to sleep . . ." He shook his head and began a new thought. "I wasn't there for Marquis on Monday, but I'm damn sure going to be there for him now."

I didn't want to soften, but how could I not? I could hear the anger and the misery and the grief all rolled into his voice every time he spoke. Now my anger was just a fraction of what it'd been when he walked through the door.

He said, "Janice, I know you're not happy with any of this. I wish you could be by my side as I fight for everything right for Marquis. But I get that you can't. At least not yet. Not until we bury our son.

"But for me, his burial doesn't mean what it means to you. In my head, I can't see the funeral, I can't see burying him, I can't see anything except the justice that's due to my son. That's all my eyes can see."

I got that.

And I got it even more when he stepped closer to me. "I just want you to remember that I love you. I love you so much."

Before I could show him that I loved him, too, the doorbell rang. And the corners of his lips twitched.

I leaned away from him and folded my arms across my chest. Was Tyrone getting ready to smile? How could he smile now when I wasn't sure that I'd ever smile again?

He took my hand. "Come with me," he said.

I wanted to snatch my hand away and stay in my mad state of mind, but when the doorbell rang again, curiosity made me slide off the bar stool and let him lead me.

Tyrone held me with one hand, and with the other, he opened the door. And there stood Raj.

I growled.

Raj stepped aside and then, I burst into tears.

My best friend was a teeny tiny little thing—at least compared to me. I dwarfed Syreeta's five-foot-two-inch frame with my own, which had me standing just a little over five seven. And last week at this time, I weighed a good one-sixty, one-seventy. That was before death had taken more than my heart; it'd stolen my appetite, too.

But no matter what I weighed, I still jumped into Syreeta's arms as if she were the larger of the two of us.

"What are you doing here?"

Syreeta gasped as if she were struggling to breathe. "What do you think?" she said, sounding like a frog.

"I'm sorry," I said, even though I wasn't. I pulled her into the house. "How did you get here?"

"Well"—she followed me inside—"they have this new invention called the airplane."

Tears still rolled from my eyes when I laughed and turned to Tyrone. "You knew about this?"

"He knew about it; he arranged it," Syreeta answered for my husband. "I mean, I was coming anyway, but Tyrone got me on that red-eye last night. He said you needed me."

She had barely explained it all before I had my arms wrapped around Tyrone. "Thank you," I whispered into his ear.

Syreeta said, "And then I couldn't fly into Philly because all of those flights were full. So I flew to New York and Raj picked me up early this morning."

I had forgotten about my brother-in-law, seemingly forgiven by all except for me. But I was proud that I was able to get "thank you" out of my mouth, then stop there without adding a curse word.

Turning back to Syreeta, I hugged my best friend again. "I am so glad you're here."

"There is no place else I'd want to be right now." Leaning away from me, she added, "Jan, I still can't believe this." Her words were a trigger, shooting tears into her eyes.

I sat on the second stair and she lowered herself next to me right as Tyrone's cell phone rang. I hardly noticed when he and Raj stepped away from us and into the living room.

She held my hand when she asked, "How are you getting through this?"

I shook my head. "I don't know. I'm really shocked that I'm still breathing, and the world is still spinning without Marquis. Kind of feels like everything should've stopped."

She nodded. "I couldn't stop thinking about Marquis on the plane. I kept remembering when he was born, and when he was five, and when I got him his first Hot Wheels set, and then, when I bought him his first cell phone. How can he be gone?" she wailed. "And for what reason? His life was taken away for nothing."

Syreeta's words had been my thoughts all night long.

"And Raj said that the medical examiner still has our baby."

But then, Tyrone rushed from the living room to where we sat. "They don't have our son anymore," he said.

Syreeta and I looked up with matching frowns.

Tyrone reached for my hand, pulled me up, and as he wrapped his arms around me, he said, "We don't have to wait anymore, baby. We can go see our son."

I didn't dare lean away to ask him if his words were true.

Because I would've been so hurt if somehow his words had gotten jumbled in my head and he hadn't just told me that I could see Marquis.

"Are you saying that the ME has released him?" my best friend asked for me.

Tyrone leaned back just a little so that he could look at me, but at the same time, he still held me as if he knew I needed his strength. "Yes, I just got the call. This is one of the things we've been working on, but I didn't want to tell you. Didn't want to get your hopes up."

"So you got the police to release him? For real?"

"We did," Tyrone said, glancing at Raj. "It just took a little bit of—"

I didn't even let him finish before I wrapped my arms around his neck. I wanted to say thank you aloud, but I couldn't get words past the clog in my throat. "Where is he?" I asked. There were tears in my eyes and a smile on my face, the manifestation of all that I was feeling: elation . . . I was going to see my son . . . devastation . . . I was going to see my dead son.

"They sent Marquis where I told them . . . to Marshalls Funeral Home. That's where you wanted him, right?"

I had never thought about where I would send the body of anyone that I loved. But Marshalls was a staple in our neighborhood.

"That's fine," I said. "Can we go now?"

"Yes."

That was all I needed to hear. I didn't even look around for my purse. Tyrone would be with me; I wouldn't need a wallet, I didn't need makeup. I just needed to go.

Spinning around, I was the first one to the door, but as I grabbed the knob, three voices behind me shouted, "Wait!"

I turned around and frowned. As long as I'd waited, I couldn't imagine why these people were standing there, telling me to wait.

It was my best friend who stepped up. "I know this has been tough, girl. And I know your heart is broken. And I'm going to be with you all the way." She paused. "But I am never going to go anywhere with you while you're dressed like that!"

Her words didn't make sense. Until I looked down, and took in my bathrobe and slipper-covered feet.

Really? If they hadn't been here, would I have walked out of the house dressed like this?

I looked back up, then down again. And when I raised my head and looked into their faces, I laughed. I mean, I really laughed. I leaned my head back and let go of a big one. I laughed in a way that I'd never thought would happen again. I laughed until tears came out of my eyes.

Chapter 10

I waited for the appropriate time. I waited until after Vincent and Pamela Marshall met us at the door of their funeral home and led us into a room where Tyrone, Syreeta, and I sat on one side of the table and the funeral-home directors sat on the other.

I waited until the Marshalls gave us their appropriate condolences and then waited through all of their promises of how they were going to take care of us and our son. I let them get through all of that, not really hearing too many of their words, before I asked the only question that was important to me. "Is Marquis here now?"

"Yes." Pam nodded solemnly. "He arrived just an hour ago," she said as if my son had come to her place of business of his own volition.

Again I let an appropriate moment pass. Then, "I want to see my son."

Vincent Marshall nodded. "We're thinking that we'll just need a few days. We'll work straight through the weekend and you can have the funeral on Monday. I know that's soon, but you've been waiting so long. And it would be a week since." He paused, and when neither Tyrone nor I responded, he asked, "Is Monday a good day, or do you want a little more time?"

I shrugged because I hadn't thought about any of that. There was only one thing on my mind. I said, "We haven't decided." Then I looked at Tyrone for confirmation. When my husband nodded, I continued, "What I'm saying is that I want to see Marquis. Like right now."

I startled both Mr. and Mrs. Mortician. At least that's what I thought by the way they pushed back in their chairs, then with wide eyes glanced at each other as if my words were blasphemous.

"Well," the wife began.

"That's quite unusual," the husband finished. "Marquis is not ready for you. We have to prepare him. And like I said, we're willing to work over the weekend."

He went on to explain all the things a mortician had to do, and it all sounded like blah, blah, blah to me. Didn't he realize that I didn't care about the length of time my son had been dead and the need for embalming? He didn't need to be cleaned up for me.

I wanted to see Marquis, hold Marquis, kiss Marquis before they drained the blood from him. I had to see my dead son for myself.

When the mortician paused, I said, "I know this is unusual, but I really want to see Marquis before . . . before . . . before he's not there anymore."

Now the morticians didn't just glance at each other. They looked at Tyrone and Syreeta as if they were asking for help. As if they were trying to say that one of them needed to explain to me that my son was already gone.

But I hadn't lost my mind. These were the thoughts of a mother.

My husband said, "We'll only be back there for a few minutes," as if he understood my need. "Just take us to our son."

I could've hugged him, kissed him, but all I did was thank him with a squeeze of his hand.

There was another round of glances, but they could have looked at each other all day. I had waited all this time. A few more minutes, a few more hours, a few more exchanged glances didn't mean a thing to me.

Mr. Marshall tried one last time. "We just want him to be ready for you."

"He's my son. He's ready now."

With a sigh and a nod, Mr. Marshall stood, and his wife did the same. Tyrone held my hand as we followed them, but it wasn't until we were at the door that I realized that Syreeta was still sitting at the table.

"Come on," I said, wondering what she was waiting for.

She shook her head. "No. This first time. This is for you and Tyrone."

Now I shook my head. "You loved him, too. Come with us."

I knew without even looking at Tyrone that he was nodding his agreement. When Syreeta stood, I was relieved. I wasn't going to be able to do this without her and Tyrone. I'd need them both, one on each side to hold me up.

It was the longest walk down that hall, to the room at the end. Mr. Marshall paused for a moment, as if giving me a final chance to change my mind. I nodded and he opened the door.

I would never be able to recall what the room looked like or what else was in it. Because my eyes focused right away on the long table at the far wall in front of us. A table with a body covered to his neck by a white sheet.

The place where my son lay.

Like I had hoped, Tyrone stood on one side and my petite

friend was on the other as we made the slow jaunt down the center of the room.

As I walked, my eyes didn't even blink.

Even though seeing Marquis was all I'd been able to think about, I'm not sure what I expected. Sure, I figured that plenty of tears might fall, and I might even pass out.

But it wasn't like that at all.

"Marquis," I whispered when we finally stood over him. "What happened?"

The heat of my emotions were behind my lids, but not a tear dropped, though my heart cracked. I knew that I would never be the same.

But even with all of that pain, there was something else.

There was an angelic peace over Marquis. He looked like he was asleep. He looked like he was happy.

He looked like he'd seen the face of God.

And with that, there was nothing for me to cry about.

I tried to lean forward but Tyrone and Syreeta each had their own vise grip on me.

"I'm fine," I said, shaking from their grasps. When I was free, I waited just a moment, then leaned down and lifted my baby's head and held him to my chest.

He was so cold, he was so stiff, all the things I imagined a dead body to be. None of the ways that I ever expected to see my son.

"I'm so sorry," I told him as I rocked him, even in that awkward stance. "I'm so sorry that I wasn't there to save you."

Closing my eyes, I set my mind free and I saw all the hopes and dreams I had for Marquis: his graduation from high school, then college, probably graduate school. Eight years from now, he would've had his doctorate, though never once had Marquis said anything about a Ph.D. But now, as I held him in this state, I could see that.

I saw the doctorate that he would never receive, the run for president of the United States of America that would never happen. I saw his wedding and then his children, my grandchildren who would never come from his loins. I held my son and imagined his destiny, a destiny that would never be.

As the first tears warmed my cheeks, I said a little prayer thanking God. Because even if God had told me on the day that Marquis was born that he was going to walk this earth for this short while, not even living to celebrate his eighteenth birthday, I still would've told God to bring him on. Because these had been the best seventeen years of my life.

Thank you, Lord, I said inside. Thank you so much for what you gave to me.

"Jan," Tyrone whispered in my ear. "Come on, baby. Come on."

Tyrone wanted me to let Marquis go and I knew that it was time. So I kissed the top of his head, then gently rested him back onto the metal table before I stood up straight.

With the backs of my hands, I flicked every single tear away. I didn't want to cry anymore. Tears didn't ease the pain anyway. Tears only drained me, and now I needed to get myself together. Because over the next few days, whatever I did would be my very last acts for Marquis.

So, no tears. Just strength.

"Okay," I said to Tyrone and Syreeta. My eyes were still on my son when I said, "I'm ready."

With a final kiss to Marquis's forehead, I turned and hooked my arm through Syreeta's.

She sobbed as we walked toward the door, and now I was the one who held her up.

But then . . . I'd taken at least a dozen steps before I noticed that my husband wasn't by my side. "Tyrone?" I whispered his name.

Together, Syreeta and I turned and saw Tyrone right where we'd left him—standing over Marquis. His shoulders shook, and for just a moment, he wailed.

"Oh, God!" Syreeta tried to pull away from me, but I didn't let her go.

"I'm going to get him," she cried.

I shook my head. "No. He needs time with his son."

Syreeta hesitated as if she wasn't sure that she should trust my words. But then she stepped back and held my hand as sobs raked through my husband's body. Just like Syreeta, I so wanted to go to him. But just like Tyrone knew what I needed, I knew what he needed. Even though he wasn't really alone, it was just him and Marquis. Father to son. Man to young man.

There were things he had to say, and really, if I had been stronger, I would've left the room altogether. Given him complete privacy. But I couldn't leave. I had to be here for Tyrone . . . just in case.

Time passed, though I didn't count the seconds or the minutes. I just watched my husband until he finally stood erect. His back was still to us, but I could see that he was wiping his tears away before he turned and faced me.

Now I could move toward him, and he moved toward me. We met in the middle and he grabbed me so hard and squeezed me so tight . . . it was just what I needed.

He sighed and leaned back.

"Are you okay?" I asked.

He shook his head. "No." But he took my hand anyway, and we turned toward the door.

I held out my other hand to Syreeta, and the three of us left the room, though I was the only one who paused and looked back. And said a silent good-bye to my son.

Chapter 11

It was the peace that God had given me that allowed me to have enough strength to sit. To sit and listen to the morticians talk about the next steps.

But sitting was all Mr. and Mrs. Marshall were going to get from me. Because once we left Marquis and returned to the conference room, all I could do was sit. And nod as Mr. Marshall asked all kinds of questions about caskets, and programs, and flowers—all of which came at a high price.

It was surprising the way Mr. Marshall spoke about death. As if it were an everyday occurrence. I guess for him, it was.

After what sounded like a soliloquy, Mr. Marshall pushed back from the table. "Well, now that we have all of that down, let's take a look at caskets."

He moved, his wife moved, Tyrone moved, Syreeta moved . . . and I stayed. When they looked back at me, I shook my head. "You do that, Tyrone."

He nodded, then kissed my forehead. "Stay with her," he directed Syreeta.

As they left the room, she sat next to me and held my hand.

She said nothing, at first. Then, "You sure you don't want to go back there?"

I shook my head. "I can't."

She waited a moment. "Okay. But you know, Tyrone doesn't have the best taste. I'm just sayin'. I don't want to see my godson in some green casket that looks like we're burying Shrek."

At first, my eyes widened, but then when I took in the seriousness of her expression, all I could do was giggle. And she giggled, too. The two of us were a giggling glob of a mess when the Marshalls and Tyrone walked back into the room.

Their confusion was in their frowns and Syreeta and I did our best to straighten up.

Tyrone's eyebrows were still bunched together when he sat down and said, "I picked out a nice one, baby."

That was it! The two of us busted into a laugh that shook the funeral home's walls.

The Marshalls and Tyrone stared at us as we buckled over with laughter. And every time I tried to stop, all I could think about was Shrek.

But finally we were able to sit up straight and our laughter turned to snickers, then just a few giggles. The Marshalls and Tyrone sat like they were the only adults in the room, and when Syreeta and I finally got it together, Mr. Marshall continued, as serious as he was before. "The last thing we have to cover is where will the services be held? At your home church?"

That sucked every remnant of laughter out of the room.

Tyrone said, "We don't have a home church," in a tone that made me wonder why I hadn't addressed this with the Marshalls alone.

Because every time our home church was mentioned, every time Tyrone was reminded of my infidelity, no matter where we were, no matter how good our marriage was now, it felt like we went straight back to that time when my marriage was closer to being over than surviving.

"Well, you are more than welcome to have the services here. Would you like to see our chapel?" he asked as if he were about to take us on a tour of Disneyland.

"I'll let you know what I decide." Tyrone spoke without conferring with me. On every other inquiry, we were a team. But on this one, Tyrone was the head of the household. His words were enough; my opinion didn't count.

Because of my unforgivable sin.

"We'll have to know as soon as possible," Mrs. Marshall said. "We have to put the location on the program, and if you want to have it here, we have to be prepared," she explained, as if she were readying herself to host a party.

"I'll let you know. Tonight," my husband said. "We'll either have it here or at my mother's church."

Tyrone pushed back from the table, the signal that this meeting was over. When he reached for my hand, I breathed again. And when he held me close, I thanked God.

There were handshakes and good-byes and more condolences before Tyrone, Syreeta, and I stepped out of the room.

The halls of the funeral home were as silent as . . . a graveyard.

But then we stepped outside. And were accosted by shouting voices and blinding flashes. By the time my eyes adjusted, I saw four, maybe five people in front of us. With cameras. And microphones. Only one I recognized—Clarissa Austin.

"Mrs. Johnson!" she said. "I'm very sorry for your loss, but did you ever expect to find yourself in the center of one of these cases?"

I'd always told Marquis that there were no dumb questions, but

I wanted to turn back into the funeral home and go tell my son that I was wrong. Because this was one of the dumbest questions ever asked.

And I wanted to tell Clarissa that, too.

But Tyrone put his arm around me. "No comment," he said as he led me with quickened steps around the side of the building.

"Are you working with the Brown Guardians to force the police to release the name of the man who shot your son?"

Tyrone shoved me into our car while Syreeta jumped into the back. Before I could catch my breath, Tyrone was in the driver's seat, gunning the engine before he sped out of the parking lot.

As we drove away, I watched Clarissa along with the other reporters become smaller and smaller in the side-view mirror.

"What was that?" I asked, once I couldn't see them anymore.

"Hold on." We were about two blocks away from the funeral home when Tyrone pulled over to the curb. The car was still running, but he grabbed his cell, scrolled through his messages, then slapped his hand against the steering wheel. "Yes!"

"What?" Syreeta and I asked at the same time.

"Clarissa Austin, one of the reporters back there, worked with the Guardians and now the police are going to release the name of the man who murdered Marquis. They still haven't said when, but we're close, babe, we're close. And once we know who it is . . ."

Tyrone reached over and hugged me and I hugged him back. From the backseat, Syreeta clapped.

But while the two of them were thrilled, I wasn't so sure. Because once they had a name, what would the Guardians do?

Chapter 12

Almost eight hours had passed since Tyrone had dropped me and Syreeta off.

And once again I told him, "I wish you would stay home with me."

"You have Syreeta."

"But I want you."

"And I want to be here, too," he said. "But I can't stay here without our son, Jan. I can't lay my head on a pillow in this house." Then he kissed me and made a promise. "We're getting close. And we're not gonna stop."

Then he dashed out the door, but like he'd said, at least this time, I wasn't alone.

Even though Syreeta was the perfect person to be with me, I wanted my husband. So now I stood in almost the same place where he'd left me. Just standing. Just staring. Just praying.

"That's not going to bring him back any sooner."

I glanced up at my best friend, who'd changed hours ago into jeans and a T-shirt. She sauntered down the stairs the way only an I-would've-been-a-model-if-I'd-been-a-foot-taller woman could.

"Come on, get away from that door." She guided me into the family room. "Let's take the load off, and maybe have some wine. You got some Moscato, right?"

I nodded as I flopped onto the couch. "We have wine, but Tyrone refuses to buy Moscato. He says that's for colored girls only."

She laughed. "He's probably right. But never fear!" She turned and sprinted from the room.

I had no idea where Syreeta was going, but I was too tired to care. I leaned back, closed my eyes, and wondered if I could stay this way till Monday.

Our trip to the funeral home had been exhausting enough, but everything that followed had stripped away what little strength I had. From finding out that the police were going to release the man's name, to going to Delores's and arranging to have Marquis's funeral at her church, to sitting in her crowded house with friends and church members all wallowing in the sadness of this occasion, it was too much.

And it really went over the top when Raj and a couple other Guardians rode up, in full regalia, looking like they were going to war.

That was my cue; I didn't even ask Tyrone if he was ready to leave. I just stood up and he and Syreeta followed me.

In the car, I once again gave Tyrone all of my facts and all of my opinions about the Brown Guardians. He just nodded, and said nothing. Until we got home—then he explained, then he left me again.

"Okay, you don't have to stand and give me an ovation," I heard Syreeta say. "A simple thank-you will be enough."

I opened my eyes and could do nothing but smile. She held two wineglasses in one hand and a blue bottle in the other.

"Don't tell me you brought Moscato all the way from Germany?"

"Nope." She handed me a glass. "This is better. Eiswein. Once you've had this, you'll never drink American again!" She filled my glass, then filled her own before she sat next to me.

We clicked our glasses in a silent salute. This was no celebration, though, so we said nothing.

I sipped and then frowned. "This is really good. Smooth."

Syreeta just smiled.

We sat and sipped in silence for a few minutes. Until Syreeta said, "This doesn't seem right."

"What? Me sitting here drinking wine while my son is lying in a funeral home?" I shook my head, then leaned back. "I should have started drinking a few days ago."

"I agree. I'm surprised you didn't drink your way through your entire wine cellar."

"I don't have a wine cellar."

"But if you had one . . ."

We chuckled together.

But then the laughter left her. "I'm talking about this." Syreeta waved her hand like she was a *The Price Is Right* model. "You shouldn't be here all alone."

"Uh . . . check this out. I'm not alone; you're here."

"But it's just me. This house should be filled with people supporting you."

"They're all over at Delores's house, remember?"

"Oh." She took a sip. "Yeah." Then she took a large swallow and giggled. "All them old ladies; I guess this is best, huh? Just you and me."

I nodded. "The way it's always been."

More silent time passed before she rested her glass on the table and then twisted her body to face me.

"I want to ask you something. And it's not that I will ever be able to understand what you're going through. But there is something I don't understand and I want to understand you." She took a long breath and asked, "Why are you so against the Guardians going after that man and making him pay for what he did to Marquis? He murdered your son."

I let her words settle for a moment. "I want that man to pay. I want him to rot in jail before he rots in hell."

"So then let the Guardians fight for that."

"I don't like the way they fight." Now I let my words settle on Syreeta. "Here's the thing. In a couple of days, I'm going to bury my son, and this will be the very last thing that I will ever do for him. I wasn't there to save him, but now I can protect him. If the Guardians get involved, what will that look like for Marquis?" I didn't give her a chance to answer. "You know what it's going to look like. The police will drag my son's name through the thickest mud. And then, Marquis will always be associated with the man who didn't get tried in the courts, but who got tried in the streets. And if he ended up d—" I paused. I didn't even want to speak that word into the atmosphere. "If he ends up with something happening to him, what kind of legacy will that leave for my son?"

I let her think on that for a moment and she nodded a little bit.

I said, "No one else may ever understand, but I do want justice. I want a mother's justice. I want the kind of justice that comes in the right way. The kind of justice that will show that Marquis was a wonderful young man who had his life stolen. I want the kind of justice that when people look back, Marquis's name will stand for something. Because this was handled in the right way."

It took her a few moments, but then she nodded again. "I get it. I never thought about how you would feel as his mom, hearing what we know the other side will say about Marquis. Now that you mention it, I don't know how those other mothers have handled it because I'm just his godmother and if I heard anyone say anything bad about Marquis"—she shook her head—"I might have to cut somebody!"

"See? The Guardians have you talking all kinds of mess. I'm more likely to cut someone than you will ever be," I said, dismissing her threat with a wave of my hand.

"Okay, maybe. But I'm just saying that I understand the Guardians, too. I get Tyrone and Raj. They understand that street justice is the only kind of justice you can get sometimes. That's something that Raj used to always say to me."

I gave her a sideways glance. "Speaking of?"

"What? Justice?"

"Raj!"

"Oh!" Even though her glass was half full, she grabbed the bottle and filled it to the brim. Then she took a swallow that half emptied the glass, sat back, and said, "Ask away."

If she didn't think that I would go in, Syreeta didn't know me. "How could you—"

She didn't even let me finish. "I know," she said, holding up her hand. "I know what you're thinking, but Raj really has changed."

I chuckled, though it wasn't because I found her words funny. "You do know that there are cemeteries full of women who've said the same thing?"

She stared at me long and hard before she rested her glass on the table. "Let's not go there right now."

"I know it sounds harsh, especially now. But maybe it's because of what's happened and I can't stand the thought of losing someone else that I love. Women die because they wanted to believe their abusers had changed. Women who went back over and over again. Women who never left."

"First of all, no one said anything about me getting back with Raj."

I looked at her like I didn't believe her . . . because I didn't.

"We're just friends again," she said. "And I think people deserve a second chance."

"He used up his second chance with you. His second, and third, and twenty-seventh and fiftieth."

"Okay, it wasn't that much. He didn't beat me that many times."

I raised my eyebrows. I wanted to ask her if her mother knew that she had somehow gone crazy.

She said, "Really, you know it was just five times."

I slapped my hands on my thighs. "*Just?* You do realize that was five times too many, right?"

"Yes. And that's why he and I will never be a couple."

I twisted my lips.

"Plus, he paid for his crime," she said, sounding like she was sad that he'd eventually been charged with simple assault.

That's why I asked her, "You're not sorry about that, are you?"

She said no, though her tone didn't change.

"Well, to me, he got off easy."

"I know that's what you think."

"He didn't even serve the full year."

She nodded. "But those anger management classes really did help him."

"I can tell. He came right out of jail and joined the Brown Guardians."

She said, "Well, if you're gonna be angry, at least channel it in the right way."

"Yeah, instead of beating up women, just kill men."

She held up her forefinger and then wiggled it with her words. "There has never been any proof that the Brown Guardians have killed anyone."

"You don't believe that, do you?"

"No, but there isn't any proof. And if they did kill someone, it's always been about justice. They don't go around mugging old ladies or beating up old men. There hasn't been a single case"— she raised her hand in the air—"where that person didn't deserve that justice."

"And that's the definition of 'vigilantism,' which is barbaric in addition to being illegal."

She shrugged as if that was all right with her. But it wasn't all right with me.

"I don't think they're vigilantes," she said. "I just think they make wrongs right, and I respect that. And that's where it begins and ends for me and Raj. I respect how he's turned his life around, I respect what he's doing with the Brown Guardians, I respect him, but we will never be together again."

"I don't know how you do it because it's hard for me to even look at him."

"Well . . . that's not just because of what went down with me and him. It's because of what went down between the two of you." She let a moment pass, then, "So . . . how is Caleb?"

That was a quick left turn. I waited a moment before I told her, "I spoke to him the other day."

"What!" Her body shot up straight. "Seems like I'm not the only one who has some explaining to do."

I held up my hands. "He called when he heard about Marquis. He was the one who told me about it being on the news."

"And that's all he said?"

"Yes."

"So he didn't try to get the two of you together or anything?"

"No. Well. Maybe."

"Oh, lawd." She fell back hard against the sofa's cushions.

"Just to pray," I explained. "That's all he wanted to do. Get together to pray for me."

She looked at me for a moment and then busted out laughing.

"That's what he said."

"Yeah, okay."

"Well, it doesn't matter because I love Tyrone and I'm not going back down that road." I paused and thought about that time. "For the life of me, I still can't believe that happened."

"It was a crazy tangle of situations," Syreeta said. "You supporting me. Tyrone supporting Raj. Tyrone mad at you. You mad at Tyrone."

I nodded. "I know it was my fault, I know I was wrong, but I will always say that if Tyrone hadn't moved out, I would never have been with Caleb."

She nodded. "I know."

"I just wanted the right thing done. Raj needed to be arrested."

"I should've been stronger," Syreeta said. "I should've been the one to call the police." She shook her head. "There are still times when I can't believe that you turned in your own brother-in-law."

"Well, you're my girl; we support each other. That's just what we do."

"I know." Then she paused. "So, if Raj were to apologize to you . . ."

She left her sentence unfinished, so I filled in the words for her: "It would mean absolutely nothing."

"Oh, come on! Why not?"

"Because what he did to me, he was just being dirty."

Her eyes got wide. "Only after you made sure he was arrested and charged."

I sat up. "So that was a reason to destroy his brother's marriage?"

"Uh . . . yeah. You tried to destroy his life. And really, he was just trying to protect his brother. I mean, yeah, there was a part of him that wanted to get back at you. But I think there was also a part of him that was just looking out for his brother. Just like you were looking out for me."

Of course, what Syreeta said made perfect sense. But I preferred to believe what I'd been telling myself for the last three years—that Raj was a low-down, woman-beating, dirty dog.

Syreeta said, "With what's happened to Marquis, we all need to realize that life is more than too short, it's too precious to waste on being mad at people you once loved." She shrugged. "Tyrone and I found a way to love each other again; I hope the same for you and Raj."

I said nothing, but Syreeta did get to me—a little. She laid her head on my shoulder and said, "We're going to make it through this, right?"

I nodded, and without even looking at her, I knew that she was crying . . . just like I was.

"I'm so glad you're here," I whispered.

"Me, too." She sniffed. "'Cause I would hate for it to be Caleb that you were sitting with like this right now."

She laughed, and I laughed, too, though she didn't know how true her words were. I really was glad that she was here because with Tyrone never coming home, and with my heart so broken, I don't know what I would have done . . . if Caleb called again.

Chapter 13

There should have been more to do; at least I would have expected more to do when planning the funeral for my son. But it was all taken care of by the funeral home. And whatever they were missing, my mother-in-law and her pastor filled in. Sure, they tried to include me.

The first call came in yesterday morning:

"Hi, baby, I know it's early," Delores had said.

I confirmed her words when I glanced at the clock. Yup, seven on a Saturday was too early to be calling me—before. But this was now. And I never minded waking up. So that I could fall asleep again and pray that Marquis would come to me in my dreams.

Delores said, "What picture of Marquis do you want us to use for the program?"

I had no idea, so I'd rolled out of bed and had gone across the hall to the guest bedroom and awakened Syreeta. Then, the two of us sifted through all the photos on my phone. But that quickly became a gargantuan task. How was I supposed to choose one that was worthy of being part of the final tribute to Marquis? One that would represent all that he was? There was no way for me to decide.

So I left that choice to Syreeta, who texted a couple to Tyrone. Then a few hours later, Delores called back.

"What scripture do you want to be read?"

I was no Bible connoisseur, but I loved the fourteenth chapter of John. That always gave me such hope, even in the middle of talk about death. "Can someone read that?"

"Whatever you want, baby. It's about whatever you want."

What I wanted was for time to slow down so that I didn't feel as if it was rushing to the moment when I'd have to say my final good-bye to my son.

But time paid me no mind and Saturday turned to Sunday much too quickly. And so, today, I decided not to get out of bed, hoping that would slow down the quickening ticks of time passing by.

So when Delores called and told me that she thought Tyrone and I should at least go to church this morning since Marquis's services were tomorrow, I told her, "No thank you," and I didn't move. When Syreeta came to my bedroom and told me to come down to the kitchen for breakfast, I said, "No thank you," and I stayed in bed. And when Tyrone called hour after hour, checking on me, asking me if there was anything that I needed, I didn't say too much. Really, after the third or fourth or fifth time, I even stopped telling him that all I needed was him.

But even though I tried to slow down time, it still moved. And now it was the evening before what would be another worst time of my life.

Those were my thoughts as I sat in the middle of my bed with my legs crossed in front of me. Syreeta had brought up a tray of Chinese food, trying to convince me that she'd prepared it, even though I could almost smell the paper cartons that the food had been delivered in.

Syreeta had been chatting away, but my thoughts kept words from my mouth. My thoughts were all about what tomorrow would bring.

"Are you going to eat that egg roll?" Syreeta asked, though she had already grabbed it from my plate before I had the chance to tell her no. Then she chowed down on it and was halfway done when she said, "I hate to sound like a cliché, but you know you have to eat something, right?"

I nodded. "I will. One day. Soon. Maybe." I pushed the tray away.

"Is that all you got for me?" Syreeta asked. She rolled off the bed and grabbed the TV remote from my nightstand. "If you're not going to talk, maybe I can find some ratchet show that will make me laugh and make you curse, or something."

She aimed the remote at the television, clicked it on, and pressed the channel button, then paused.

I didn't look over at Syreeta, but I'm sure her expression was the same as mine as we stared at the image on the screen.

"He was my grandbaby," Delores said. Her eyes were on the camera, so it looked as if she were talking straight to me. "And I'm glad we now know who killed my grandson. I'm glad that now there will be justice."

I got on my knees and crawled to the edge of the bed as if that would give me a better view.

"Thank you, Ms. Johnson," Clarissa Austin said, then turned to face the camera.

"That was Delores Johnson, the grandmother of Marquis

Johnson. And, as she said, the funeral for the seventeen-year-old is tomorrow. We still haven't had a comment from Marquis's parents, but the Brown Guardians have asked that we respect their privacy at this time. And we will."

"That must be why there's no one knocking down your door," Syreeta whispered.

I nodded; at least the Guardians were good for something.

Clarissa continued, "But as we just reported, we have confirmed that seventeen-year-old Marquis Johnson"—and then a picture of Marquis filled the screen, the picture we'd sent to Delores yesterday—"was shot and killed by Wyatt Spencer." Now a new photo. Of a white man. A dirty-kind-of-blond-haired white man. A kinda-dark-blue-eyed white man. That photo stayed on the screen until Clarissa signed off with, "We will bring you more as it comes in. Back to you in the studio."

"Rewind that," I told Syreeta.

And then seconds later, I listened to it again. Then I had her rewind it again. And again.

After the fourth time, Syreeta handed the remote to me and I let the segment play again, this time freezing it on the picture of the dirty-blond-haired, dark-blue-eyed white man.

Sitting shoulder to shoulder with my best friend, I stared at that picture. I stared even as I heard the front door downstairs open and close. I stared even as I heard the footsteps on the stairs and then in the hallway. I didn't look up even as I felt Tyrone come to our bedroom door.

He stared, too. At me and Syreeta. And then his eyes shifted to the television screen. After a few moments, he moved and took the remote from my hand before he clicked off the television. Then he pulled me up and into his arms.

I can't tell you exactly when Syreeta slipped from the room. But by the time Tyrone laid me down on the bed, she was gone.

And my husband held me, wrapping his protective arms around me. My back to his front. He never said a word, and neither did I.

It was early, just eight o'clock or so. Too early to go to sleep. But not too early to be held by my husband. To be held by him in our bed for the first time since Wyatt Spencer had taken our son away.

Chapter 14

It wasn't until I was actually sitting in the front pew, the seat of honor that had been reserved for me and Tyrone and those who loved Marquis the most, that I realized I didn't want to be here.

Not that I ever wanted to attend anyone's funeral. But my own son's? I just knew, I just knew, I just knew that this wasn't happening.

If my mind had been right, I wouldn't have let Delores plan this service without me. All of these people shouldn't have been here. This should have been private. Just me and Tyrone. Maybe Delores and Syreeta. And because we were sitting in this church and I was feeling benevolent, I would've even let Raj attend. Maybe.

There should have been only three or four or five of us burying my dear son, without the spectacle that this had become.

Since the news report last night, this story had played over and over on just about every station.

At least that's the way it felt this morning as we got ready. Tyrone had the television on, and the whole time, a picture of Marquis was plastered on the screen. While Tyrone sat on the edge of the bed watching, I dressed, trying my best not to look and then I got out of there as quickly as I could.

But I couldn't escape, because downstairs in the kitchen, Syreeta had the TV on, too.

Apparently now, Marquis Johnson's death was newsworthy since it had all the elements for good media drama: a white man, a black teen, a gun, a dead black teen.

"For the scripture reading," Pastor Davis said in his singsong preacher's voice, "turn in your Bibles to the Gospel of St. John, the fourteenth chapter, and the first verse. And read along with me."

I closed my ears because I didn't want anything to interfere with my eyes that stayed on the silver casket. I didn't want to hear any part of this service. I wanted to dwell only on Marquis, though my mind kept drifting back to when we first arrived at Harmony Hearts Baptist Church.

Our town car had barely hooked around the corner when I saw all of those newspeople. So many that a spot across the street from the church had been cordoned off for them.

That had been shocking. But as Tyrone and I walked into the church with camera lights flashing behind us, I was stunned to see all the people before us.

Reverend Davis led the processional and we followed him down the center aisle as he recited the Twenty-Third Psalm as if it were a ballad. But my focus was on all the people. Every one of the two thousand seats was filled, and I scanned the crowd of mournful, unfamiliar faces. Until I saw . . .

Heather!

Oh, my God. I'd forgotten all about her, and now, as she stood in the center of the sea of black faces, her cheeks already damp with tears, I wanted to take her hand and bring her to the front with me.

But I didn't.

Because just as I thought to reach out to her, another face came into my view. Just a row in front of Heather.

Pastor Caleb Brown!

He caused me to stumble and Tyrone held my arm a little tighter.

"You okay?" my husband whispered.

I nodded, because not only couldn't I speak, but I needed all effort to pray that Tyrone wouldn't see Caleb. Funeral or not, an encounter between the two wouldn't end well.

Didn't Caleb know that? Why was he even here? Why would he take that chance?

We'd made it to the front pew, and now here I sat, with my eyes riveted on Marquis's casket. In an hour, this would be all I would have. Just these memories. I wished that my glare would bore a hole through the steel casing. If I'd had my way, we would've kept the casket open for this entire hour. This final hour. My last sixty minutes with my son.

The choir stood to sing. The song—"My Help Cometh from the Lord"—was one of my favorites. But today I didn't hear the tune or the words that in the past soothed me. Right now all I heard was Marquis.

"Mommy, are you going to be okay?"

I nodded.

"Then why are you crying?"

"Because . . ."

"I promise I'll come home right after kindergarten is over, okay?"

"Okay," I said.

And then, while he held the hand of one of the teaching assistants, I watched him march into that classroom for the first time like the big boy that he'd told me he was. When the assistant and Marquis stopped by one of the small tables, he glanced up, smiled, blew me a kiss, and then waved, letting me know that I was dismissed.

I left only because my son wanted me to, but I sobbed all the way home, like he was going off to war.

A single tear rolled down my cheek at that memory and I wiped it away with one hand as Tyrone squeezed my other hand.

"Now we will hear tributes for Marquis," Pastor Davis said. "And remember, please keep your remarks to under two minutes."

My view of the casket was obstructed by bodies passing by. So much so that I wanted to tell everyone to keep my view of the casket clear.

Then, from the corner of my eye, I saw the white man step to the podium and I had to look up. Four other young men stood behind him, one black, one white, one Hispanic, and one Asian. The United Nations that was Winchester Prep Academy.

Mr. Preston, Marquis's music teacher, began. "Marquis Johnson was a remarkable young man . . ."

I studied the boys who stood with the teacher. All of their faces were etched with sadness as their glances fell to me and Tyrone.

I smiled, I nodded, but I didn't listen. I didn't have much time, so I took my mind away again. Just me and my son. I thought about the time that he'd left for his first overnight Boy Scout trip and I'd cried like he was never coming home. I thought about his stellar performance at his first piano recital, and I thought once again about last Sunday, Mother's Day. Marquis's last full day alive.

"Do you want to say anything?" Tyrone whispered in my ear.

"What?" I asked, dragging my mind back to this place where I didn't want to be.

He repeated his question and I almost asked him to say it again.

He couldn't be asking me if I wanted to stand up there to speak. How was a mother supposed to do that? I had to save all of my energy to breathe.

I shook my head and Tyrone nodded, and then I watched with big eyes as he stood, buttoned his jacket, and made his way to the altar.

Beside me, Delores sniffed, but I was too shocked to cry. Tyrone hadn't told me that he was going to speak. He must've just decided.

There was no way I'd be able to watch him and not pass out from sorrow. So I took myself back to that safe place again, this time with Marquis and Tyrone.

"Where have you been?" I asked as my three-year-old waddled through the door and into my arms.

"With the airplanes!" Marquis cheered.

As I unzipped his coat, I looked up at Tyrone. "Where did you two go?"

He grinned. "He just told you. We were with the airplanes."

I tilted my head and Tyrone laughed.

"Tell your mama what you did," he said to Marquis.

"I jumped high, and touched the airplanes. Right, Daddy?"

"Yes, son." And to me, Tyrone explained, "I took him out near the end of the runway at the airport. And you should've seen me and Marquis jumping up. We almost touched a couple of those planes."

I shook my head. That didn't sound like much fun to me. "So that's where you've been? For three hours? In the cold? Out there jumping up, having my son thinking that he could touch a plane?"

Tyrone shrugged. "Yeah. We had a great time. I was teaching him that he's gonna be a giant among men. Because only giants can almost touch airplanes." He raised his hand and Marquis gave him a high five.

Tyrone laughed, Marquis giggled, and my heart swelled with so much love because of the lessons my husband was teaching our son.

My eyes were bright with tears when Tyrone sat down, but not because of the words he'd just spoken. I cried for the lessons he'd taught Marquis in the past that would never be part of his future.

While Pastor Davis gave Marquis's eulogy, I let my mind race through the rest of Marquis's life: from when he learned to tie his sneakers after hours and hours of practice to when he learned to write his name after hours and hours of study.

Now, I sobbed and Tyrone put his arms around me, though I'm sure he thought my cries were because of the two attendants from the funeral home who'd stood and removed the cloth from the casket. Then, in a slow, solemn move, they lifted the casket's lid.

After Friday, I'd chosen not to see Marquis until this moment, and from the side, my baby looked like he was sleeping. And that cover of peace that I felt when I first saw him, blanketed me again.

The ushers beckoned the people to come and say good-bye, and row by row they marched up. Just about everyone stopped to give me, Tyrone, and Delores their condolences, but all I did was nod at the nameless faces.

Until Heather came before me. And I stood. When I pulled her into my arms, she cried the same way she had the morning after.

"I'm so sorry, Mrs. Johnson."

"I know, baby," I said. I didn't want to let her go, but I had to, so that people I didn't know could speak to me.

The procession of strangers continued, and it was hard for me to concentrate. Because at any moment, I expected to see Caleb. But as rows and rows of people filed by, I soon released the stress weighing down my shoulders. Caleb wasn't going to make an appearance.

Then the row behind us stood and I began to shake.

There were a few people from my job, Delores's best friend, several of the men from Tyrone's shop.

The moment was getting closer and closer.

And then the moment came.

Raj stood first with Syreeta. He held her around her waist as they moved to the casket. A tissue was pressed to her nose and I watched her tears drip onto my son as she stood over him. Not even a minute passed before she and Raj turned away.

Next was Delores, and Tyrone stood with his mother. He hooked his arm through hers as she stood over the casket, though she looked like she could've done it alone. Yes, she wept, but she stood tall, she stood strong.

Her lips moved, though I heard no sound. I didn't know if she was speaking to Marquis or maybe saying a prayer.

Tyrone led his mother back to the pew, and once she sat, he reached for my hand. For a moment, just a moment, I wanted to tell him no. Not because I didn't want to see my son, but because I wanted to prolong the moment until the inevitable good-bye.

But I took his hand and let him just about carry me the twenty or so feet to where Marquis lay.

My smile was instantaneous as I looked down at my sleeping son, my handsome son. Tyrone had chosen well, dressing Marquis in the gray pin-striped suit that he'd worn eight days ago. He called it his first grown-up suit since it wasn't purchased from JCPenney or Sears. Tyrone had taken him to the Men's Wearhouse and spent one hundred and fifty dollars.

"I look good, Mama, don't I?" he asked that Mother's Day morning.

"Yes, you do," I said, straightening his tie.

I leaned over and straightened his tie now, then smoothed away invisible wrinkles.

Water burned my eyes, but these were my last moments and I couldn't waste them with tears. So I leaned over once again, letting my face get close to my son's.

"I loved you before you were born," I told him. "So you being gone now doesn't change anything. I will love you until my last breath on earth, and then I will join you in heaven and love you some more.

"I hurt so much because of all that I knew you would be. But I am grateful for the years that we had together. You were an amazing young man, and I will get down on my knees every day and thank God for you.

"God bless you, baby. God. Bless. You."

I pressed my lips against his forehead, and kept them there until my back began to ache and I was forced to stand erect.

I stood with Tyrone as he spoke to Marquis, though his words were silent. But I imagined his heartfelt good-bye from the tears that rolled from his eyes.

I don't know how long we stood there. Maybe it was too long, because Mr. Marshall finally came up behind us.

"Would you like to close the casket?" the mortician asked.

"No," I said.

"Yes," Tyrone said, then looked at me. "We'll do this together."

He held my right hand tighter with his left, and then with our free hands we touched the top lid of the casket. Together we lowered it slowly, but we'd only moved it a few inches when I said, "Wait."

We stopped.

"I don't want to close this," I whispered. "Because we'll never see him again."

"We have to close it, baby," my husband said, his voice shaking. "We have to."

"Can I have one more moment?"

He nodded. But then my moment turned into two, and three, and by the time too many moments passed, though my hand was still on the casket's lid, it was Tyrone who closed it, taking my son away from me forever.

Tyrone led me back to the pew, but my knees wouldn't bend. So I stayed standing and my husband stood next to me. Soft cries and sniffles filled the air of the sanctuary as the attendants sealed the casket, twisting the keys, locking each of the corners.

Pastor Davis raised his hands, and finally everyone in the church stood with me and Tyrone.

The pallbearers lined up, then carried my son out and Tyrone held me once again as we followed the casket and Pastor Davis down the center aisle. The sorrowful air was so thick I felt like I was going to choke on it.

It was so hard to breathe. Or maybe it was that I didn't want to breathe. Because breathing was for life. So I didn't need to take any more breaths.

What for? It was official; now my life was over.

W‌ould you like some water?" Tyrone asked me as he handed me a small bottle that was in the side of the town car.

I shook my head.

More minutes passed as the car rolled up the interstate.

"That really was a beautiful service," Delores said.

"Yes, it was," Tyrone answered.

Even Syreeta and Raj mumbled something.

But I hadn't been able to say a single word since we'd closed the casket. And then, once they laid Marquis into the ground at the cemetery, I was sure that every word inside of me had been buried with my son.

When the car came to a stop, it kinda surprised me. Not that I thought we'd be driving forever. It was just that I had been looking out the window, but I guess I saw nothing.

The driver turned off the motor and trotted around to the side where Tyrone sat. When he opened the door, Tyrone got out first, and then Raj slipped out next.

Delores slid to the end of her seat. "Well, this is where I get out," she said. She paused as if she were waiting for me to speak. When I said nothing, she added, "Come on in, Jan. I want to make sure you get something to eat."

I shook my head.

"You have to eat."

And then I was forced to say my first words. "I just want to lie down."

"You can lie down here," Delores said in a tone that sounded like she was insisting.

I knew having me in her home would help her feel better. Give her something to do—she could take care of me. But I just couldn't say yes. Because there would be people here.

In my home, I'd have peace. No, let me rephrase that, because I would never have peace again in this life. But I'd have peace's partner. I'd have quiet. That's what I wanted.

Delores surrendered and hugged me. Told me that she'd call me later. And then, when she slid out of the car, it was just me and Syreeta.

In that quiet.

Then, because I guess Syreeta figured out that I was never going to say anything, she said, "I was going to go back with you, but I'm wondering if I should stay here for a while."

I gave her a blank stare. There was no way I could figure out what she should do when the only plan I had for my future was to lie down.

She said, "I was thinking that you and Tyrone could use some time. Right now. Together. Alone."

I nodded.

"Is that okay?"

Again, all I had in me was a nod.

Syreeta hugged me, too, but she held me much longer than Delores had. She held me so long that I could've taken a short nap. When she finally leaned away, she said, "I'll give you a couple of hours, okay?"

"Yes," I whispered only because I felt like she deserved a word. At least one.

That pleased her. I could tell by her smile.

Then I sat in the car alone. I tilted my head, taking in the scene outside. Syreeta followed Delores into the house, but Tyrone stood on the lawn with his brother, their heads close together. It was apparent that they were whispering, plotting. Then, together, they glanced at the car.

They couldn't see my frown through the tinted window.

Not more than a minute passed before Tyrone stepped away and slid into the car at the same time as the driver.

"Where to?" the driver asked.

Tyrone wrapped his arm around me. "Take us home. Take me and my wife home."

Chapter 15

I'd been right—there was so much quiet in our home. I welcomed and savored it.

But I'd been wrong, too. Because though I didn't expect it, I also found a bit of peace here. It was a different kind of peace, not complete, but enough peace to give me hope. I knew this peace came from God, through Tyrone. I found peace in my husband's arms.

We'd lain together like this in bed so many times over the years of our marriage, but I'd never felt this close, never this intimate with my husband. We were fully clothed, but our hearts were exposed, bleeding sorrow.

As I cried, Tyrone wiped my tears away, and as he cried, I did the same for him.

Though every part of me ached, this is where I wanted to be. If Marquis had to be gone, if there was no way for me to get him back, then I wanted to be here with Tyrone. Just the two of us wading through this together.

We'd been this way for hours, lying in the quiet of the peace with only the dimming brightness of the sun to show the passage of time. I had no idea, really, how many hours had passed. It seemed like it might have been six o'clock, seven o'clock. It was still light outside, the days longer now as we moved toward summer.

Summer.

Marquis's favorite time of the year.

I sighed and rolled over and Tyrone pulled me close. My back to his front.

"Are you okay?" he asked.

"No. But I will be. I hope. One day."

I felt his nod behind me. "We're going to make it. Together." And then he pulled me even closer as if he were trying to make the two of us one.

More quiet. More peace.

Just minutes and hours of it.

Then Tyrone said, "The Guardians are arranging some protests."

I stiffened, but Tyrone didn't let me go.

He said, "Today, they're protesting over at the Montgomery courthouse. They're there right now."

Slowly, I rolled back over so that I could look into his eyes. Maybe seeing him would help me to hear better, because surely, my ears were doing that deceiving thing.

When I looked into Tyrone's eyes and he said nothing else, I told him, "We just buried Marquis!" because clearly, my husband and everyone else had forgotten that fact.

"I know, but with the news on us, with this focus, we have to move now for the greatest impact. Public sentiment is on our side. Did you see how many people were at the funeral?" he asked as if he were actually a little bit happy about that.

I blinked.

"That was because of the work the Guardians have put in. This is the perfect time to show the police and district attorney that the people are with us. We want the world to know . . ."

See? Right there was the problem. The world to know?

The world was beginning to know my son's name, but no one in the world knew my son. And that's why the Brown Guardians couldn't be part of this. Because then the world would judge my son by those thugs.

But I didn't want a fight, not even a debate, so I pressed my lips together. Saying nothing was the safest, easiest way.

Tyrone said, "I'm not going to the protest tonight. I want to be here with you." He paused and I already knew what was coming. "But tomorrow, I'm going to be there and I want you with me."

"No." I couldn't say it fast enough. Then, "I don't like the way this is going, Tyrone. The police are starting to do their part. They've released his name—"

"Only because of the Guardians."

I acted like I didn't even hear him. "So why not wait for the police to handle the rest of it?"

"Because why should we wait?" His tone told me that he thought his answer was obvious. "The Guardians are all about being proactive, not reactive. They're going to stay within the system because I've told Raj how you feel. That's why they're setting up protests and rallies rather than . . ." For a moment, he stopped speaking, and for that same time, I stopped breathing. "We know that's what you want," he continued, "so the Guardians are going to do it your way. But we are not waiting for the police to do what's right."

"I don't trust the Guardians."

"I don't trust the police."

And there it was. Our impasse. There wasn't anything I could ever say to a black man about the police.

So I tried what I knew would tug at Tyrone's heart. "If we turn this into a black-and-white thing, do you know what they'll do to Marquis?"

Right away I saw that strategy didn't work. His frown was so deep when he lifted and tilted his head as if he needed to get a good look at me. "The worst possible thing has already been done to our son. We had to put him in the ground a few hours ago," he said, as if I needed the reminder. "So now? It's whatever. I don't care. There's nothing they can say, nothing they can do to hurt Marquis now."

Clearly, my husband hadn't watched any of the other situations on television. Or maybe he had. Maybe he just hadn't watched with a mother's eye. Or maybe I was the only mother who had this kind of eye. I didn't know. But while it was true that the worst was done, I knew more bad could come.

But Tyrone was right. We'd just put our son into the ground and all I wanted to do was hold Tyrone and have him hold me and have our hearts connect, and think of the boy that we had created.

So I leaned forward and pressed my lips against his. He opened his mouth and accepted my truce. And then he rolled over, and this time, I held him. His back to my front.

And we lay that way. Not saying another word. I'd have plenty of time to tell him no—tomorrow.

Chapter 16

Morning came. And my first thought when I rolled over was, I wonder how the night had been for Marquis?

Crazy, I know. But I was beginning to accept crazy. Especially once Tyrone rolled over, kissed my cheek, and started up again about what he was going to do with the Guardians. He hadn't even brushed his teeth, but he was riled up and ready to go.

It sounded all kinds of crazy to me.

"That man has to pay" was Tyrone's mantra.

I agreed with that; I just wanted to make sure that while Wyatt Spencer was paying, no one I love was caught in any kind of cross fire.

Tyrone rolled to the edge of the bed and looked over his shoulder. "Wanna take a shower with me?"

I shook my head and his eyebrows rose. When had I ever passed that up?

But while I needed my husband so bad, I wasn't ready to take a shower with him. Not yet. Leaning toward him, I gave him another soft kiss. Telling him everything was all right when we both knew that it was all wrong.

I stayed in bed until Tyrone was locked inside the bathroom, then I wrapped myself inside my robe and went to the bedroom across from ours.

Before I knocked, I pressed my ear to the door, not wanting to wake Syreeta. I hadn't heard her come in, so I had no idea how late she'd been.

But I heard the soft drone of the television, so I knocked.

"Come on in," she said in a voice that sounded like she'd been up for hours.

I took two steps inside and asked, "You just getting in?" as I looked her up and down.

"No. Why would you ask me that?"

"Uh . . . because it's barely eight and you're not only up, but . . ." I took in the T-shirt, jeans, and brown blazer she was wearing. With her hair pulled back in a ponytail and no makeup, she barely looked like she was out of her teens.

She reached for the remote, and as she muted the TV, my eyes glanced at the screen and got stuck there.

It was the first time I'd ever seen myself on television. But there I was holding hands with Tyrone as we walked into Harmony Hearts Baptist yesterday.

"I'm going to go with the guys." Syreeta's voice pulled me away from the television. "I'm going to the protest with the Guardians."

I sat on the edge of the futon that doubled as a bed for our overnight guests, my attention now fully on my friend.

She leaned back against the dresser and crossed her arms with an expression on her face that looked like she expected to do battle with me. She said, "Tyrone told you about the protests, right?"

I nodded.

"Are you going?"

"No. And I'm surprised that you are since you know how I feel."

She lowered her arms. "But there's not going to be any violence. Last night, that's all they talked about. How they wanted to do things differently because of you. I was really impressed as I listened to them at Delores's. They have a plan and it's not about the Guardians at all, it's about Marquis and all the young men who've been hunted and shot down in the streets."

I shook my head. "Even if I could trust them, which I don't, the Guardians are going to turn Marquis into a cause."

"So? What's wrong with that? If he were here, Marquis would be proud of what the Guardians have put together in his name."

Now I folded my arms.

"Think about it, Jan. Think about what they've done so far. Without any kind of threats, without any kind of violence, they got the ME to release Marquis's body early, then they got the police to release that man's name. Now, if it were the old Guardians, that man's house would have been firebombed already."

"Dang, Syreeta!"

"I'm just saying. That man and his family would've had to move to another planet. But do you know what the Guardians did? They put the word on the street, to all the homies in the hood, that Wyatt Spencer is not to be touched. And they're not playing. Raj is making sure that it's all handled the way you want it."

"The way I want it? How many times do I have to say I want it handled in court?"

She threw up her hands as if what I was saying was absurd. But couldn't my friend see that sure, the Guardians would be peaceful today, maybe tomorrow. But there would be a point when the violence would start.

After a couple of huffs, she sat down next to me. "Seems like there's nothing I can say to you, and there's nothing that you can say to me. So I tell you what: I'm going. Period. And you're not. Another period. But I'm going for you. I'm going to stand in for you . . . and Marquis."

I felt like I was being deserted, but how could I hate on what she'd said? She was wrong, but it wouldn't take long for her to realize I was right. Once these protests started, she'd see the Brown Guardians' true colors, and then, she'd leave them alone.

Maybe today. Maybe tomorrow. Definitely soon.

I hugged her, stood, and once again my eyes locked on the television, now focused on an image of the empty steps of city hall. Syreeta clicked the remote, fading the screen to black.

She put her arm around my shoulders as we walked into the hall and then down the stairs. Tyrone walked out from the kitchen just as we hit the last step.

"Hey, Syreeta," he said.

"Hey." Then, she said, "I drove Raj's truck here last night since he was gonna ride his motorcycle over to the courthouse this morning with . . ." She paused, but it was too late; I already had the image in my mind—of dozens of black men in brown fatigues rolling their motorcycles onto the courthouse steps. She asked Tyrone, "Wanna ride with me?"

"Yeah," he said to her, though his eyes were on me.

Without another word, Syreeta stepped outside, leaving me and Tyrone alone.

"Are you sure?" he asked me.

I nodded and asked him, "Are *you* sure?"

He nodded and pulled me into his arms.

I muttered a quick prayer for protection, begging God to keep my husband safe.

It felt like Tyrone's arms were still around me, even as he stepped back and kissed my forehead.

"I'll be back as soon as I can."

I followed him to the door, and even though I only had on my bathrobe, I stood on the step outside. May's morning sun was bright and warm, welcoming me to the first day of my life after my son's burial.

I watched Tyrone open the driver's-side door, but before he slid inside, he held up his cell phone and I nodded.

And then he blew me a kiss.

I stayed in place as Tyrone rolled Raj's truck to the end of the driveway. And even once they were out of sight, I stood outside, marveling at how the day could bring such beauty in the midst of such sadness. And then I stepped inside and closed the door behind me, leaving all the warmth outside.

As I looked around my home, memories screamed from every corner. My eyes settled on the stairs and I could see Marquis bouncing down.

"Mom, I'm late. I gotta get to the bus."

"You have to eat breakfast."

"No time."

But then, he stopped long enough to give me a kiss.

He always stopped, always kissed me good-bye.

I sighed and moaned at the same time as I ascended the stairs, pausing at the top to catch my emotions more than my breath. Then, I moved a few more feet and paused again outside of Marquis's room.

My hand held the knob on the door before I pushed it open. Then, I took a tentative step to the edge and inhaled. It was faint, but I relished the scent, a blend of Old Spice and old sneakers.

"You need to open the windows," I said.

"Ahh . . . Mom!"

"'Cause there's kid funk in here."

That had sent my twelve-year-old into a fit of giggles. He thought I'd been kidding; I was not.

I took another step in.

"I'm scared, Mom. Suppose no one likes me at Winchester?"

"Everyone's gonna love you." I sat on his bed.

"You have to say that 'cause you're my mom."

"But I'm your smart mom, and your honest mom. And everyone is going to see what I see. That you're a smart, funny, talented, amazing young man who's as cute as a button."

"Mom!"

"Okay, not cute. But as handsome as his father. I'm telling you, you're going to thrive."

Those memories made me brave and I stepped all the way into his bedroom. After a moment, I walked around, letting my fingertips graze the edge of his bookcase. I paused in the corner and felt the tops of his golf clubs and then I picked up his saxophone, cradled it actually. I held it the way I used to hold my son.

I sat down and remembered the Christmas when Marquis had busted into our bedroom hours before sunrise to thank us for the saxophone that he'd found under the tree. And then, he started blowing into that thing, sounding more like he was playing a bullhorn.

Gently, I placed the saxophone back in the corner, and I lay down on Marquis's bed and listened to the sound of silence until it became too loud.

Reaching for the remote, I turned on the television, wondering if the protest had started.

Instead, the screen was filled with the image of that photo again. That man. That man who killed my son.

Then the photo became smaller, a small square pushed up in the corner. I'd been so focused on the picture that I didn't even realize someone was speaking.

A man.

With hair the color of ginger.

And a build like a block of ice.

I turned up the volume.

"We know that once the police investigation is complete, my brother will be exonerated, completely shown to be without blame. It was Marquis Johnson who was the aggressor. Marquis Johnson who got out of his car in front of my brother's house. It was Marquis who attacked my brother with a baseball bat."

My eyes widened.

"Busting his nose."

I sat straight up.

"It was Marquis Johnson who forced my brother to protect himself. He had to do something to make sure that he wasn't the one having a funeral today."

"You're lying!" I screamed.

"My brother is a good man, a devoted husband, a loving father, and he's been an asset to this community. And yes, he's a Christian. Killing Marquis Johnson was the last thing that he wanted to do, but Marquis Johnson was a known thug."

"Oh, my God!"

"And ask yourself this. If you find yourself face-to-face in the middle of the night, with a known thug holding a baseball bat, what would you do?"

He paused for just a moment as if he was trying to make eye

contact with each of the reporters. Then he turned around and strutted away as if he'd just delivered a presidential address.

I couldn't move, but I looked up; I didn't even realize I was standing, with my hand clasped over my mouth, until I saw my reflection in Marquis's mirror.

And I saw my tears. But this time, I wasn't crying from sadness. Now, I was pissed.

This man had just told lie after lie about my son, lies that had been broadcasted across the nation. And now, who was going to speak up for my son?

Before I even answered that question, I ran out of Marquis's bedroom and into my own. By the time I was in front of the bathtub, I was already naked. Under the heat of the water, I remembered that man's lies.

"Marquis Johnson was a known thug."

I scrubbed harder.

"If you find yourself face-to-face in the middle of the night, with a known thug holding a baseball bat, what would you do?"

I was trembling when I jumped out of the tub. There was no way for me to move fast enough. I tore into my closet, slipped on a black shell and black pants. I would've put on a black veil if I'd had one.

I wanted America to see me in my black.

Dressed, I dashed down the stairs, then paused only to grab my purse and keys from the table before I raced through the door.

This was not a fight that I wanted, but I would fight to the end now. That man had spoken my son's name in vain.

Now he would have to deal with me.

Inside the car, I bobbed and weaved through the streets and then took I-76, but once I exited and hit Main Street, I was stuck in traffic.

What was all of this on a Tuesday morning?

I circled the streets of the courthouse in search of a parking space. But there was not one available—except for the five or six spots in front of fire hydrants.

"If you find yourself face-to-face in the middle of the night, with a known thug holding a baseball bat, what would you do?"

I parked in front of the hydrant that was closet to the courthouse. Let them tow me away!

I locked the car after I jumped out, then ran down Main Street. But the crowd thickened as I crossed Cherry, and when I got to Swede, it was hard to press forward. I could see the Montgomery County courthouse in front of me. An old building that always reminded me of the Supreme Court in Washington, DC.

But though I could see the building, I couldn't get there, not through the thick crowd.

Was this all for Marquis? It couldn't be. Just an hour ago, the news cameras showed empty courthouse steps. But now there were throngs of folks. Mostly black, but a lot of white people, too.

"Excuse me," I said taking baby steps forward. "Excuse me," I said as I inched through.

I clawed my way to the front of the steps, but now the people were packed so close together there was no way that I was going to make it any farther, no matter how many times I excused myself.

But then behind me, I felt the gentle hand of someone touch my elbow. Turning around, I faced a man in a brown beret and brown fatigues.

I'd never seen this man before, but from his eyes, I could tell that he knew me. Without a word, he cupped my arm in one hand, and then with his other, he cut through the crowd.

"Coming through."

It was like he was a "crowd whisperer," making the masses part. It was more than that, though. Whenever anyone looked up and saw the uniform he wore, they stepped aside.

With this man by my side, I climbed the stairs, and even once I could see the top, where Tyrone stood, my Guardian escort did not let me go. I was about halfway up when Tyrone looked down.

His expression was not what I expected; I'd been sure that my husband would bust out in a grin. But as he trotted down the steps, his eyes filled with tears.

I understood.

And I grinned at him.

I was handed off to my husband, who grabbed me into the tightest embrace. Then, as Raj's voice boomed through the speakers that were all around, Tyrone held my hand and we climbed to the top together.

The first one to greet me was Delores, and after her hug, she passed me to Syreeta. Even Raj gave me a nod, though he didn't miss a beat as he delivered his speech about justice for all.

"We've had enough of this!" he shouted. "Enough!"

And the crowd chanted back, "Enough!"

I stood next to Tyrone and looked down at all the people. It was more massive than what I'd seen below.

Tyrone whispered, "They're all here for Marquis, baby. This is all about our son."

"We want justice for my nephew," Raj kept on. "And justice is more than an arrest; we have to put an end to this law that allows murderers to hide. We have to get rid of this law that is not about giving people a chance to protect themselves; this is about giving people a license to kill!"

"Enough!" the crowd shouted.

Raj said, "Think about it. This law isn't asking adults to use reason; our country is saying go ahead and act on the emotion of the moment. We're saying, 'Go ahead and shoot to kill! Ask questions later.' This is legal murder!"

"Enough!"

"We've had too many murders, too many of our boys dying in the streets. And so this is the time. Wyatt Spencer must be put on trial for murder and this law must be repealed."

The steps beneath my feet felt like they were vibrating with the way the crowd stomped and cheered.

Then Raj raised his fist in the air, and the hundreds that had gathered did the same.

"Enough," they chanted. "Justice for Marquis."

After taking the deepest of breaths, I raised my fist. And I chanted, "Enough!"

I chanted that over and over, even as I cried.

PART TWO

Meredith Spencer

I WISH . . .
I COULD
HAVE BEEN THERE . . .
TO STOP HIM

MAY 20, 2014

Chapter 17

Say the T-word," Newt shouted as he punched his cigar through the air, emphasizing each word he spoke. "Come on, the T-word."

I wiggled a bit, more from the discomfort of Newt's words than the hard cushion of the hotel's chair.

But even as my husband's attorney roared as he bounced on the edge of the sofa, my eyes stayed locked on the television screen.

"Come on, Wally," Newt shouted as if my brother-in-law could hear him through the TV. "Say the T-word."

Then . . .

"Marquis Johnson was a known thug . . . If you find yourself face-to-face in the middle of the night, with a known thug holding a baseball bat, what would you do?"

Wyatt and Newt sprang up from the sofa, knocking over the chessboard that was on the table in front of them. But neither seemed to notice. They high-fived and cheered the way I'd watched them do many times on a Sunday afternoon when the Eagles scored a touchdown.

Only this wasn't Sunday. And this wasn't football.

"He did it," Newt said as he grabbed my husband in a bear hug. "Wally came through."

"So it was really that important for him to say 'thug,' huh?" Wyatt asked as he muted the television.

Newt nodded, his head wobbling on his shoulders like a bobblehead. "That's the new N-word. All the white people will know what Wally meant. In their minds, they'll see that big black boy in a hoodie with his pants sagging and music blasting from a cell phone that's more expensive than theirs and probably stolen." Newt laughed. "Wally just scared every white person sitting in front of their TV. And probably a few black ones, too."

I wanted to throw up.

"So what do you think, Meredith?" my husband asked.

It was a reflex the way that once I heard my name, I arched my back, sat straighter, crossed my ankles, and blinked a couple of times. Then I passed them both the smile that had become my signature.

"If that's what Newt thinks, then—"

"Okay, so we won this first round, huh?" Wyatt said, turning away from me that fast.

Newt nodded. "And I'm hoping that we won't have too many more rounds to go." Wyatt's attorney flopped onto the sofa next to my husband. "I don't have the connections up here that I have in Texas," he said, referring to the state where he now lived. "But I've put out some feelers and I don't think you'll be charged. They don't have a case."

Wyatt released a long breath of relief.

I wanted to throw up.

My husband said, "I can't believe they gave out my name like that, though."

"That's part of the law, dude," Newt said, stubbing out his cigar.

"You oughta pay me double for how long I was able to stall them. But it's good. Your name's out, and now so is your story."

The sound of barking filled the room and Wyatt laughed and shook his head the way he did every time an incoming call sounded on Newt's phone.

Newt glanced at the screen. "Let me take this." He pushed his massive frame from the sofa, then ambled toward the small kitchen in the suite.

Wyatt stood and for the first time gave me more than just a second of attention. "How ya doing, sweetheart?"

I waited a moment to see if he really wanted an answer. When his eyes were still on mine, I said, "Fine." I couldn't maintain eye contact with him, though, so I let my gaze roam around what this hotel called the living room section of the two-bedroom suite.

"Wally did a great job, didn't he?"

I caressed the back of my neck, twisting a bit to relieve the stiffness. But I didn't say a word.

"Maybe now we'll be able to go home," Wyatt said, not noticing that I hadn't answered him. Then, "Where's Billy?"

"He's asleep," I said, so glad that my son had slept through that press conference. Even at three years old, I didn't want him to see the way his father and godfather behaved. "I'll check on him in a minute."

Wyatt smiled, leaned over, kissed me, and then patted the top of my head just as Newt ended his call.

"It seems your house is still safe."

"I'm sure it is," Wyatt said. "I'm paying a fortune for security."

"I'm not talking about security. I'm saying that no one is there. No one has even come close to your house. There's nothing. No protests, none of those stupid memorials with those teddy bears and plastic flowers. Nothing."

"Really?" Wyatt's eyes were filled with the same surprise that I felt. "What's that about?"

Newt shrugged his heavy shoulders. "Whatever it's about, it's good. I'm not saying it's safe to go home, but you might not have to stay here much longer."

Wyatt glanced around the room the way I'd done just minutes before. "Well, no matter what's going on, we're not staying here." His face was marked with disgust. "I've worked too hard to be staying in a two-bit hotel like this."

"Two-bit hotels don't have suites," Newt said. "And you're not on vacation. But like I said, you might not have to be hiding out much longer."

"Well, either we go home in a day or two or you need to upgrade us to the type of place my wife has become accustomed to."

The two of them glanced at me, then laughed as if I was the butt of their joke. Again I smiled, said nothing.

The banging on the door took all smiles away, and we were silent as Newt placed his hand on his waist. Even though his jacket covered him, I knew he'd reached for his gun, holstered to his waist. Without even thinking about it, I stood and moved to the door that led to the bedroom where my son slept.

Newt glanced through the peephole, then he inched the door open. But his hand was still on his gun until Wally walked in alone.

We released a collective breath, and just like he'd done to Wyatt minutes before, Newt grabbed Wyatt's brother into a hug. "You did it, dude."

"Yeah?" Wally asked.

"Yeah." Wyatt responded this time. "Thanks for handling that."

"It was fun," Wally said with a whole-face grin. "All those people waiting to hear what I had to say."

"How do you think they received it?" Newt asked. "You think they believed you?"

"Yeah, why wouldn't they? I was telling the truth."

"Well, except for the busted-nose part," Wyatt said as he touched his nose.

They all laughed as if the lie was funny.

Newt ran his hands through his white hair that was as much a function of his DNA as his age. I'd only met Newt eight years ago, right before Wyatt and I were married. But even in their high school pictures, Newt's hair was already turning some shade of silver.

"One thing everyone in this room needs to know is that the truth has little to do with anything. It's all about strategy if we want to keep you"—Newt pointed to Wyatt—"from having a mug shot on record."

Wyatt and Wally nodded as they sat on the sofa and I returned to the chair.

"So, what now?" Wyatt asked. "Maybe I should make a statement."

"No!" Newt exclaimed, practically cutting him off. "I already told you, not only will you remain silent, but you're going to pretend you're Casper the Friendly Ghost."

"But I was just thinking, maybe if the world saw me and my beautiful wife"—they all turned to look at me once again—"maybe that would help. That would show everyone that I'm not a killer."

But you are! I said inside. And my stomach rumbled.

"What happened," my husband continued, "was that thug's fault."

"You're not going to make a statement. There's—" Newt's words were interrupted when Wally picked up the remote and turned the television's volume back on.

"All I can tell you is that Marquis did nothing wrong," a black man was saying. "The police know this, so now it's time to do what's right. Wyatt Spencer must be arrested and brought to trial just like any American who takes the life of another for no reason."

"I had a reason," my husband shouted, though none of us gave our attention to him.

Cheers erupted from the crowd, and I moved to the edge of my seat.

To this point, all I'd seen on television were pictures of the Brown Guardians, a herd of angry black men who took away my breath even though we were dozens of miles away from our home.

Over the years, I'd heard little things about that group. They always talked about justice, but many in our circle called them homegrown terrorists who kidnapped and murdered, and who terrified me.

But this man who spoke, he couldn't have been part of them . . . I could hear his heart in his tone.

"Marquis Johnson was our son."

I pressed my hand across my chest. Marquis's father! Then my eyes moved to the woman standing beside him. Was that Marquis's mother?

"Marquis was on his way to college . . ."

"Turn that off!" Wyatt shouted at Wally, although he didn't give his brother a chance to make a move. He grabbed the remote, turned the screen black, then threw the remote, which crashed into the wall. "That man is lying!"

Newt's eyes followed the now cracked remote, then he turned

back to his friend. "Well," he began, his voice was just as calm as it was before, "we don't know that any of that is a lie. All that man said was that his son was on his way to college."

"I'm telling you," Wyatt said, pointing his finger at Newt, "the boy who came at me Monday night was not a college kid. He was a thug, I'm telling you."

"Okay. All right. Calm down. I agree with you," Newt said as if he were a therapist reeling in an off-balance patient. "I know why you shot that boy. All I'm saying is that he *might* have been on his way to college. Some technical school that his father is calling a college or maybe some barber college. You know they'll make up anything to make their son look good.

"But whatever it is, and whatever he says, we have to ride it out until the police confirm your story, and then you'll be able to get back to your life. And the way everything looks, that's going to be soon."

Wyatt sat back and took a deep breath. "I want all of this to be over."

"Well, it's only been a week, and frankly, it's been a good week for you. Like I said, you may be able to go home in a couple of days. We just want to make sure it's safe for you, Meredith, and Billy."

He nodded just as Newt's cell barked again and I rose, taking the moment to escape into the bedroom. Neither Wyatt nor his brother noticed that I had moved, and just as I put my hand on the doorknob, Newt clicked off his phone and let out a long whistle.

I paused as my husband said, "What?"

"That was Detective Ferguson."

Wyatt lifted his eyes to the ceiling. "What does that nigger cop want?"

I wanted to throw up.

Newt jabbed a finger at Wyatt. "Dude, that is one thing you're not gonna do. You're not gonna use that word."

"What?" Wyatt looked around as if he were innocent. "There's no one here but us."

"I don't care," Newt snapped. "You never know who's listening or where a tape recorder is hidden and I don't want you to get so used to saying that word that it slips out at an inopportune time." He paused. "Do you hear me?" When my husband didn't budge, Newt said, "Do you hear what I'm saying, Wyatt!" It wasn't a question; it was a demand.

Even though my husband looked like he wanted to punch Newt in his eye, he said, "I hear you!"

"Good. Make sure you really hear me." Newt straightened his jacket. "Now, what *Detective Ferguson* wants is to speak with you one last time."

"How many times are they going to question me?"

"This is standard operating procedure. They take several statements just to see if you're consistent. There's nothing to worry about; in fact, from his tone, I'd say that this is Ferguson's final act."

"The last time?" Wyatt asked.

"I think so, but it doesn't matter. As long as your story stays straight, it won't matter how many times he talks to you."

"My story is straight," Wyatt said. "Because it's the truth."

Then my husband glanced at me. A long look, a knowing look. And I broke away, almost running through the bedroom door. If I could have locked it, I would have. Not that a lock could bolt the thoughts out of my mind.

Closing my eyes, I leaned against the door for a moment just to steady myself.

But then, that image once again flashed through my mind. Of Monday, May 12.

And an intestinal volcano rumbled inside of me. By the time I felt the gurgles in my throat, I was in the bathroom, seat up, head down.

I wanted to throw up. I needed to throw up. And that's just what I did.

Chapter 18

I felt the leg on my shoulder and then the giggle in my ear. Still, when I opened my eyes, it took a few moments for my mind to remember: this was not my bed, not my bedroom. We weren't in Haverford. We were in Springfield at a three-star hotel, hiding out because of what my husband had done.

I rolled over and looked into the green eyes of the only one who could still make me smile.

"Morning, Mommy."

"Good morning, sweetheart." I pulled my son into my arms. "How's Mommy's baby?"

Billy giggled. "I'm not a baby."

"Yes, you are," I said, and tickled him, sending him into a frenzy of giggles.

He rolled around the bed, laughing loudly, and that was when I had my first real thought of my husband: Where was Wyatt? I could count the number of times in our seven years of marriage when Wyatt had opened his eyes before me.

Swinging my legs over the side, I grabbed my bathrobe and asked, "Are you hungry?"

"Uh-huh." Billy nodded. "I want cereal. Cap'n Crunch."

I cringed, but nodded at the same time. I was not a fan of all the sugary cereals that had been staples of my childhood diet, but over the last three days, I'd given Billy whatever he'd wanted—my attempt to assuage the guilt I felt from uprooting my son so suddenly and completely from his life.

I hoisted Billy onto my hip, swung the bedroom's double door open, but I didn't take another step.

All three men looked up—Wyatt and his brother from the sofa, and Newt from the chair.

"Oh!" I clutched the collar of my bathrobe, covering up what little of my chest showed. "I didn't know . . . I thought we were alone." My glance moved between my brother-in-law and our attorney.

Wyatt wore a frown as he looked me up and down. Still, his tone was candy-coated when he said, "Sweetheart, you're not dressed."

Didn't he hear what I'd just said?

"I was going to get Billy some breakfast first, and then—"

He jumped from the couch. "I'll take Billy." Our son crawled from me into his father's arms. Wyatt leaned over and kissed my cheek. "You get dressed. That cop will be here soon and we decided that you should be there this time."

"Me?"

Wyatt raised an eyebrow. "You." Then he turned to our attorney. "Newt thinks Ferguson needs to see me with you, see me as a family man so all of this nonsense can stop." He paused. This time it felt as if Wyatt was looking through me. "So you need to get ready." He spoke slowly as if he wanted to make sure I understood his words. "Ferguson will be here at nine thirty, so get ready." He stopped. "And get dressed."

I nodded and turned back to the bedroom, closing the door behind me. It was 7:48, according to the digital clock on the nightstand; I had more than an hour to get dressed, but I'd need a lifetime of hours to get ready. Was the policeman going to ask me questions? What was I supposed to say if he asked me what I knew.

I squeezed my eyes shut and remembered what I wished I could forget.

Just as I adjusted the blanket over Billy, a sudden pop cracked through the silence of the late night and made me pause. I listened to see if I'd hear it again.

Nothing.

So I let the sound slip from my mind, kissed my son's cheek, and tiptoed out of his room . . .

That night, I had no idea that the sound I heard was a gunshot. That night, I had no idea that the sound I heard would change my life.

And now, I had to talk to this detective. Of course, I didn't want to, but what excuse could I give to explain why I didn't want to stand by my husband's side?

There was nothing I could say, so I rushed to the closet, where my clothes were crushed in a space smaller than one corner of my closet at home.

I knew I needed to be understated, not only because this was serious, but because I didn't want the policeman to see me at all. Because maybe if he didn't notice me, maybe he wouldn't ask questions that I didn't want to answer.

I grabbed my navy sheath just as the bedroom door opened. Glancing over my dress, I said, "I'm just picking out what I'm going to wear."

Wyatt walked toward me and planted another kiss on my cheek. "Good morning again, sweetheart." Then, stepping back, he said, "Did you pack your green dress?"

I frowned. I had a closet the size of this suite filled with a wardrobe that had come from seven years of having an unlimited budget.

Wyatt answered my unasked question. "The emerald-green V-neck I bought for your birthday."

Now my frown was so deep I felt my eyebrows touching. "No. Why? Are we going out somewhere?"

"That's what I want you to wear this morning."

"Wyatt, that dress is evening wear."

"We're having that meeting with Ferguson," he said, as if stating a fact that I already knew was a good enough explanation.

"Well, I don't have it here." And I was so glad that I didn't.

"No problem. I'll have Newt send someone to pick it up for you."

"Wyatt!" I hoped that the way I said his name would remind him of what I looked like in that dress, which he'd bought more for his delight than mine. It really wasn't something that I needed to wear outside of our bedroom.

Like he said, he'd given it to me for my birthday, but then he asked me to wear it two nights later when we went to a neighbor's New Year's Eve party. I'd felt so uncomfortable in the neckline that almost cut to my waist and the hemline that left no room for error.

"So, it's in your closet, right?"

I shook my head. Maybe I needed to say this another way. "That's not business attire."

"And who said this was business? This is all about having the upper hand. And you, my dear, are the weapon that gives me a million upper hands." He kissed me before he moved toward the door. "You can take your time bathing. By the time you get out, your dress will be here."

I was still holding on to the navy sheath as Wyatt walked out of the room.

There were so many ways to say no, but Wyatt never heard me. He never listened to any of my protests about anything, including when it came to what he wanted me to wear.

Sometimes it was hard for me to believe that this was the man that I'd met eleven years ago. *That* man hated the exploitation of women; at least, that's what he led me to believe.

I tugged at the pink shorts the way I'd done every day for the past week. But the fabric didn't come down. The barely-there shorts were still barely there, but at least they covered up more than the cropped top. The top was already a size too small, leaving no need for imagination. My 36DDs were on display. And that was before I put on the two bras that management insisted we wear to hike up the cleavage. My cleavage didn't need a bit of hiking, but I needed this job.

Though I didn't like the shorts, and could do without the top, there was a part of my uniform that I really hated. The Hair and The Makeup.

I was a ponytail, smidgen-of-makeup kind of girl. But not at Twin Peaks. Here it was hair down—all the time. Makeup—natural, but applied to accentuate my features, whatever that meant.

But it didn't matter what I liked or didn't like. I was a Twin Peaks girl on a mission to make enough money so that I could move out of the one-bedroom apartment I shared with my mother. At twenty-two, it was time.

So I added one more coat of mascara, covered my lips with another layer of Glorious Red shiny gloss, and then fluffed my hair.

Turning sideways, I asked, "How do I look?"

"Fabulous," my new friend, Keisha, said. She'd been with Twin Peaks for over seven months, so she was the expert-in-residence. All last week, anything that I needed to know, Keisha told me.

She said, "Let's go out there and make some money."

We walked out of the locker room together, checked in with the manager, then got to work.

As I took one last glance in the mirror between the dining room and the kitchen, I was still amazed at just how ordinary my life had turned out.

Four years out of high school and I hadn't set the world on fire. Even though I'd always been told I had the looks, a modeling gig that a friend of a friend of a friend had set up for me in New York had turned out to involve no clothes and a camera. So less than a week after I'd made the trek from Philly to New York, I was back home, once again living with my mother.

I'd tried a few corporate temp jobs, but since I knew nothing about technology beyond my cell phone, I couldn't find a place to fit in the corporate world.

But there was one thing I knew how to do—wait on tables. It was in my DNA since that was the only job I'd ever known my mother to have.

Since high school, I'd worked at five different restaurants, nothing too upscale. I was still trying to put together a plan, though, because God knows this was not the way I wanted to spend my life. But what was a high school graduate with average grades and below-average scores on the college entrance exams supposed to do?

"You ready to hit it?" Keisha asked, bringing me back to my reality.

"Yeah." At least I'd gotten this gig at Twin Peaks, where the tips were way better than at other places. After my first week, I'd tripled what I'd been making in tips anywhere else.

I walked into the front of the restaurant at exactly the same time as a group of five guys barged in.

"Hi! Welcome to Twin Peaks," I said as if I were glad to see these dudes. I could tell these five forty-something-year-old men with their boisterous talk and laughter were going to be rowdy.

As the suited men sat at their round table, I glanced down at their shoes—a quick assessment that my mother had taught me when I was just eleven.

They had on the usual black business shoes shined to a high gloss, except for one; this guy wore suede ankle boots. Not at all flashy like the other guys.

I liked him already—until I looked up. I guess you could say that he was kind of cute—if you liked walruses. Because he looked like a walrus. With hair. Lots of hair. Like a mop of hair. A walrus with a mop of hair.

I didn't get much time to study him, though. They hadn't even sat all the way down when they were all over me. Not in a physical way.

It was with their eyes. They leered at me as if I were dancing naked. But I smiled like I enjoyed being ogled and took their drink orders, wondering how bad it would be once they were drunk.

Their order was simple: beers for all, except for the walrus guy, who ordered a scotch, straight, no chaser.

"And put it all on one tab," the one who was sitting closest to me said.

Ah . . . the leader. I now knew where to direct my attention.

When I returned with their drinks, I asked, "So what are you having today?"

The leader leaned forward. "What about you?" he said. "Can we all have you?" He made a circular motion with his hands, letting me know that he meant the whole group.

Four of the five laughed. The walrus guy was the only one who looked away and down into his scotch.

I kept my smile as I said, "Nope, I'm no groupie."

"Ah . . . that's pretty funny. Group, groupie, get it?" the leader interpreted for the rest as if he were the smartest.

Then he scooted to the edge of his seat and lowered his voice, as if he and I were about to have a private conversation. "So what if it's not a group? What if it's just you and me?"

Inside I sighed and wondered, Why did I have to go through this just to get a paycheck? But I remembered that I was an entertainer. And the tips. I had to remember my tip.

So I laughed (although there wasn't anything funny) and I said, "I don't do married men either."

For some reason, that was even more hilarious to all of them . . . well, except for the walrus, who was still studying his drink.

The leader actually pouted as if he'd meant what he'd said about us getting together and he was upset that I wouldn't consider it. "Well, all of us here are married." He glanced around the table and paused on Mr. Walrus. "Except for Wyatt over there." He pointed him out. "Hey, Wyatt, she's looking for a guy who's not married."

More laughter and then the walrus guy looked up. Wyatt. I was glad to have something to call him in my head besides a funny-looking mammal.

"So, would you marry him?" the leader asked, daring me to tell the truth.

When I said nothing, they cracked up so hard I thought some of them were going to start rolling on the floor. But Wyatt didn't laugh. He returned his glance to his glass and I felt sorry for him. These guys were the male version of the mean girls in school. And I hated all of them.

But—the tip. And since it was probably the intellectual leader who would be paying, I laughed, took their food order, and bantered with them for the next hour while they devoured curly fries and wings and a couple of pounds of crab legs.

The whole time, I watched Wyatt the Walrus. Though he chatted and laughed a little with them, he wasn't of their nature. Really, he seemed to be the only one who had any sense. For sure, he had respectability; at least he had my respect, because never did he join in when they talked about the way my tank top fit my "twin peaks," or the things they imagined I could do with my legs.

What was Wyatt doing hanging out with these guys?

That table worked me, making me go back for a couple more rounds of beer and more orders of fries. But I kept up with them, glad that they were pushing up the bill.

When I brought the almost-two-hundred-dollar check to the table, I left it near the leader, but Wyatt leaned across and grabbed the folder.

That made me smile. These guys might have had the big mouths, but it seemed Wyatt had the big wallet.

And . . . the big tip! When he signed the credit-card receipt, he'd scribbled "100" in the gratuity line.

My eyes widened, and when I looked at him, he winked. And he smiled. Really smiled for the first time.

I said good-bye to the other four, but I gave Wyatt a personal farewell. "Thank you," I told him when he lingered behind.

"You're welcome," he said. Then he added, "I hope you're okay with the way they talked to you the whole time."

I laughed. "That's just what happens at Twin Peaks."

His eyes roamed over me, but when he did that, it didn't feel as disgusting as when other guys did it. "And the way you're dressed."

I shrugged. "It's just the uniform I have to wear."

He nodded as if he understood, but then he said, "Maybe you shouldn't be working here."

That made me laugh harder than before. As if I had options. "I don't have anywhere else to work."

"Maybe I'll have to do something about that." He gave me another *quick scan while he said, "You deserve better than walking around half naked." Then he kinda swiveled in his suede boots and walked out of there, leaving me wondering all kinds of things about him.*

Wyatt had gained my respect that day back in 2003. I didn't know if I'd ever see him again, but I would always remember how kind he'd been. And how he cared about how women were exploited.

But then we were married and Wyatt became the Exploiter-in-Chief. He'd drag me to all kinds of business meetings, using me to close a deal with financiers, or to negotiate better prices with suppliers, or even to hire a top employee away from a competitor.

But today with Detective Ferguson—this was the lowest of Wyatt's lows. Did he really believe that he could influence someone who was investigating the killing of a young man by distracting him with his nearly naked wife?

No, this time, I wasn't going to do it. I couldn't, I wouldn't wear that dress. I was already saving Wyatt's life by not saying anything about what I knew. That would have to be enough.

Tossing the sheath onto the bed, I dashed into the bathroom. I had two hopes: one was that whoever was being sent on that errand wouldn't find the dress, and the other was that if I was already dressed before the errand runner returned, Wyatt wouldn't send me back to change in front of Newt. It would look too ridiculous, and that's one impression Wyatt never wanted to give—that he was ridiculous. Or stupid. Or anything that negated all of his country-boy-done-good accomplishments.

So I jumped into the shower. And then I prayed. I prayed as I bathed and I prayed as I dried off. Prayed through my routine; prayed for the whole hour that it took me to get dressed.

As I looked in the mirror, I knew Wyatt would approve. My

hair was blown out—full and a little bit frizzy, the way he liked it. My face was plastered with makeup that was way too heavy for daytime, especially the bright red lipstick that made my collagen-filled lips the first thing everyone saw when I entered a room.

But Wyatt liked that, too. He'd like this whole look. Once I stepped into the living room, Wyatt would realize that with my hair and my makeup, and my dress and my pearls, this was far more appropriate for a meeting with a man who could take or make his life.

I stepped into the sheath, then glanced at my reflection in the mirror. As I zipped up the back, I checked the clock—just a minute before nine.

I'd won.

That was when the bedroom door opened. Wyatt walked in, a garment bag folded over his arm. His disapproval was in his glare.

"I . . . I put this on because . . ." I pointed to the clock. "Won't Detective Ferguson be here at nine?"

His eyes didn't leave mine. "He'll be here at nine thirty."

"Oh, I thought you said nine."

"I said nine thirty." He spoke to me in the tone he used when correcting Billy.

My shoulders slumped. "Wyatt, please," I whispered.

He handed me the garment bag and then did what he always did. He kissed my cheek, then patted my head. "You'll look beautiful, sweetheart. Just like you always do." He turned and was almost at the door when he added, "Please hurry. I want you to be the one to greet the good cop at the door."

I shook my head.

He said, "All you have to do is say hello." He paused then

added, "That's all. You won't be saying anything else." He gave me another very long look.

Then he left.

And I shook.

Why couldn't I just say no? Why didn't I ever just say no?

I picked up the garment bag, slid out of the dress, and did what I always did: I acquiesced to Wyatt's wishes.

Chapter 19

I hadn't even bothered to look in the mirror. Why? Because I knew what I looked like. There was no need to be embarrassed sooner than I needed to be.

But now I was officially embarrassed.

It was the way all conversation stopped when I stepped out of the bedroom. The way Newt looked at me. And the way Wally actually licked his bottom lip.

And then there was Wyatt. Who beamed like I was a trophy.

"You look beautiful, sweetheart," he said, getting up and greeting me. I tilted my head the way he liked so that he could give me an air kiss. He wouldn't want to ruin my makeup; he never wanted to ruin my makeup.

I pressed my legs together, hoping that would bring down the hem of my dress, and then I waited for Wyatt to direct me.

"I was just sending Wally to his room with Billy so you, Newt, and I can review what we're going to do with Ferguson."

"Okay, let me get Billy dressed," I said, thinking this might be the perfect out. If I were taking care of my son when Detective Ferguson arrived, I wouldn't have to see the officer. And he wouldn't have to see me.

But Wyatt took my hand and led me to the large table in the dining area. "That's okay. He's just going next door. You can get him dressed afterward." Then, to our son, Wyatt said, "Say bye to Mommy."

Billy turned to me and reached up his arms. I normally knelt down to talk to my son at his eye level. And hug him and kiss him. And tell him I loved him.

But in this dress, I couldn't bend an inch. So I just wiggled my fingers. "I'll see you in a little while, angel. Okay?"

Billy folded, then unfolded his fingers, his language for me to lift him up. But I just slid into the chair and waved as Wally took his hand, leading him from the room.

Wyatt sat next to me, then Newt followed, wiggling into the chair across from us.

"Well, now we can get started."

Was Newt panting?

Newt "ahemmed" as if there was something in his throat. He slid a few pages from his folder, and when he looked up, his eyes zoomed right in on my cleavage. "Uh," he muttered before he forced his eyes away. "Let's go over your statement one more time, Wyatt."

I didn't want to be here, listening to this again. I'd heard Wyatt's version before. Twice—right after, and then the next morning when he returned from the police station after his all-night questioning.

I was in such shock on that night from all that had happened. But it was Wyatt's tale that was the biggest shocker. First, when he'd told it to me, and then when he'd told it to me and my mother. He'd given an account that was so different from the facts that I knew.

And now he was ready to spin his tale again.

"Okay." My husband placed his palms flat on the table before he started. "I was sitting in my living room when headlights shined through our window. I peeked out and noticed a car parked right in front. I didn't recognize the car, so I went outside—"

"Wait," Newt said, looking up. He glanced at my chest again, then turned his gaze to Wyatt. "Remember you have to say that you weren't concerned at first."

"Right. Right." Another deep breath and Wyatt continued: "I didn't recognize the car, but I wasn't concerned at first. It wasn't until I went into the kitchen, then passed back through the living room." He stopped.

Newt said, "Let's say you came back thirty, forty minutes later."

"Should I say thirty or forty?"

"Say both," Newt advised. "You don't want to be too exact. You don't want to sound like you're rehearsed."

Wyatt nodded. "It wasn't until I went into the kitchen," my husband continued, sounding like this was rehearsed, "and then passed back through the living room thirty or forty minutes later that I noticed the car again. That's when I got worried."

"Don't say 'worried,' say 'concerned.'"

"I got concerned." My husband corrected himself. "So I stepped out of the house and went down my driveway to the car. I saw a white girl sitting with a black guy."

"I told you before, don't mention their race. White people can never talk about race."

Wyatt sighed as if he thought that was ridiculous, but he nodded as if he knew that was the truth. He said, "I saw a girl sitting in a car with a boy—"

"Don't call him a boy."

Wyatt blinked as if this was all getting too complicated. "So I can call her a girl, but I can't call him a boy?"

Newt nodded. "You're white, she's white, you can call her anything you want."

"But I can't call a black boy a black boy?"

Newt shrugged his answer and added, "Not one that you just killed."

Blowing out a long breath, Wyatt continued: "I saw a girl sitting in a car with . . . a guy, but the girl was crying. And so I was worried. I mean, I was concerned, and I knocked on the window."

My husband paused, but Newt nodded for him to keep going.

"When she rolled down the window, I asked if she was all right. She shook her head, but the boy, I mean, guy wouldn't let her speak and told me to mind my business. I told him this was my business and I asked the young lady if she wanted to get out of the car. It seemed to me like she was nodding, but that's when the guy jumped out of the car. I walked toward the back, to meet him, just to calm him down, talk to him a little, but he came at me with a baseball bat."

I closed my eyes, wondering if there was a way for me to close my ears as well.

But I heard it all as Wyatt kept on. "I got scared. I was fearing for my life and I didn't have time to think and I shot him."

Newt nodded. "That's good. Let's take out the part about you didn't have time to think."

"Why? Isn't it good that it was a reflex?"

Newt lowered his head and pondered the question for a moment. "I don't know, it could play either way, and what I have to think about is how these words will sound to a jury."

Every time Newt mentioned anything about court, my heart leaped. Or my stomach gurgled. This time, I suffered from both.

My husband didn't like those words either. "But you keep telling me this isn't going to court."

"And it isn't. But I wouldn't be a good attorney if I didn't play this like a chess game and stay seven moves ahead of my opponent. I have to think in the unlikely chance that this goes before a jury, what plays best—did you think about it or not? Is a black boy's life so valueless to you that you didn't think or did you give it careful consideration before you decided to shoot him dead? Which is more believable, more salable?"

Wyatt nodded. "So, which way do you want me to go?"

"Leave it all out for now. I'll decide when Ferguson gets here. It depends on what he says." He paused, stared at me, and let his eyes rest on my cleavage again.

It wasn't until I shifted, and tugged at my neckline, that he looked away.

Newt made one of those clearing-his-throat sounds again and said, "Okay, I think we're ready." The knock on the door made him add, "And, it seems, just in time."

Newt moved to push his chair back, but Wyatt said, "Let Meredith open the door."

I didn't even try to hide the way I shook my head.

"No, I'll get it," Newt said.

Wyatt shook his head. "That dude is black, right?" The rest of his explanation he told with his eyes—when his glance roamed over me.

I rolled my shoulders forward and lowered my head, wishing there was a way for me to shrink and eventually disappear.

Newt's only answer was that he frowned.

Wyatt said, "Meredith, open the door, please."

Slowly, I stood and walked, taking the tiniest of steps. When I opened the door, the detective and I shared a frozen moment. That little bit of time when two people are faced with the grand questions: What should I say, what should I do?

I was struck by how handsome this man was. Now, I'd never been one of those white women who is into black men, but I always acknowledged attractiveness, and this man was more than good-looking. I'd only seen him on television, but in person, his features were sharper, his shoulders were broader, his presence was commanding.

I gave him my signature smile, held out my hand, and played my role. "Detective Ferguson. I'm Meredith Spencer."

He took my hand, but really only touched my fingers as if he thought touching any more of my skin might be a crime, and then he stepped into our hotel suite.

"Hello." He kept his eyes above my neckline and gave me two quick shakes of my fingers before releasing me.

I didn't even realize that Wyatt and Newt were behind me until Mr. Ferguson greeted them. I closed the door as they exchanged the social niceties expected from men of a certain age and stature.

As they did that little chat before they sat, I studied the detective.

Many men and women looked at me and assumed that with my blond hair and green eyes I wasn't very bright.

That was my advantage.

And I had a feeling the same was true for Detective Ferguson. If I didn't know better, I would have taken him for a twenty-years-past-his-prime jock, who stayed in shape, and fought hard against the pounds that came with age. I would have thought him to be more athletic than intelligent, because he was black.

And there was his advantage.

"Let's sit down," Wyatt said finally.

They all waited until I sat, then they joined me.

The detective started. "I don't want to take too much of your time. We're wrapping up our investigation."

"I'm glad," my husband said. His voice was so solemn I had to look at him twice. "I really want this to be over. Not just for me, but for that poor lad's family, too."

Lad?

I was able to keep a straight face at that ridiculous word, but I guessed it was better than "boy." Newt did some more of that clearing of his throat.

Detective Ferguson pulled a pad from his pocket, the way policemen did on TV.

"First, thank you, Mr. Spencer," he said, looking at my husband, "for doing this with me one last time."

"You're welcome, although I was surprised, since you have all of this on tape already."

"Yes, but I have a few questions I can't ask the tape." And then the detective chuckled as if this questioning was not a major deal.

My husband and Newt chuckled along. And inside, I smiled. Newt and Wyatt just didn't know.

"Plus, I want to make sure we have everything before we turn this over to the state prosecutor."

It was so smooth, the way he said it, that if I hadn't been listening carefully, I might not have heard it. But I heard it, and Wyatt and Newt did, too.

"What?" my husband said, looking between the detective and Newt. "Turn this over to the prosecutor? For what?"

Newt gave my husband a long look that was meant to shut him

up before he turned to Detective Ferguson. "You're not saying my client is going to be prosecuted?"

"Oh, no, but you know how this works." He shrugged a little bit. "There are steps we have to take and procedures we have to follow . . . This is normal."

Newt stared at the detective before he turned to Wyatt. "This is all procedural," he said.

"Great! So let's get started," Detective Ferguson said. "So tell me again, what happened that night?"

If the detective had meant to take a little bit of my husband's confidence away, it worked. Because I heard just the slightest bit of unsteadiness when Wyatt began, repeating the story that he'd just rehearsed.

He talked about being concerned, he didn't mention the "lad's" or the girl's race, never said the word "boy," and he added the "thirty to forty minutes." He repeated the story verbatim, sounding more like a well-oiled machine than a human, and he paused only when he got to "I was scared. I feared for my life."

The policeman, who'd been jotting down notes, looked up. "That's it?"

Newt jumped in. "That's it. As you can see, my client acted only on reflex. It was a fight-or-flight impulse, and in this state, you have a right to stand and fight."

The detective nodded. "So they say."

Newt's eyes narrowed. "Yes . . . they say. This was self-defense."

Again the detective nodded. But this time he said nothing, which seemed to unnerve Newt more.

Newt added, "Wyatt was standing his ground. And in this state, as long as he saw a weapon and feared for his life, he could protect himself."

"So the law says," the detective said.

"Wyatt saw a weapon; that kid came at him with that bat," Newt said. "And he told you he feared for his life."

Another nod from the detective, but this time it was accompanied by a bit of a smirk.

My husband didn't seem to notice that little toe-to-toe exchange between the detective and the attorney. Wyatt said to Detective Ferguson, "So you understand. I had to protect myself." He reached over and touched my hand. "And my wife and son."

The detective's only response was to glance down at his notepad once again. "Well, I think I have everything that I need."

That was too quick. And clearly, my husband thought so, too. Wyatt said, "That's all?"

The detective nodded, moved to stand, but when he was halfway up, he stopped. "One more thing," he began while he was still slightly bent over, "did Marquis say anything before he swung the bat at you?"

"What?"

"Did Marquis say anything?" the detective repeated.

Wyatt's eyes turned to Newt, but with the detective having a good view of both of them, Newt wouldn't be able to play ventriloquist. "Uh, I'm not sure," Wyatt said. "I think he called me something."

"You think?"

"Yeah, I kinda remember him saying something." He glanced at Newt again. "He . . . he called me something."

"He called you a name? Did he call you *by* your name? Did he recognize you? Did you know him?"

His questions were like rapid fire and I was sure that this was some kind of technique. Especially the way it had my husband shifting from one side of his chair to the other.

"No, I didn't recognize him. I didn't know him. That's why I shot him."

"You shot him because you didn't know him?"

Newt moaned.

"No! I shot him because he threatened me," my husband shouted.

"With a stick."

"No, it was a bat! I told you that. He swung that bat and I wasn't about to get hit in the head."

"Okay." The detective's voice seemed to be several decibels lower than it was before. Or was I just imagining that because Wyatt had raised his voice to one degree below a shout?

Now Detective Ferguson was standing straight and my husband and Newt were sitting down, looking up. "Again, thank you for your time." He took two steps toward the door and then turned back to me. "Mrs. Spencer, were you the one who called 911?"

"She didn't call," Wyatt said, now acting like my ventriloquist. "But you know that already," he said like he was making an accusation. "You know that I called from my cell phone. When I went back outside."

The detective frowned as if he didn't understand. "Back outside?" He let a beat pass. "Oh, yeah, that's right. You had to go back into your house to get your cell. That's so curious to me."

My husband's eyes darted from the policeman to Newt then back to Mr. Ferguson.

"Why?" Wyatt began slowly. "I didn't have my cell so I had to go into the house to get it to call 911."

Detective Ferguson nodded.

Then, just when relief filled my husband's face, the detective asked, "So . . . the first time you left your house, when you went to see who was sitting in the car, you left your cell inside, but you took your gun?"

"Detective Ferguson," Newt said, now standing.

"Usually their cell and wallet are the first things someone reaches for," the detective continued as if Newt hadn't spoken.

"I wasn't going anywhere, I was just checking—"

"But you took your gun to check?"

"Because . . . Look, I have the right to carry a gun. I told you I have a license."

"Yeah, we checked that out."

"So I did nothing wrong!" Now Wyatt was shouting.

Detective Ferguson was not fazed. "Nothing wrong except that a young boy is dead."

"That's not my fault. He deserved—"

"Wyatt!" Newt shouted, his face now crimson. Then he turned to Ferguson.

But the detective continued his questioning. "So back to the phone. You went into the house and where was it?"

"Where was what?" Wyatt frowned and shook his head.

"Your phone? Where do you keep it?"

"On the table, by the door."

"Is that where it was?"

"Yeah!" Wyatt said clearly agitated. "I told you . . ."

"Detective," Newt jumped in again. "I'm going to have to stop—"

But the detective held up his hand. He said, "I think I have enough . . . for now. Thanks again."

We didn't take a single breath as the detective walked toward the door. But then, before he put his hand on the knob, he held up his finger as if he were remembering one more thing. "Did you witness any of this?" he asked me.

"No, she didn't." Again Wyatt spoke for me.

The detective's eyes bored through me, and if he had even an iota of Superman's powers, he would have seen the secret I kept.

As if my husband hadn't spoken, the policeman said, "Mrs. Spencer?" and then waited for the answer to come out of my own mouth.

I shook my head. "I was in our house." That was the truth.

He said, "So you didn't see anything out of the window?"

"No." Another truth.

"Did you see anything at all?" the detective asked me.

"I told you," Wyatt jumped in, stopping me from having to tell my first lie. "She didn't see anything! She was inside; I was outside."

"Detective Ferguson, this has been traumatic for everyone. I think my client just wants to protect his wife."

"Because she has nothing to do with this," Wyatt said. "I shot that boy."

The detective let a couple of beats of silence go by before he said, "Yes, you did."

The detective's eyes narrowed, but my husband glared back. I always thought of Wyatt as such a bright man. But he wasn't smart enough to realize that he couldn't intimidate a detective. This man wasn't like the black teenagers who stuffed cheesesteaks between bread or senior citizens who swept the floors at Wyatt's Cheesesteak Castles.

Finally, though, it was Ferguson who gave a slight smile. And now, I felt that if I had Superwoman's powers, I would be able to see the secret that the detective held.

He said good-bye to all of us and gave me a look that had nothing to do with the dress I was wearing.

Detective Ferguson closed the door behind him, and seconds

ticked . . . one, two, three . . . seven, eight, nine . . . before Newt spoke up.

"You let Ferguson rile you up and set you up."

"What are you talking about?" Wyatt barked.

"You forgot what you said when they taped you down at the station. You said you went upstairs to get your cell phone. That's why your call went in to 911 three minutes after the girl's, remember?"

"I forgot." Wyatt shrugged. "What's the big deal?"

"It's a major contradiction that Ferguson didn't have before he walked in here. There was always a hole in your story, Wyatt, about why you didn't call the police right away. Why was there that big gap of time? And if your cell phone was right by the front door, there wouldn't have been a three-minute gap."

"So what? I just forgot."

"That might've worked if your contradiction wasn't coupled with your temper." Newt blew out a long breath. "Before he walked in here, it was over."

Wyatt folded his arms. "I was tired of answering the same questions."

"The police can ask the same question one hundred times. You always have to answer."

This time, all my husband did was huff.

Newt laid his arms on the table and sighed. "I have a feeling that we're in a fight now. And if that was round one, I think we lost."

Chapter 20

I glanced at the closed bedroom door where Wyatt had been hunkered down since the meeting with Ferguson yesterday, watching every news report about Marquis Johnson and Wyatt Spencer. I couldn't believe the nonstop coverage; it was too much to me. But even when the news shifted to another story, Wyatt stayed in front of the television, since he recorded every segment with the TV/DVR that he'd had Newt bring to the hotel.

"What does the NAACP have to do with this?" I heard Wyatt shout.

Leaning against the wall that was right across from the bedroom, I slid down until my butt hit the floor, then crossed my legs in the lotus position. I needed to meditate, so that I would be ready for whatever happened next.

I closed my eyes and saw the events from May 12 again, as if they were on a never-ending repeat reel.

This was not working. I opened my eyes, stretched out my legs, and stared at the bedroom door.

I wanted to remember something different. So I took myself to a different day, a better day, another time, when Wyatt had changed my life.

Even though I would always remember Wyatt the Walrus some-where in the recesses of my mind, he was all but forgotten until I walked into Twin Peaks for my shift the next day. He was almost block-ing the door when I stepped into the restaurant.

"Hi," I said, at first glad to see him. But then my mind went straight to that tip—had he realized how much he'd given me and was here to take it back?

But he knocked that fear right out of my mind with, "I came back to see you. I wanna have lunch, but told them I'd wait for you."

"Okay." I'd never had anyone do that before, but it worked for me. "Where are your buddies?"

"Those guys aren't my friends; they're business associates. So today, I came alone." Then, his voice got shy-soft. "I wanted to see you."

"It's good to see you, too. I'll be right back," I said.

His smile twisted into a grin.

"I just have to change into my uniform."

His grin twisted into a frown.

"They don't let us wear them to work."

"That's a good thing; you can't walk around the streets looking like that."

I nodded. "Don't go anywhere."

That brought his grin right back, but I was only saying it because if he tipped me today like he tipped me yesterday, then I'd be one hundred dollars closer to my goal.

I dashed to the back, determined to dress in record time so none of the other girls could get near Wyatt.

Seven minutes after he greeted me, I was back on the floor; he was seated at a table and had put in an order for a Cobb salad and a scotch on the rocks.

"*So what's a nice girl like you doing in a place like this?*" he asked when I set his drink in front of him.

It didn't surprise me that he couldn't come up with a better line. Even though I could tell his suit was kinda expensive (the Macy's kind of expensive rather than the Rittenhouse Row expensive) and he was well groomed, looking like he'd recently had a manicure, there was a part of him that seemed out of place. Like he wasn't really all that comfortable in that suit . . . or his skin.

But still, I answered his question. "I actually just started working here."

He shook his head. "Walking around like that." Like the day before, his eyes roamed over me, but not in a sneering, leering kind of way.

"It's my job," I said.

"Why don't you look for another one?"

"Because I like it here." I was getting annoyed. I mean, why was he coming down on me for being a waitress at Twin Peaks? At least it was an honest way to get a day's pay.

He must have sensed my attitude because he held up his hands. "I was just thinking that you're such a beautiful woman and I can tell that you're smart."

Now, that was a pretty good cleanup line. "How can you tell that?"

"By the way you handled my associates yesterday. A person has to be smart to be quick."

"Well, thanks for the compliment. Let me get your food."

By the time I served his salad, the lunch-hour crowd had packed the place and I was working four tables. So I couldn't chat anymore; I just hoped that wouldn't affect my tip.

It didn't.

Wyatt left me another one hundred dollars; this time, the tip was more than his bill. I rushed into the locker room just so I could let out a whoop.

When I showed Keisha my tip, she cheered with me. "Dang, girl. What do you think Pops wants from you? Did he ask for your number or something?"

I laughed. "Pops?"

"Yeah, he's old."

"How old do you think he is?"

"I dunno. Like forty, fifty."

"Yeah, that's what I think, but he didn't ask for anything. He's definitely not interested in me that way. He just doesn't like us walking around in these uniforms."

"Yeah, all right." Keisha laughed. "Trust me, if you weren't wearing that, he wouldn't be giving you one-hundred-dollar tips. Let's just hope that he comes back."

And Keisha's hope became my reality. Day after day, Wyatt showed up for lunch. And day after day that turned into week after week, I served him.

I began enjoying our talks, or rather I enjoyed his interest in me because our talks were always just a series of questions.

"So, did you go to college?"

"No, I wasn't that kind of student."

"I can't imagine that. You probably didn't have the right guidance."

Then:

"If you could be anything that you wanted to be, what would you choose to do?"

"I don't know. I guess be a doctor."

"Why?"

"'Cause they make the most money."

"I'm not talking about money; I'm talking about what's in your heart. What would you do from your heart?"

I thought for a second. "I'd wanna be a good wife and a great mother. I wanna have a family." I stopped because I had never thought of that before. Is that what I really wanted? I guess I did—people always wanted what they never had.

I got so used to seeing Wyatt that I stopped counting the consecutive days (stopping at thirty-three) that he'd shown up, though I didn't stop counting those tips. One hundred dollars every day, five days a week—serving Wyatt was the best gig I'd ever landed. I'd never had more than fifty dollars in my bank account at any given time, but now I had over three thousand dollars. Because of him, I started looking in the paper for affordable apartments.

But then he stopped. Without a word or a warning, he didn't show up one day, which turned into two, then three and four. By the fifth day, I knew that I wouldn't see him again.

And I missed him. It was more than the tips. It was that I'd never had anyone show any kind of interest in me—ever.

I got to that point where I forgot about him. So of course, that's when he showed up three months later. I was heading out of Twin Peaks and he was heading in.

"Hi!" I said with all kinds of glee in my voice. "Where've you been?"

"You didn't think that I was going to eat Cobb salads for the rest of my life, did you?"

I laughed. "You can order something else."

He took a quick peek inside the restaurant and said, "Nah, I only came by to see you."

That made me shift from one foot to the other. Now that I thought *about it, wasn't it kind of weird for someone to be at a restaurant every single day? And now he just happened to waiting for me outside of Twin Peaks?*

But then in the softest, kindest, gentlest voice, he said, "Why don't you have dinner with me?"

"Thanks, but we're not allowed to fraternize with the customers."

He frowned. "How would they know?"

That was a good question. And actually, no one had explained that rule in the employee manual to me.

Still, I didn't know a thing about this guy. But then I thought about all the tips. And though I didn't think he'd given me those tips for this purpose, I said, "Instead of dinner, what about a cup of coffee in that Starbucks across the street?"

"Okay, that's good enough for me."

After we ordered—hot chocolate for me and a black coffee for him—we parked at one of those café tables and talked and talked and talked.

Just like in the restaurant, Wyatt asked me questions about everything.

"So what do you do for fun?"

I said "I take on as many shifts working as I can."

That made him frown. "I know your life is more than that. A beautiful girl like you. You must have dozens of suitors lined up waiting to take you home every day."

"I don't know what's funnier," I said, chuckling. "Dozens or suitors? My mom uses that word and it always makes me laugh."

The way the corners of his lips turned down a little bit, I felt like I'd hurt his feelings.

"But I like it. I mean, I don't have dozens of suitors. I don't have any. Guys just don't ask me out."

"Is there something wrong with you?"

I laughed again.

He said, "Because that can be the only reason; I mean, look at you."

"Awww, that's so nice, but no, there's nothing wrong with me. Guys have told me that I'm unapproachable, though I don't know what that means. I once heard Halle Berry tell Oprah that the hardest thing for her to do was get a date on Friday night. And I understand that."

He shook his head. "These young guys don't know what they're missing."

"Young guys?" I took a sip of my hot chocolate. "How old are you?"

He raised his eyebrows. "Don't you know you're never supposed to ask a man his age?"

I laughed. "I thought that was only for women."

"Oh, yeah, you're right." He paused, as if he didn't want to tell me. As if he were calculating in his head, trying to come up with some number that I would believe.

I did my own calculations, figuring he was forty-one, forty-two.

"I'm forty-eight."

"That's how old my mom is."

The corners of his lips turned down once again. Dang, if I kept hurting his feelings, he'd just get up and walk out.

That's when I decided it was time for me to go. We'd sat in this Starbucks from the end of my shift at five until the sun had bowed to the summer night.

"Well, this has been great, Wyatt." I made a move like I was about to rise up from my chair.

"Before you go, I have a proposition." And before the frown could completely take over my face, he added, "It's about a job."

A job? I sat all the way back down. "What kind of job?" I asked, thinking that this might be my chance to really rake in some good *money. Two jobs: Twin Peaks and whatever Wyatt was talking about.*

He said, *"Well, it's not just any job. You'd first have to go back to school."*

"Like college?" I shook my head before he could even answer. "Then that job is out because I'm too old to go to college, not to mention the money it would cost to do it."

"How old are you?"

I laughed. "Don't you know you're not supposed to ask a woman her age?"

He chuckled, but the way he kept his eyes on mine let me know that he expected an answer. "I'm twenty-two."

He shook his head. "And that's too old?"

"The kids who were in high school with me are graduating from college this year."

"So?"

"Well, even if you don't think it's crazy for me to just be starting college, I don't have that kind of money. So if this is a job that needs a college degree, I'm not your girl."

"You are my girl." The way he said that made me sit back a little bit. "I mean, you're the girl for this. I own a couple of restaurants," he said. "And I'm looking for a good manager."

"What kind of restaurants."

"Cheesesteak Castles."

"You own those? That's cool. But they're not exactly the kind of places I'm used to working."

"I'm not looking for a waitress. I have three restaurants now and am looking to open more. So, I need an on-site manger to help with the day-to-day operations. And I want to begin a foundation, something for inner-city kids. You're young; you can help me with that."

That was impressive, but still, I wondered. "Why me?"

"Because I've seen you work."

"Oh, I get it." I nodded. *"That's why you came in there every day. You were checking me out."*

He only answered with a shrug and a smile and then went on to tell me everything about his business: how he didn't attend college, but with the insurance money he received after his father's death, he'd done something he'd always wanted to do: he opened up a business five years ago. A year later, he opened his second location and a year after that, his third.

I was impressed. There was a Cheesesteak Castle right around the corner from me and I ate there all the time. And now here I was talking to the founder. Wyatt didn't say it, but I had the feeling that he was making millions, especially when he told me he'd just bought and renovated a house in Haverford. Those houses over there were already like mansions; what had he turned his house into?

"Your wife must be really happy she married you."

"I don't have a wife . . . yet."

I was thinking that at forty-eight, that "yet" was probably getting kinda close to never. But that was none of my business.

What was my business were the plans that this man had for me, because it got even better when he told me that the training part of the program would be an all-expenses-paid ride to the Community College of Philadelphia.

"You're kidding!"

"I'm not. The scholarship even comes with a small apartment that's close to the main campus, so you can take classes and really take advantage of college life."

My own apartment? That was my life's dream!

He said, "Then during school breaks, you'll be working at the main Cheesesteak Castle—in the back office with me."

"I can't believe this." Then I rolled back all of my happy feelings. *"How do I know this is real?"*

"You say yes, and I'll draw up a contract. With everything in it. From your tuition being covered to your rent being paid."

It was that apartment that made those happy feelings once again bubble and burst. *"When do you want me to start?"*

"Right now."

"Okay. I'll give my notice tomorrow and start in two weeks."

He shook his head. *"I meant right now."*

That didn't make any sense. Everybody knew that an employee had to give notice.

He kept on: *"It's now or never. You start with me today and I'll write you a check for the first installment on your stipend, and within a week, you'll be in your apartment. The fall semester begins in a month, so you'll have time to get settled, and pick your classes."*

"This is kinda fast."

"I'm in the fast-food business; this is how I make my money, and this is how I live my life—fast."

I had been searching for a way to change my life and this would be more than life-changing: this would be forever-changing.

Still, I wondered . . . but I talked myself out of my questions. It was true that I didn't know this man, but I knew Wyatt better than I'd known any of my past employers.

So we shook hands, and the next day, I called Twin Peaks, apologized for leaving them, and prayed that it worked out with Wyatt because I'd never be able to use Twin Peaks as a reference.

That began my journey of a life with Wyatt . . .

It had been quite a ride—in the beginning. Wyatt had done every bit of what he promised, making me feel like I was the star in my own *Pretty Woman* movie.

I had my own furnished one-bedroom apartment, and I majored in English at Wyatt's request, though I thought business management was more appropriate. But he said he wanted his manager to be well rounded, learning language and culture—whatever that meant. Since he was paying the bills, I did what he said, went to school, aced my classes, and during school breaks, I worked by Wyatt's side.

But it wasn't all work with Wyatt Spencer. He exposed me to a life that I'd never known existed: we went to New York to see plays on Broadway and to the Kennedy Center in Washington, DC, to see the ballet. And right in Philadelphia, we went to the Kimmel Center for the Performing Arts to see the Philadelphia Orchestra.

We did all the things that my mother called highbrow, all the things that I'd never really thought someone like Wyatt would enjoy. But he did, and so did I.

But the best part for me . . . was always the shopping sprees.

Never ever did I think I'd get to buy a purse from Louis Vuitton. Or own a pair of Jimmy Choos.

I always told Wyatt that it was too much, but he insisted that not only did it bring a smile to his face, but it was part of the program.

"You have to be glamorous and sophisticated," he told me. "The way you look is important to what I'm building."

So I said, "Okay," and accepted his generosity.

In the beginning, there were moments when I wondered about Wyatt's motives. I mean, was anybody in the world really this kind?

But I pushed my apprehensions aside because Wyatt did have me working, really learning the business. And never did he try anything with me—not a touch on the hand or a kiss on the lips. Never any impropriety on our overnight trips—we always had separate suites.

So I settled into believing that I'd been blessed with the best of two worlds: a chance to be a career woman, and the opportunity to be cherished by a surrogate father, loved for the very first time in my life by a man.

But what I came to learn was that everything was not what it seemed and now that truth was playing out in my life.

Another shout from the bedroom made me jump, made me come all the way back from my memory.

"That's not true!" Wyatt yelled again.

I didn't know what he was talking about, but I did know one truth that the world did not know.

The problem was if I stood up and told that truth, my husband would be in prison for the rest of his life.

Was I willing to do that? Was I willing to give up the man who'd given me everything? Would I be able to live with that? I didn't know. I just didn't know.

Chapter 21

Okay, Wyatt," Newt said as the black SUV made a slow turn onto our street. "You have your instructions, right?"

"Yeah, yeah, you want me to stay in the house."

"I'm not kidding," Newt said, sounding like he was admonishing a child. "I don't want you going to your office, don't go to your restaurants. I don't even want you going to church."

"This doesn't make any sense." Wyatt slapped his hands against his thighs. His voice was strained, as if he were working hard to control his rage. He said, "If it's safe for me to go home, why isn't it safe for me to go out? "

Wyatt and Newt were in front of me, in the second row of the SUV. But even from where I sat, I could see the muscle beneath his jaw twitching.

"How will they know where I'll be? I just don't understand why I'm being treated like a prisoner. I should be able to go where I want. Nobody knows me."

"It's just because you're stressed that you're not thinking, but do you really think that once your name was released, people didn't run to Google? They know where you live, they know that you're the owner of the Cheesesteak Castles, and they know where every single one is located. Hell, they know where Billy goes to pre-school," said Newt.

Those words made my stomach gurgle again.

"Look," Newt continued. "I know what I'm doing. Trust me; I'm keeping you, Meredith, and Billy safe."

Wyatt glanced over his shoulder as if Newt had reminded him about his wife and child. I smiled, but that went away as soon as his eyes left mine.

My husband bounced back in his seat and crossed his arms. But after a few moments of silence, he said, "Okay," in a much calmer tone. "I'll do what you say. But can we get this resolved soon? My life can't stay on hold forever. I have a family to take care of."

"I'll get this resolved as quickly as I can," Newt said. "And we're keeping the security detail with you."

Wyatt shook his head. "That's fine if you want to, but I don't need security. I already . . ."

I cringed and thanked God that Wyatt didn't finish his thought.

When the SUV rolled to a stop in our driveway, I unhooked Billy from his seat as Wyatt, Newt, and the two guards (one black, one white) who'd rode with us unloaded our luggage.

I'd packed five suitcases when Newt told us that the police were giving us a three-hour heads-up before Wyatt's name was released. For our safety, the police advised us to spend a few days away from our home.

Never did I believe we'd be back this soon, just a week rather than the months that Newt had told us we might be away.

"You might have to sell your home and move," he'd even warned.

It seemed that we wouldn't have to do that—at least not now.

Holding my son's hand, I followed Wyatt and the men across the walkway. The moment Billy got to our front door, he broke away and dashed inside, heading straight for his playroom, which was in the back, with a wall of windows that looked out onto our pool.

Wyatt led each of the men up the circular staircase to our bedroom, and as I stepped over the threshold, I paused.

I did this often when I entered and took in the opulence that greeted me. It always took me back.

I may have been one of the oldest graduates at twenty-four, but I wore my cap and gown as proudly as any of the twenty-year-old graduates. And after the ceremony, I walked into Serendipity, Wyatt's favorite restaurant, with my head high and my diploma in my hand.

Of course, Wyatt had a private room set up for my graduation celebration, even though it was going to just be me, Wyatt . . . and my mom.

Yes, my mother.

That was the only thing that might possibly take the sunshine out of this day.

Gloria Harris.

Not that I didn't love my mother. It had always been just the two of us for my whole life, since I didn't know my father. It wasn't that my mother was trying to keep him from me, she just couldn't tell me his name. At least not exactly. She'd been honest and given me the names of three men who could have fathered me.

"It's kinda like a multiple-choice test. You can pick an answer, but I don't know if you'll be right."

That was just one of the crazy moments with my mother, but she had really done the best she could. It hadn't been easy for her; with only an eighth-grade education, only minimum-wage jobs were available to her and she settled mostly for waitress gigs in diners and dives.

It had always been a struggle for us, which was why when Wyatt asked me to invite her, there was a part of me that was glad. I wanted her to see that the little she'd done had been enough. I was on my way to being a career woman.

But then, she was Gloria Harris. Did I really want her around my boss?

"There's my baby!"

I heard her squeal before I saw her. Wyatt and I had just sat down and were checking out the menu, when my mother scurried into the room.

At first, I wondered why she was walking like a geisha. But then I saw the pencil skirt that she wore, so tight, she could only take the tiniest of steps.

Wyatt and I stood at the same time to greet her and she hugged me tight.

"Thanks for coming, Mom," I said, when we stepped back from our embrace. Then I turned so that we were both facing Wyatt. "This is Mr. Spencer, the man who made this all possible."

My mother did that little two-step scurry to the other side of the table and embraced Wyatt as if she'd always known him.

"It is so nice to finally meet you." She held on to his hand as she added, "Thank you for taking care of my baby girl."

Wyatt's eyes stayed on my mom. "I can certainly see where she gets her beauty."

My mom waved her hand in front of her face and . . . was she blushing?

"You go on," she said, sounding like she was sixteen.

And I wondered . . . wouldn't it be wonderful if Wyatt and my mom clicked?

From that point, it was really comfortable. As we ate, we chatted, or rather Wyatt did his thing and questioned my mother. And like me, she just fell into it and shared everything: from how she'd raised me in Section 8 housing to how she'd felt like she'd never find success in life or love.

"Well," Wyatt began. "Maybe I can change all of that."

That made me pause—was Wyatt interested in my mom?

"Really?" my mother said. "What? Do you have a job for me, too? Are you going to send me to college?" She rested her hand on his arm and giggled like a schoolgirl.

But his expression stayed stiff. "I'm not talking about a job; I think you've worked enough."

"I'll be working till the day I die."

He shrugged. "Maybe you won't."

My mother and I probably looked like twins the way we stared at Wyatt with questions in our eyes.

Without a word, Wyatt reached into his jacket and pulled out a box.

"Oh," my mother said, looking from Wyatt to me, and then back to him. "Is that a graduation gift?"

"In a way."

This was a surprise. I wasn't expecting yet another gift from Wyatt. He'd already given me a credit card and told me that I had no limit.

As he stood and came around to my side of the table, I imagined what was inside the box—a watch, a necklace, or maybe a diamond tennis bracelet that I saw a year ago but couldn't bring myself to buy, not even with Wyatt's money.

But when he knelt beside me and opened the box, my mother gasped. Or maybe I was the one who made that sound.

"Meredith, I have come to love you and I want to marry you. I want you to be my wife."

Wasn't I just imagining Wyatt with my mother?

"Oh!" My mother clapped.

But I said nothing, did nothing. Because this was crazy.

Now, color me stupid, but I'd had no idea that Wyatt was interested in me in a romantic way. How could he be? Our relationship was so far to the left on the platonic scale that he really could have been my father.

"Aren't you going to say something?" Wyatt asked.

"Uh" was all I could get out.

"She says yes!" my mother shouted.

Her words made Wyatt smile, though he kept his eyes on me. "I'd like to hear that from Meredith."

"Uh . . ."

He waited a moment before he asked, "Is that all you have to say?"

My words finally came to me. "Wyatt . . ." *I whispered his name.* "Maybe we should have talked about this. And not here." *I made a sideward glance toward my mother.*

"In front of Gloria?" *he asked.* "I thought this was the perfect place and the perfect way. I know how important she is to you, and I know that when you and I are married, she's part of the deal."

"I am?" *My mother pushed back her chair and scurried over to stand behind me.*

"I'll take care of her, too," *Wyatt promised.*

"Really?" *There was so much joy in my mother's voice.*

With her behind me and Wyatt in front of me, I was trapped.

But how could I feel trapped by the only two people in the world who really knew me? Who really cared about me? If I'd ever been loved, it was only by these two.

While Wyatt stayed on bended knee, I replayed the last two years in my mind; they'd been the best years of my life. And if that was any indication of what my future would be, why would I say no? Except for the fact that . . . I didn't love him.

And then he asked the question I was thinking. "Don't you love me, Meredith?"

"Of course she loves you," my mother answered as if I'd discussed this with her.

"Uh . . ."

My mother bent over and hissed into my ear, "Meredith!"

Inside her tone, I heard all kinds of warnings. And saw all kinds of images—my life with Wyatt, my life without Wyatt.

"You don't love me," Wyatt said with his eyebrows raised high on his forehead. "I just hoped . . ."

His eyebrows drooped and now there was sadness written all over his face.

That made me touch him for the first time. Made me take his face between the palms of my hands. Made me lean forward and gently press my lips against his. For the first time.

I stayed like that for only a moment, then leaned back. "Yes, I'll marry you, Wyatt Spencer. I want to be your wife."

There were tears in his eyes when he slipped that ring on my finger. "I will always take care of you, Meredith. And I will love you forever."

When he hugged me, I thought about the fact that I wasn't in love with him in the way I expected to love a man. But while I wasn't in love, I did love him; so all I needed was a little emotional shift.

I could do that. After all that Wyatt had done for me . . .

"Meredith!"

I blinked and made the nine-year mental trek back to the present, and looked into the eyes of the man who'd once been the centermost of my dreams.

"Why are you just standing there?" Wyatt asked. His eyes were filled with concern. "Are you all right with us coming back here?" he asked, as if my opinion counted.

"Oh, yes." I nodded. "I was thinking how great it is to be home."

The worry lines faded from his forehead. "Yeah." He kissed my cheek, then patted the top of my head.

"So . . ." I looked up as Newt came down the stairs. "I'll check in with you guys every few hours." When Newt stood in front of us he said, "Just remember what I said. No—"

Wyatt held up his hand. "No need to repeat it. I'll stay low-key."

Newt nodded his approval. "Good, because I don't need you out there making news if this does go to the state prosecutor."

Wyatt shrugged and nodded at the same time.

"Okay," Newt said. "And, if I don't hear anything from Ferguson or the prosecutor within the next few days, I know we're home free on that side. We'll just have to wait for it to die down with the Brown Guardians, but that shouldn't take too long. Something will happen somewhere else, and all the attention will shift away from us to the next shooting. Hopefully something will happen in Florida and they'll forget about this little thing here in Pennsylvania." Newt embraced Wyatt like the longtime buddies they were. Then he turned to me. "Take care of this dude, will you?"

"I'll try." He hugged me, too, holding our embrace for one moment past comfortable. I was always the one who pulled away from him.

Wyatt closed the door behind his friend. "I'm going to go into the office. Why don't you go upstairs and unpack."

As I stepped toward the staircase, I glanced out the windowed wall that covered the entire back of our house. And I paused. Even from that far away, I saw a wineglass and a plate on top of one of the tables by the pool.

"Who's in the backyard?" I asked Wyatt, wondering if I should be afraid. But even before he answered, I figured it was one of the security guards taking a break and I hoped I hadn't just gotten someone fired.

He frowned and walked toward the back. I followed him because Billy was back there, too.

But we'd only moved a few feet before Wyatt's frown turned upside down. And I did just the opposite.

Because it was my mother.

Chapter 22

Wyatt slid the glass doors apart and stepped outside. "Hey, Gloria. What are you doing here?"

The pool chair faced us and she tilted her sunglasses up to give herself a better view. "Did you think I would let my favorite son-in-law and daughter come home without someone here to welcome them?"

As Wyatt leaned down to hug my mother, I rolled my eyes and it wasn't just because of what she said. I couldn't believe that while we were in hiding at a hotel that was two steps above a motel, my mother was lounging around our pool like she was in Saint-Tropez.

"Meredith?" My mother said my name as if she were asking a question.

And when all I said was, "Hello," she swung her long bronzed legs over the side of the chair, stood tall, and planted one hand on her hip.

It was a stance of expectation, like she was waiting for me to give her the same greeting that Wyatt had.

My mother stood there in all of her itsy-bitsy-teeny-weeny-white-on-black-polka-dot-bikini glory. Looking fabulous, I had to admit. Anyone trying to guess her age would be decades off.

Still, though, she was my mom, and as usual, just a bit past over the top. A fifty-nine-year-old woman needed to be more covered up, no matter how fantastic her body.

When I didn't make a move toward her, my mother did one of her model strolls toward me, one perfectly toned, shaped, tanned leg in front of the other. Of course, she strutted in her four-inch sandals because she never went anywhere (not even to a pool) without her stilettos.

After giving me an air kiss on each cheek, she asked, "Where's my grandson?"

"He's in his playroom," I said, then asked, "Why are you hanging out back here?"

"I already told you," she said, glancing at Wyatt, who still stood there with a grinning face. "I wanted to welcome you home and enjoy this absolutely fabulous day."

"It's not even seventy degrees, Mom." Giving her a once-over with my eyes, I asked, "Aren't you cold?"

That was supposed to be a hint for her to cover up, but subtlety never worked with Gloria Harris. All my words did was make my mother step back and pose once again, this time with her hand on her other hip. "Do I *look* like I'm cold?"

"I think you look beautiful," my husband said.

My mother giggled and I had another one of those moments when I wanted to throw up.

Not that I was ever concerned about their constant flirting. This was the only way my mother knew how to interact with men. Wyatt, her son-in-law, was the same as Roger, the grocery store clerk. And for his part, Wyatt would never be unfaithful to me with my mother. They were the same age; she was much too old for him.

Wyatt said, "Well, I was heading into my office; I want to check the mail, make some calls." He kissed my cheek, then said, "Good to see you again, Gloria."

"I'm going in, too. I need to check on Billy and get unpacked."

"You go on upstairs," Wyatt said. "I'll hang out with our son."

As Wyatt and I moved toward the door, my mother scurried in front of us. "I'll go with you," she said. She did a little skip walk so that she would enter the house first, then she put a little extra into her stroll so that her boobs would jiggle and her booty would joggle.

Even after we stepped inside, Wyatt watched me and my mother walk up the stairs as if he were our security detail. She didn't stop her little wiggle walk until we stepped into my bedroom. Then she flopped onto my bed.

I went right to my closet and tossed her one of my silk robes.

"Thanks, sweetheart, but I don't need this," she said. "I'm fine."

"No, you're not." Then I gave my mother a look that I often gave to my child. "Stop it, Mom."

She sighed and slipped the robe over her shoulders. "I can't believe I raised such a prude."

"I'm not a prude. I'm just tired of you flirting with my husband."

She laughed. "As if! You know I don't want Wyatt. I just love that he appreciates a woman like me."

I waved my hand. "Just cover up."

"All right. All right." She slipped her arms through my robe. "Now, tell me the latest."

"The latest?" I unzipped one of the suitcases.

"Yeah, with the shooting and everything. With you guys hiding out." Her tone held a bit of excitement.

Stepping back from the bed, I folded my arms. "Mom, this is not gossip. This is not the *National Intruder*," I said, referring to my mother's favorite source for news.

"Well, something is going on," my mother said. "Haven't you been watching TV? Wyatt's picture is everywhere and they keep playing Wally's interview." She paused for just a second. "I wish you and Wyatt had asked me to do the interview instead of Wally."

"And what in the world would you have said?"

My mother flipped her blond extensions over her shoulder. "I would have done exactly what Wally did, only it would've sounded better coming from me. I would've told them what a wonderful man my son-in-law is. In fact, I think I'm going to let Wyatt and Newt know that the world needs to see me."

"No, Mom."

"Why not? We need to show the world that Wyatt Spencer is loved not only by his immediate family, but his extended family, too. They need to see a woman speaking up for him, someone who's not a blood relative and someone who is a mother."

Her idea worried me because I knew Wyatt would agree with her. And putting Gloria Harris in front of a camera was the worst thing we could do.

"What we're trying to do is let it all die down. Newt doesn't want us saying a word."

"Why not? Those black people are talking. Every day on every channel. Well, except for Fox. But even Fox keeps replaying that boy's funeral like he died a dozen times."

"To his mother and father, it probably feels that way."

"And speaking of his father . . . his father and his uncle always have something to say. They're out there every day with those black champions."

"Black champions?" I frowned; I paused. "You mean the Brown Guardians?"

My mother waved her hand. "Whatever. It's all of them, all the time. The only thing they haven't done is drag his mother to the stage."

That made me stop altogether. I hadn't seen any of the recent news stories, but every day I thought about Marquis's mother and I wondered why she hadn't spoken.

Although if anyone had taken Billy away from me, especially with the way Marquis had died, I wouldn't ever get out of bed. So she was way ahead of anything that I would've been able to do.

My mother didn't give me much time to stay in my thoughts. She said, "So far, the news coverage has been all about them. I think it's time for this to be about us."

"We're riding it out, okay?"

"As long as there will be no charges and this whole thing is dropped, I'll be fine," she said as if this were in any way about her.

"We're not sure what the police will do," I said. "I don't know how they can just ignore what happened."

"They already know what happened." As if she were telling me something for the first time, she added, "It was self-defense. Wyatt was protecting himself, you, and Billy. That's what he told us and that's what they said on Fox." She kept on because, of course, now she was an expert.

"When it's self-defense, you can stand your ground. You don't have to retreat." A pause and then with a wave of her hand, she finished with, "Anyway, this will all be over soon because there's a witness."

My eyes stretched wide as I slowly walked around the bed to the side where my mother sat. I said nothing at first because it was hard to speak when my heart was blasting its way through my chest.

There was a witness? Someone who knew what I knew?

I sat down, then forced myself to speak before my heart attack claimed my life. "Who . . . who is the witness?"

She looked at me as if I'd just asked the dumbest question. "Wyatt! He was there."

I pressed my hand against my chest, trying to push my heart back inside, and with my other hand, I wanted to shake my mother for scaring me like that. "Really, Mom? Really?" I jumped up. "Wyatt cannot be his own witness."

"Well, he's the only one who was there."

"He's the only one who was there who is still alive. The other witness is dead."

My mother put her head down, then flicked her fingers against the robe as if she were removing lint. "Well, that boy shouldn't have been in the streets acting like that. Threatening people. I bet this is not the first time he did something like this. Wait until they pull up his police record. I bet you he has one ten pages long. He just came upon the wrong man this time."

"How can you talk like this when a boy is dead? You sound like it's no big deal."

"Because it's not a big deal to me if the choice was either that boy or your husband. I, for one, am glad with the way it turned out."

For a second I closed my eyes. May 12. That image.

She said, "I just wish there *had* been another witness besides Wyatt, because maybe then, all of this foolishness would have already stopped."

Again I sat down on the bed. I waited a moment before I said, "I'm not sure that there aren't any other witnesses."

Her eyes grew wide and round. "What do you mean?"

In the moments that passed, I thought about my secret. It felt like it was getting bigger by the day, a burden that had grown into a boulder and was becoming too heavy to carry.

Maybe I could tell my mother.

"Meredith, what are you talking about? What witness?"

Could I, should I tell her? I wanted to, but I wasn't sure where my mother's loyalty lay. She loved me, but she really loved Wyatt. Because like he promised, he'd made my mother's one-bedroom Section 8 apartment part of her history. She was no longer a woman on welfare, no longer on food stamps.

I'd married up; she'd come up. Gloria Harris was a "kept mother-in-law" with a condo, a car, and a credit card.

"Meredith? Did someone come to you and tell you something?"

"No." I shook my head. "No one else." I paused. "But I . . . I may have seen something."

The way my mother's eyes moved, I could tell she was searching my face, studying me to determine what I was trying to say.

Then her tanned face drained of all its color, turning her skin porcelain as her eyes widened with all kinds of understanding.

Now she was the one to jump off the bed and she glared down at me. "Were you out there with him?"

"No," I said, though she already knew that.

"You were in the house when this happened?"

"Yes." She knew this part, too. She knew it all, except . . .

"Then you didn't see anything," my mother stated as if it were a fact.

"But I did. I saw—"

She held up her hand, stopping me. "You saw nothing. And even if you did, a wife can never testify against her husband."

That surprised me, a little. I guess my mother's study of the law, which came from watching *Law & Order*, was paying off. "But," I began, determined to now tell her.

My mother spoke over me. "You are not going to say anything to anyone. You're not going to tell me; in fact, you're not going to think about it anymore; you're not even going to dream about it."

"But suppose I know something that's really important?"

"Didn't I just tell you what you know?" She spoke to me as if I were nine years old. "You know nothing." But then she sat down on the bed and didn't say anything for a long time; she just held my hands. But after a while she said what I'd been thinking.

"What do you think will happen to you, to Billy, if Wyatt goes to prison?"

"I'm his wife," I said, as if that were the answer to every question that would come if I told what I knew.

"His wife who would be responsible for him getting convicted of murder!"

I was surprised that my mother assumed that what I'd seen could do that.

She continued, "If Wyatt goes to prison because of you, he will make sure that you have nothing."

I shook my head. "The courts will make him pay . . . something. He has a son."

"He'll make sure that his family gets custody of Billy."

"They won't take him away from me," I said, with a surety I didn't feel. I was shocked that my mother would think that, yet I knew what she said was true and I was horrified.

It was just Wyatt, Wally, and their eighty-three-year-old mother, who lived in Vancouver with her eighty-eight-year-old sister. I'd only seen Wyatt's mother once, when she made the cross-continent trip to attend our wedding. She'd never met Billy, not wanting to return to the States too much after her husband's tragic death from early-onset Alzheimer's. Not to mention the twenty-four-hundred-mile trip was too much for her elderly bones, no matter how she traveled.

And Wally . . . even Wyatt said that his brother was a waste of skin. He was in his fifties, yet he'd never held a job outside of the positions that Wyatt gave him, and he couldn't even hold on to any of those.

Would a judge allow Wyatt's brother or Wyatt's mother to raise Billy? And would Wyatt even want that for his son, no matter what I did?

Shaking my head, I said, "No, Wyatt wouldn't do that."

She raised an eyebrow. "Then I know your husband better than you do."

"I'll fight him in court."

"With what money, Meredith? You don't have anything without Wyatt."

And there it was.

The truth.

She looked around my massive bedroom and I knew what she was thinking. This space where I only slept and bathed and dressed could hold the entire apartment where I'd grown up. "Do you see where you live? Have you checked out the credit cards in your purse? What about the clothes in your closet?"

She was asking all the questions aloud that I'd already asked myself. "So I'm just supposed to live with what I know?"

"Yes," my mother said, like she had no doubt. "There's nothing you can do to bring that boy back."

I took a breath, and was reminded that Marquis would never take a breath again.

For good measure, my mother added, "I'm telling you, that boy did something that made Wyatt do what he had to do."

My stomach rumbled.

"Promise me that you'll do what I said."

I didn't move.

"Promise me!" my mother demanded.

"Promise you what?"

Wyatt's voice made both of us jump, and for a second, there was silence as my husband studied me and my mother.

My mother crossed her legs and gave her son-in-law a seductive grin. "I was telling my daughter to promise me that she was taking good care of her husband."

"Oh, really now?" Wyatt said as his lips spread, showing how much my mother's words pleased him.

My mother nodded.

And I sat there with a rumbling, tumbling stomach. I sat there until I couldn't sit there anymore. I rushed past Wyatt and into the master bathroom, past the double sinks, past the Jacuzzi tub, past the steam shower.

I made it to the commode in time to close the door behind me. And then it was seat up, head down.

But even when I was empty, I stayed on my knees. I was in the right position to do what I didn't do often—I needed to have a conversation with God. About my secret, though now I suspected that I held more than one.

Chapter 23

I stood on the balcony off of the master suite and looked down onto the pool.

Billy's giggles rose as he and Wyatt splashed my mother while she lounged in her usual chair wearing a Stars and Stripes bikini, her tribute to this day.

"Hey," she squealed, sending her grandson into another fit of laughter.

This was our Memorial Day celebration, though I seemed to be the only one in our family who realized there wasn't anything to celebrate, though there was much to remember.

Today was Monday. Two weeks after May 12. I wondered what kind of Memorial Day Janice Johnson was having.

Turning away, I stepped inside and took in the display that I had sprawled across our bed: my platinum Visas, my gold MasterCards, and my black American Express.

"Have you checked out the credit cards in your purse? You don't have anything without Wyatt."

Sitting on my bed, I picked up the cards and counted them: four platinums, four golds, one black. Nine. And these didn't include the accounts that I had at Gucci and Chanel.

With a sigh that came from deep within me, I gathered the cards and returned each to its designated slot inside my lambskin wallet.

I sank onto the duvet and leaned back, resting on the pillows. I'd gotten so used to living here that I no longer noticed all the symbols of wealth. But the signs of our affluence were everywhere—I was sitting on a duvet that cost over five thousand dollars, leaning on mulberry silk pillows, holding a wallet that would have paid my rent for a year when I was growing up—everywhere I turned, I had the best of everything. The way I'd lived these last years overrode every past hardship. How could I go back to that?

Years of living this life with Wyatt had made it ordinary to me. But this was so far away from ordinary and I needed to remember that. I needed to go back to being grateful the way I was the first time I'd come into this house.

On May 12.

But it was a different May 12 from the one that I remembered now. The May 12 of two weeks ago was about death. The other May 12 was about life, a new life.

May 12, 2007 . . .

"Where are we going?" I asked, peeping through the tinted limousine window.

Wyatt didn't answer. Instead, he tossed a couple of hundred-dollar bills into the driver's hand. "We'll see you in the morning," Wyatt told him. "We have to be at the airport three hours early for the international flight."

I was still sitting inside the car when I asked, "Are we staying here?" Wyatt hadn't told me anything about our wedding night or even about our honeymoon. I imagined that we'd stay in the Ritz-Carlton, or maybe the Rittenhouse Hotel before we took a flight tomorrow to places unknown, at least unknown to me. All I knew about our destination was that I needed my first passport.

But this wasn't a hotel; it looked more like a house. It wasn't Wyatt's home, though. I tried to get a better glimpse, but it was difficult to see in the darkness of midnight.

Wyatt took my hand and helped me to maneuver out of the limo through what felt like miles and miles of the sequined organza of my Vera Wang gown.

As he led me up the walkway, I asked again, "Where are we?"

Wyatt's response: he swept me up and into his arms, then carried me over the threshold into even more darkness.

But then there was light when he said, "Welcome home, sweetheart," and the circular-shaped space became illuminated.

I slipped from his arms, but all I did was stand there, mouth open, eyes wider. The marble floors, the circular staircase, the chandelier that hung as high as the sun.

Questions swirled through my mind, but I was too stunned to focus on a single one.

So Wyatt answered what I couldn't ask. "I bought this house just for you."

"A house?"

"For you."

It was hard to wrap my mind around anything this wonderful. Even as Wyatt took me on a tour of the already furnished, six-bedroom home that felt more like a country club than a residence, I knew this couldn't be real, this couldn't be for me.

With my dress hiked up as high as I could handle, I ran from room to room, marveling at the ceilings that reached to the heavens, the French doors throughout, and marble and crystal everywhere.

"All for you, sweetheart."

In the twenty-six years that I'd been on earth, I'd never been inside a house like this, let alone imagined that there would ever be a day when I called a place like this home.

"Tennis courts?" I exclaimed when Wyatt took me out by the pool and showed me the rest of the grounds.

"All for you."

Wyatt saved the master bedroom suite for last, and when we stepped inside the already candlelit grand room with a circular bed that was as wide as the ocean, I almost cried.

"Who did this for us?" I asked.

His answer was a kiss on my forehead, and the way he held me, I knew that I was so loved. It was hard to hold my tears when he slowly unzipped my wedding dress, then unwrapped the fabric from my body as if I was the precious gift that he'd told me I was.

I trembled with anticipation because in the two years of our engagement, Wyatt still had never touched me in that way.

He had explained it to me: "You're so precious. I want to honor you and save that wonderful moment for our wedding night."

It had sounded weird then, but it felt so wonderful now. When we lay down on our bed, and Wyatt made slow, wondrous love to me, I knew for sure that waiting had been the best thing. These were moments to be remembered and treasured.

I was so blessed; an ordinary woman about to live an extraordinary life.

That had been an amazing night, though a few years later I came to understand that being Wyatt's wife wasn't what I thought it would be.

But what had remained from that time was the grandeur around me. I had this home, this money, this life. Could I go back to the way I used to live? There were lots of women who raised their children alone. My mother had done it, though she hadn't done it well. But I wasn't my mother. I had an associate's degree. So I could get more than a minimum-wage job and take care of myself and Billy.

As I thought of him, I heard the delight in his laughter rising up from the pool.

Closing my eyes, I tried to imagine what life would be like with just me and Billy. But all that came to my mind when I thought about my son was that night.

Just as I adjusted the blanket over Billy, a sudden pop cracked through the silence of the late night and made me pause. I listened to see if I'd hear it again.

Nothing.

So I let the sound slip from my thoughts, kissed my son's cheek, and tiptoed out of his room.

My first thought was to go to my bedroom. But then I wondered if I could entice Wyatt to have a glass of wine with me. To celebrate our anniversary, since he hadn't remembered.

So I moved toward the stairs. And at the top of the landing, I stopped. Why was the front door open?

Sighing again, I wished so much that I could go back to that night and not see what I saw. Because now, I didn't know what to do. Though that wasn't completely true; I knew what was right.

I was a mother, I had a son, and I wanted to lay my head down every night and sleep in peace.

So I had to do right by Mrs. Johnson. I had to do right for her son and set the example for my own.

Billy and I would be just fine.

And to prove it, I rushed to my side of our bed, grabbed my

iPad, opened an app, then typed a list of everything I would need to live on my own with Billy: rent, food, utilities. I'd need child care, someone to take care of my son while I worked. And a new car because I was sure that Wyatt would see to it that when I left, I left with what I'd brought with me. Which meant that I'd need clothes, too.

I typed in numbers, added them up, and wondered where in the world I would get a job that would cover expenses of five thousand dollars a month. I deducted a couple of things, brought down the cost of my car, the insurance, and even lowered food to just two hundred dollars a month for the two of us, figuring that I could go without a lunch or two.

Still—over three thousand dollars?

I could do it! That was my thought, that was my hope, at least.

Then, something stirred inside of me, taking my breath away and my hand moved to my belly.

It could be just the stress of what was going on that had me so sick, that had my irregular period even more erratic.

Looking down at those numbers, I thought about what another child would mean. Many of these numbers would double. And what about health care? I'd have to have insurance for me and my babies. Wouldn't that cost a fortune?

It seemed like so much, but didn't I have to do this? But do it for whom? Would doing right for Mrs. Johnson mean that I was doing wrong for my own children?

Children. That was so different from just one child.

Switching over to the Internet, I signed in to my doctor's portal, then searched for her next available appointment.

Tomorrow. At two o'clock.

I hadn't expected anything that soon, but maybe this was a sign. Before I could change my mind, I logged in my information, noted the reason for my visit, set the appointment, then closed my iPad.

Going to see my doctor was better than taking a home test. More accurate and there was no chance of Wyatt finding out.

Chapter 24

I took a breath before I knocked on Wyatt's office door, then stepped inside. He was stretched back as far as his executive chair allowed, his eyes unmoving, staring at the television.

When he hadn't been outside at the pool, he'd been inside, sitting here, catching every bit of the news. Again.

"Wyatt . . ."

He held up his hand, stopping me, and I was forced to do what I hadn't yet done. I glanced at the television and saw the man that I'd seen almost a week ago. The caption below his image said: *Tyrone and Janice Johnson.*

I took a tiny step closer and squinted so that I could get a clearer picture of her.

Janice. That was her name, and she was my reason.

"We are going to do this every single day until an arrest is made," Tyrone Johnson said. "And if the powers that be in Montgomery County are expecting to wear us down by allowing time to pass, they need to know that won't happen. Don't mistake our peacefulness for passiveness. There will be justice for our son. Wyatt Spencer will be arrested. That's all we're asking. For justice . . . through the system. But the system needs to start working. Because we have had enough."

Then, the crowd chanted, "Justice, justice. Enough is enough!"

Wyatt muted the television, but his eyes were still on the TV as he spoke. "I don't know why that . . . man and all those others have to constantly say my name."

My inside voice said: Because you killed his son. Aloud, I said, "Sweetheart, I just found out that I have a doctor's appointment."

He frowned. "What?"

"I have an appointment. With my gynecologist. For a Pap smear."

He peered at me as if he were seeing straight through to my lie. "You just had a Pap smear a few months ago."

I wondered if this was normal. Did all husbands watch their wives so closely that they knew when they had their gynecological exams?

I nodded. "Yes, but Dr. Leach just called this morning. She wants to do it again."

He swiveled the chair so that his whole body faced me, as if now I deserved all of his attention. "What's wrong?"

"Nothing," I said, needing to assuage his worries. I paused, trying to determine what would be the best lie to keep Wyatt from calling my doctor and blowing this all up.

My decision was to say, "There was a problem in the lab and some of the tests were lost. So she wants to do mine again—just to have something for the record. She knows nothing's wrong . . ."

The way he shook his head I wondered if the other lie would've been better. The lie that said there were some abnormalities and she wanted to test me again.

But with all that was going on in our lives, I didn't want to put something like that out there in the atmosphere. Plus if Wyatt believed there was a problem, he'd want to go to the doctor with me.

He said, "I hope she's not going to charge you for this visit."

I was amazed and relieved that money was his only concern.

"Of course not," I said, rather than reminding him that his insurance was so stellar, we didn't even have to pay for office visits. "It's just going to be a quick in and out."

"Wait a minute," he said. "Newt doesn't want us going out of the house."

"I know, but I was thinking that I'll have one of the security guards go with me. He'll drive me, and if you want, I'll even have him wait in the reception area while I have the test."

He thought about it for a moment.

I added, "I'll be fine; no one knows what I look like." Then I shrugged. "And even if they did, would anyone be waiting for me at my doctor's office?"

I needed Wyatt to believe that this was no big deal. Because I had to get to the doctor. I had to know today so that I could put an end to my indecision.

A few more pensive moments and then, "All right. I'll send both guards with you."

"That's not necessary, Wyatt. I really want one guard to be here with you."

He grinned. "You're worried about me, huh?"

I nodded, though I wasn't worried about Wyatt. Everyone knew what he could do with a gun. My concern was for anyone, like the postman, who might by mistake come to our door, and who might then, after an encounter with my husband, end up dead.

My husband needed supervision.

Wyatt reached out his hand, and when I took it, he pulled me onto his lap. I paused for just a moment before I laid my head against his chest and sighed.

I lived for these moments with Wyatt. When he reminded me with no words that he really did love me. He held me close, for the first time since this madness started. Then, when he kissed me, leaned back, and said, "Do you really have to go to the doctor now?" I wanted to take back all of my lies. Just tell him the whole truth. Then go upstairs so that we could make love and figure this all out together.

But I couldn't back away now. So with a sigh, I told him, "I have to go to the doctor."

He nodded. "I know you do. Maybe when you come back."

I had no idea what life would look like when I returned. Had no idea what I would know or what I would do. So I just wrapped my arms around him and told him that I loved him. Because I really did.

When I stood, he said, "I'll have Andre go with you. The black guard. No one will bother you if you're with him. What time are you going?"

"Now. I want to do this and get back to Billy . . . and you."

He gave me that grin again as he pushed himself up from the desk. "I love it when you show me that you care."

"Of course I do," I said, uttering some of my first truthful words of the day. "I really do care about you and love you."

He kissed my cheek, and as he left to set up my ride, I checked in on Billy before I grabbed my purse and jumped into the SUV that was a permanent fixture in our driveway.

As Andre took off, I leaned back, closed my eyes, and tried to rest my mind. But, of course, my thoughts would not stop.

This time, though, my thoughts were all about the doctor and this baby that I might be carrying.

As scared as I was, thinking about being pregnant was the only thing that made me smile. I had no idea how Wyatt would feel. Which is why I couldn't tell him until I knew for sure. I couldn't tell him until I knew what I was going to do.

"Mrs. Spencer?"

I'd been so deep into my thoughts that I hadn't realized we had arrived. Andre was already standing at the open door, holding out his hand. He helped me out, then locked the doors with the remote.

But when he turned to follow me into the medical complex, I shook my head. "Just wait for me down here."

He shook his head. "Mr. Spencer told me not to leave your side."

"Really?" I frowned as if I were confused. "I don't think he meant that literally." I leaned closer and whispered, "I'm going to see my gynecologist and I know you're not interested in seeing my legs hanging up high in stirrups."

His eyes and mouth widened at the same time. "Uh . . . I'll wait . . . down here."

With a smile, I rushed into the building, but inside when I punched the elevator button for the fifth floor, all I did was lean back and pray. The only thing was, I wasn't sure what I wanted to ask God—did I want to be pregnant or not?

I greeted Dr. Leach's receptionist, signed in, but before I could even sit down, the nurse told me that the doctor was ready for me.

There had never been a time when I'd come to my doctor's office and seen her so quickly. Yet another sign, though I had no idea what any of these signs meant.

Two minutes after I stepped into the examination room, my doctor walked in. After her greeting, she said, "Your husband called me."

"Oh, God!" I didn't mean to say that aloud.

Dr. Leach held up her hand. "I didn't say a thing—doctor/patient privilege. But he kept asking about new charges for a Pap smear. I told him that I would discuss it all with you."

"Thank you, Doctor," I said, so grateful that she'd said the right thing to Wyatt.

"So, you think you're pregnant?"

"I think so."

She nodded. "And you don't want your husband to know because . . ." Then she paused as if she wanted me to fill in the blank.

But what was I supposed to say? That I wasn't sure if I would ever tell him about this baby because I was thinking about going to the police and telling the truth, so Wyatt might not ever see this baby anyway?

I said nothing, of course, so the doctor finished her sentence: "Because of what you're going through."

I nodded, though I hadn't thought about my doctor knowing what was going on. Of course, everyone in the country knew.

"I really am sorry about what's happening with you and your husband. I didn't even put it together until I heard about the Cheesesteak Castles." She paused. "How are you doing?"

"We're hanging in there."

"Well, if you're pregnant, you know you're going to have to watch the stress, right?"

"That's why I wanted to know. Know for sure."

"How late are you?"

"About a week, though you know I've never been regular.

I didn't have a period last month, but I've never skipped two months."

"Well, you know the drill." She handed me a small plastic cup. "Leave your urine sample in the bin in the bathroom. Then come back, strip down, put that on," she said, pointing to the paper robe on the examination table. "I'll do a pelvic examination, too."

I nodded.

"Don't look so solemn," she said. "This just might be the news that you and your husband need."

Not even ten minutes later, I was on my back, legs up and open, eyes focused on the ceiling. It didn't take too many minutes before she rolled the stool away, snapped off her plastic gloves, and told me to give her a few minutes. I dressed, then sat and waited. And when Dr. Leach returned, it was her smile that told the story before she said a word.

"We're about to have another little Spencer in the world."

My lips smiled because I was happy. My heart pounded because I was scared. Both of those feelings were equally real to me.

"So, are you glad about this?"

"I am . . . it's just that . . ." I stopped as if I'd given her a complete thought.

"I know." She nodded. "But I really think everything is going to be okay. Now, I'm going to have the nurse come in and get some blood work on you."

I slid off the examination table. "Can I come back?" I had what I needed to know. Everything else could wait.

"Okay, but I don't want to put this off. I want to get that work in, determine how far along you are, and get you on prenatal vitamins and a nutrition plan. Remember, you didn't gain enough weight with Billy."

I promised her that I would return next week, smiled as she once again offered me congratulations, and then stepped out of the room. But not a second passed before I turned back around.

"Dr. Leach, I need a couple of days . . . I'm not going to say anything to my husband yet."

She nodded. "You forgot about doctor/patient privilege. I won't say a word."

I didn't allow myself to think until I was settled in the SUV. Then I thought about my son and the child I now carried.

And then I thought about Janice Johnson. Right away, tears came to my eyes. I had wanted to do right, but now, there was no way that I could.

Chapter 25

I came to the conclusion that there was a way for me to lay my head down at night in peace. My hope centered on the police.

If the police couldn't charge Wyatt with a crime, then why should I say anything? If the case was never going to court, why should I feel guilty about keeping my secret? If the police determined that my husband had just cause, who was I to accuse Wyatt?

Without a case, I would be set free.

This was my final hope.

But my hope didn't take away my anxiety. My stress was off the Richter scale now, especially since I'd taken to watching the news as much as Wyatt.

For the last five days, I'd watched everything about Marquis Johnson. And in five days, I'd seen his image a thousand times.

The news stations all used the same picture. Marquis was posing in what looked like a boxing stance, like he was ready to fight. His hands, large hands, were balled into fists that half hid his face. But his fists weren't large enough to hide his dark eyes, or his flaring nostrils or his lips, big lips that were twisted, almost contorted, and that highlighted his anger.

And then there was the hoodie that he wore, a black one where the hood covered his whole head and part of his forehead.

Every time I saw that photo, I trembled. In the daytime, it scared me; I couldn't imagine what it would be like if I'd seen Marquis at night.

But on the other side, there was his mother. Janice. They never showed a photo of her; I only saw her image as she stood by her husband's side. Every time. He never spoke alone.

She was so regal, not in terms of the clothes that she wore. In my years of marriage to Wyatt, I'd learned the difference between discount and designer. She was definitely a Target or maybe a Marshalls shopper. The kind of shopper that I'd once considered upscale.

Her elegance was beyond her clothes. It was in the way she stood, head high, chin forward, eyes wide and clear, even as people around her spoke of her dead son.

And it was in the way she carried herself, she moved with grace, looking as if her feet barely touched the ground. She held her husband's hand. Every time. He never walked alone.

She was the kind of woman that I wished I knew, the kind of woman I wished I could help.

"Sweetheart!"

I blinked my thoughts away and focused on my husband standing right beside me. I hadn't even heard him come into the kitchen.

He frowned before he planted a kiss on my cheek, then gently patted my head. "Are you all right?"

I nodded.

"That's all you're having for lunch?"

I looked down at the chicken broth and crackers. "It's all I want. I'm not very hungry."

He shook his head. "I know what this is about."

My heartbeat galloped. Had Dr. Leach broken her promise?

He said, "You're tired of being cooped up in this house. Because," he continued, "I know I'm going crazy and so is our poor boy. This is just plain ridiculous." He opened the refrigerator and grabbed a beer. "Ten days. We've been home for ten days and we can't do a thing." After a long swig from his beer bottle, he said, "I hope Newt brings some good news soon."

I nodded; I agreed.

"They're not protesting as much anymore, just like Newt predicted," Wyatt kept on. "So I don't think it will be too much longer."

The sound of chimes filled our home and I rolled my eyes.

Even though I hadn't said a word, Wyatt laughed. "You think that's Gloria?"

I nodded. "I don't know why she feels like she has to come here every day." That's what I said, though I suspected that my mother came by so often to check on me. She was making sure that I kept my promise never to say a word.

Wyatt grinned. "Gloria is our only entertainment, since I sent Wally to visit my mother."

As he went to answer the door, I tried to come up with some excuse that would send my mother home. But my thoughts turned from my mother when I heard the heavy footsteps.

"Hey, Meredith." Newt came over to the island where I sat and kissed my cheek.

And my stomach did a triple backflip.

It was the sternness of his expression, the stiffness of his shoulders, and the fact that he was here on Sunday that kept me silent. But whatever I saw in Newt's countenance, my husband didn't see the same.

Wyatt gave Newt one of those buddy slaps on the back. "So, you've got good news for me?"

"I have news." A long pause. "And it's not good." Another pause. "There may be charges."

"What?" Both Newt and I jumped a bit when Wyatt pounded his fist on the counter. "What kind of charges? How could there be charges? You told me there wouldn't be."

"Well," Newt began, his tone sounding so calm alongside my husband's rage. "There are a couple of challenges. I spoke with the district attorney. They've interviewed the young girl who was in the car and she's telling them that Marquis had no weapon."

"He had a baseball bat!" Wyatt screamed.

I stuffed two crackers into my mouth.

"Well, that's another thing. There were no fingerprints on the bat."

"What?"

"No fingerprints. Marquis's fingerprints were not found on the bat."

"Well, whose fingerprints were on there?" Wyatt asked.

Newt shook his head. "They said they found no prints."

"That's impossible," my husband shouted.

"I know. Look, I'm just telling you what I know so far."

My glance went back and forth, from Wyatt to Newt. And I kept eating crackers.

"So based on this girl, they're going to charge me?"

"Based on her and the bat, it looks that way. But"—Newt held up his hand—"there are things that we can do before they make a final decision."

Wyatt's lips hardly moved when he said, "Whatever we have to do, we need to do it."

Newt nodded as if he was steps ahead of Wyatt. "We're going to begin putting on our defense. I've hired a firm to start spinning our story, doing a publicity campaign."

"Is that legal?" I croaked.

Newt nodded. "Everybody does it, especially with these kinds of cases." Turning back to Wyatt, he said, "We're going to dig into Marquis's background and his father's and mother's."

"Oh, God!" I pressed my fingers against my mouth.

Only Newt looked my way; my husband didn't even hear my cry.

Newt kept his eyes on me for a couple of seconds before he continued. "We're digging into everything about the Johnsons: their lifestyles, their social media accounts, we're going to find their police records—the son or the father probably has something. We're checking out if Tyrone Johnson has ever had an affair, anything we can use to show that they're not the victims, you are."

Wyatt nodded as if all of this sounded like a grand idea to him.

I ate the last cracker.

"And then the second thing is going to be this girlfriend."

"Okay. What? What do I have to do? How much money do we have to offer her?"

Newt held up his finger. "Don't ever say anything like that again. Do you know the penalty for witness tampering? You'll go to jail for sure."

"Witness tampering? That's not what I was talking about."

Newt shook his head as if he thought my husband didn't have a clue. Still, he went on: "There may be something that we can do to stop her from testifying. Her name is Heather Nelson. She's the daughter of Richard Nelson."

"Richard Nelson? Who's on the board of my Raising Up Boys foundation?"

Newt nodded and that made Wyatt grin.

Wyatt said, "I'll just talk to Richard, tell him what his daughter needs to say."

This time, all Newt did was shake his head. "Listen," Newt began, "just let me handle this case. You don't talk to anyone unless I tell you to."

"Okay, okay."

"So . . ." Newt went back to explaining his plan. "We're going to figure it out with Heather, either get her not to testify, or get her to admit that Marquis was angry when he got out of that car and went after you."

"Good! 'Cause that's what happened."

"And," Newt said, "we are gonna play up your foundation. When everyone hears how you work with inner-city kids, they'll get a better understanding that you're not this white man hunting black boys that the media is making you out to be."

"Good. Good. I don't know why I hadn't thought of my foundation," Wyatt said.

I had to admit that Newt had a good strategy there—at least with the foundation. The foundation that Wyatt and I started together did do good work, training teenagers so they could find jobs in the fast-food industry, teaching them how to be good employees, and after they held a job for two years, they could enter a special program that prepared them to own a franchise, if they could ever raise the money.

"And what about the fact that most of my jobs go to those kids?"

Newt chuckled. "You give most of your jobs to those kids 'cause nobody else will take them."

"Look, a job is a job. And ninety percent of my workforce is black kids."

"Someone is going to point out that all of those jobs are minimum-wage positions."

"So?" Wyatt shrugged. "They're still working, right?"

"We'll figure out how to spin it. But the key to all of this is making sure the Johnsons don't look like angels and making sure that Heather Nelson doesn't take the stand, or if she does, that she'll say what we want her to say."

"Okay, okay!"

My husband was cheering up with excitement as tears came to my eyes. They were going after the Johnsons, people who had already suffered.

"Just know, Wyatt, that we're going to take care of this," Newt said. "And so many people are on your side because this could be a precedent-setting case. Our office is being inundated with calls from television stations, radio shows, corporate executives—all asking how they can support you. Everyone knows what's at stake."

I wondered if that would be the case if everyone knew the truth.

Wyatt nodded. "Just do what you have to do, buddy. Money isn't an issue; whatever, however much it takes." He held up his hand. "And I'm not talking about tampering with any witnesses. I'm talking about paying for whatever services we need."

"Okay." Newt was a little more relaxed than when he first walked in. But his tone was still stern when he said, "I want you to understand, though, that this could happen. I want you to be prepared." He turned this glance from Wyatt to me. "Both of you. This could go to court."

Now my stomach swirled and twirled. And that must have shown on my face because Newt added, "But, if that happens, I will get you off."

"How . . . can you guarantee that?" I said, sounding as if I were speaking through stones in my throat.

"I have my ways. But with what they have now, this isn't going anywhere. There wouldn't even be any charges if there wasn't all of this social pressure. This is all about satisfying the black community. So I'm not worried. Let them do what they think they have to do. And unless some witness comes forward, you have nothing to worry about."

I was barely able to jump up and charge out of the kitchen to the downstairs bathroom in time to assume the position—seat up, head down.

I heaved and heaved until I was empty and spent.

There was a quick knock on the door. "Sweetheart, are you all right?"

"Yes," I squeaked, hoping that Wyatt didn't open the door and find me sprawled out on the tile. "I just . . . had to go to the bathroom."

A pause and then, "Okay. Newt wants to talk to us some more; we'll be in my office."

"Okay," I said. But I didn't want to hear anything else Newt had to say. He'd already said enough for me.

Unless some witness comes forward.

You have nothing to worry about.

That was so not true. My husband and Newt had so much to worry about. And they didn't even know it.

Chapter 26

It felt like a whirlwind of hate to me. But that's not what Newt called it.

"We're just exposing people to all of the facts," he said.

And the facts began to roll out the day after Newt told us of his plan.

It was Monday, June 2, three weeks after May 12. And I was sitting in Wyatt's office with Newt and two other lawyers. These were the men who would actually be representing Wyatt if he was charged since Newt didn't have a license to practice in Pennsylvania.

I didn't want to be at the meeting; I didn't want to hear anything that was going to upset my stomach or my baby. But Wyatt had insisted. Early this morning, he'd awakened me and told me that Newt was coming over for a strategy session and he wanted me to be there.

There was no way for me to protest, so I agreed, and then I made sure that I didn't eat a thing. The only way to handle all of this was on an empty stomach.

My strategy in their strategy session was to sit as far away as possible, giving myself the illusion that I wasn't really part of this effort to destroy the Johnsons. I sat by the door that led to our son's playroom.

"So what do you have?" Wyatt asked once they were all around the circular table that seated four.

"We have plenty," Newt said, sounding like a kid who was about to tell someone's secrets. "First, Marquis Johnson was suspended from school back in April." Newt's grin became wider when he added, "For possession of marijuana."

Newt stopped and Wyatt paused, too, as if he were waiting for more. "That's it?" he finally said. "That's all you got?" He shook his head as if Newt had failed him. "If every teenager who had a joint on them were suspended right now, America's schools would be empty. Trust me, I work with these kids. Smoking weed to them is like smoking cigarettes for us."

Then Newt puffed up his chest. "You must not remember who you're working with. That's *the fact*. But *the spin* is going to be that Marquis Johnson was suspended from his upscale private school because he was caught with marijuana *and* because he was suspected of selling drugs to other students. We're going to say that there is some information that might also connect him to one of Philly's top drug dealers."

"Oh, my God." I pressed my hand against my stomach. "Is that true?"

Their faces, when they looked across the room, made me think they'd forgotten that I was there.

Newt answered me. "No."

I frowned. "It's not true?"

"No."

"So you're just going to lie?"

"No."

I think Newt would have left it there if he were only talking to me. But Wyatt had as much of a question on his face as I did, so

Newt continued: "This is what's called spinning, Meredith. We're taking the truth—that he was suspended from school for possession of marijuana—and we're spinning the rest.

"We didn't say that the other things are facts. We're saying that he was *suspected* of selling drugs to other students and *there's information that might* connect him to a drug dealer."

"Oh, I get it," Wyatt said, now grinning, too. "This is brilliant."

Well, I didn't get it and I thought it was rather stupid. And immoral, and really should have been illegal. No matter what you called it, it was nothing but lying.

But the team went with it, and that night, as I sat with Wyatt in our media room, we saw the spinning begin. Wyatt had the three televisions all tuned to a different news station. And all three stations reported the story. It ran so much on the conservative channel that it felt like this story about Marquis Johnson being suspended from school was the most important news of the day.

The next morning, Newt and his team returned to our home at nine o'clock sharp! With a new report. This time, it was about Marquis's uncle, Raj Johnson.

That night, the news anchor spoke the words that Newt had read to us that morning.

"We've just received new information pertaining to the Marquis Johnson shooting," the reporter said. "Apparently Marquis's uncle, Raj Johnson"—a picture of a black man wearing a scowl and a beret flashed onto the screen, and lingered as the anchor continued—"is a member of the Brown Guardians, the motorcycle gang that some call vigilantes and others call terrorists. Johnson, who has been arrested several times for domestic violence, is also a suspect in several unsolved murders in the Philadelphia area. And there are reports that he was grooming his nephew, Marquis, for a role with the motorcycle gang. Several people inside the Brown Guardians say that Marquis was on his way to a meeting the night that he was shot and killed."

Then that picture of Marquis flashed next to his uncle's. It was the same picture of Marquis, and each time that I saw it, he looked more dangerous to me. In that moment, I wondered if maybe Wyatt *had* been terrorized that night.

Wednesday's report was about Tyrone Johnson and his auto mechanic shop. Several patrons suspected illegal activity (or so the report said) and an ex-employee (who admitted to being recently fired) said that he'd once bought a gun from Tyrone.

While Newt and Wyatt chuckled over the spinning, I wanted to cry with the Johnsons because I was sure that's what they were doing. I tried to imagine Janice. What was she thinking, what was she feeling when she heard these "spins" about her husband and son?

And then Thursday came.

It was only because Billy wasn't feeling well that Wyatt didn't summon me to the meeting that morning. As I held Billy in my arms, I was grateful to be away from the Think Tank, which was what Wyatt now called their daily meetings.

I didn't ask Wyatt what the attack was going to be about tonight. But maybe I should have. Or maybe it was better that I saw the report cold—the same way Janice Johnson had to see it.

"It seems that every day there is new information about Marquis Johnson and his family," the news anchor said on Thursday night as I sat in the media room. "And the latest is that Marquis might not even be Tyrone Johnson's son."

My mouth was wide open when the anchor tossed the story to the reporter in the field.

"Yes, Jefferson," the reporter began. "According to a friend of the Johnsons, there has long been speculation that Marquis might not even be Tyrone Johnson's son. Mrs. Johnson is said to have been involved in a long-term affair with her pastor. And there are questions as to whether the pastor is Marquis's father . . ."

It wasn't until Wyatt released a whoop that I remembered that I was not alone. My husband leaned back in the recliner and laughed so loud anyone outside would've thought we were watching a comedy show.

But if they'd seen my expression, they would have known for sure that this was no comedy—it was fantasy at best, and horror at worst.

For a long time, I sat there, staring at the television, and the reporters went back and forth, one asking questions, the other offering speculation, and then I turned my glare onto my husband.

But Wyatt didn't notice or even remember that I was there as he got on his cell.

"This is the best one yet," he said.

I suspected that he was talking to Newt. "And you thought you were going to find something on the husband!" He laughed again. "And these people wanted to come after me?"

I stood and moved like a zombie from the media room around the corner to the staircase then up the steps. I waited until I was in my bedroom, waited until I sat on the edge of my bed, before I cried.

If this was how I was feeling, I couldn't imagine what Janice Johnson was going through.

From what I'd learned over the past few days, there was always some semblance of truth to these stories, but not enough to go after a family who'd already lost their son.

But no one working for Wyatt cared about that. It was all about winning at any cost.

"Meredith, what's wrong?"

Tears still rolled down my face when I looked up. I'd forgotten that my mother was here, helping out with Billy today.

She frowned as she walked over to me, dressed in jeans and a top, and not some bikini, for once. She sat next to me and in a mother's voice asked, "What is going on with you?"

Then she put her arm around me; I laid my head down and sobbed into her shoulder.

"What is it?"

I waited until I could form a few words. "This is all too much."

"What?"

"Everything. Especially what we're doing to the Johnsons."

My mother stood and frowned. "This is about them?" She shook her head. "Have you forgotten that they're trying to put your husband in prison?" she said, as if the Johnson family didn't have a reason for wanting that.

"Wyatt killed their son."

"He had to."

"No." I shook my head. "He didn't!"

My mother's eyes were wide as she stood there for a moment, then she rushed to close the door. She was silent when she came back and just stood over me as if she were trying to intimidate me with her presence.

"Listen to me," she hissed, as if I were the one who'd done something wrong. "You better get yourself together. I told you, never say that to me or anyone ever again."

I squeezed my eyes shut, wishing that I could blink myself to some other place, some other time. Maybe even blink myself back to May 12 so that I could have stopped Wyatt.

My mother said, "Are you willing to give up your life for people you don't even know?"

She waited for me to answer; I didn't.

"If you don't care about anyone else, think about your son, Meredith. Think about Billy and figure out a way to stand by Wyatt's side without all of these"—she waved her hand in the air as if she were trying to figure out a word—"emotions."

"You just don't know what I know."

"And I don't want to know. But I know other things," she said. "I know that Wyatt Spencer gave you more than a chance, he gave you love. He gave you more than a home, he gave you a life. Think about where you would be without him."

"And you," I couldn't resist saying because I was sure a major part of her concern was what would happen to her life if Wyatt were tried and found guilty.

"Yes, and I don't mind admitting it. I don't have anything to be ashamed of. Just because I was smart enough to recognize a great opportunity for you and for me."

When I shook my head slightly, she sat back down.

"I just don't know why you can't see this," she said, her voice lower now. "Why can't you see what you have here, what you're risking by not standing by Wyatt."

"I didn't say—"

"You don't have to say anything, it's how you're acting. And if this goes to court . . . you're not ready. You can't be standing next to Wyatt weeping for the other side."

The door busted open and my mother and I looked up. "There you are," my husband said. "You okay?"

My mother stood and greeted Wyatt at the door.

"She's okay," she said. "Just a little emotional now. You know, female stuff . . ." And then my mother paused, as if she had a thought.

She was still standing next to Wyatt when her eyes asked the question.

I nodded so slightly, and subtly pressed my index finger against my lips.

My mother's nod back to me was just as subtle. And because Wyatt never paid attention, he didn't notice our exchange.

"Female stuff, huh?" was all he said, not figuring out what my mother had.

"Yeah," I said. "I'm a woman and I feel sorry for the Johnsons."

He shrugged. "They started this fight," he said. "As soon as they back away, and get the DA off my back, we'll back away, too. But until then . . ." He shrugged. "I don't think it will be too much longer, though. Newt says all of this stuff is working."

My mother clapped. "That's good, isn't it, Meredith?"

I nodded.

"Yeah, he said public sentiment has definitely shifted our way," Wyatt said. "I'm going to check on Billy."

"And I'll go with you," my mother said.

Only my mother looked back at me as the two of them stepped out of the room.

Once alone tears burned my eyes again, but not so much for Janice. This time I wanted to cry for myself. There had never been a time in my life when I'd felt more like a hypocrite.

Chapter 27

For the past ten days, it had been Newt and his team, arriving promptly at nine every morning. Today, Newt stepped into our home alone without a word, without a smile, and my heart stopped beating.

Like always, Wyatt didn't seem to notice anything unusual. He trotted down the steps and greeted Newt with his buddy hug and loud exclamation: "What's going on, dude? What do we have today?"

But when Wyatt moved toward this office, Newt said, "Let's talk in the living room." And then he turned as if this were his home.

And we followed, as if we were his guests.

How my legs held up I would never know. But my limbs stayed strong enough for me to stagger to the sofa. I sank into the cushions and Wyatt sat beside me.

I knew that my husband finally got it; I knew that he was reading Newt's unspoken message when he reached for my hand and held me.

I was thankful because I wanted to hold on to him, too.

Newt didn't waste a moment. In his all-business tone, he said, "The state prosecutor has decided to press charges." A pause and a blink. "First-degree murder."

Wyatt gasped and I cried out.

"I've arranged for you to turn yourself in tomorrow." He paused again, this time as if he were waiting for Wyatt to say something.

And I waited, too.

But Wyatt sat as still as I was.

Newt took his silence as permission to continue. "I want to do this first thing in the morning. This way, we have a chance of having bail set tomorrow. Normally, the bond hearing isn't until the preliminary arraignment, but I've already talked to the DA and we may be able to get a few concessions because of who you are."

All my husband did was nod. I expected more, I expected rage. But then, I realized that Wyatt was shell-shocked. And I understood. Because I'd convinced myself that his and Newt's strategy, as foul as it was, was going to work.

Now I couldn't believe that it hadn't worked. All of that tearing down of Marquis and his parents. For what? For nothing!

As if Newt heard my thoughts, he said, "Now, I don't want you to think that what we've done so far has been in vain. The momentum had totally swung in our favor. It's just that in this political climate . . . and with Barack Obama as president . . . when in doubt, it goes to the blacks."

This time, Wyatt nodded and grunted.

"My plan is for you to be in jail for just a few hours. Overnight, tops."

Those words woke my husband up.

"Jail?" he said. "I can't believe this is happening to me."

"Don't panic. Remember I told you last week that this could happen. But we've got it under control. I'm thinking that there may not even be a trial. I'm thinking that a good part of this is symbolic."

"What do you mean?" I asked.

"Well, tomorrow is June twelfth, a month later . . . you know."

"Are you sure that I'm going to get bail?" Wyatt asked.

"In Pennsylvania, every defendant has the opportunity for bail. You're white, no other offenses, you're not a flight risk, you'll get bail. It may be high, though."

Wyatt raised his eyebrows.

"Don't worry," Newt said. "You'll be able to handle it. About a million, though I'm going to get it as low as possible because it has to be in cash."

"I don't have that kind of money sitting around. It may take a few days."

"We'll handle it. I'm not going to let you sit in there."

Wyatt released a long breath and held his head in his hands.

"Listen to me, buddy," Newt said. "I need you to be strong. Because it's important that you show nothing but confidence. Everybody has to believe that you know you're innocent. And then everybody will know that, too."

"Okay. Okay."

I closed my eyes because I didn't know it.

Newt said, "It's going to be a simple case, a self-defense case."

"Good," Wyatt said. "I wanna tell everyone that I was standing my ground."

"That's not a defense. Self-defense is the legal defense, and we'll talk about Stand Your Ground as part of that."

"Okay. Okay."

"The other side wants to put this law on trial, but they're making a mistake. They have no basis for attacking Stand Your Ground. As soon as Marquis brought that bat out, it was over. There was nothing else that you could do."

"Right. Right." And then, my husband added, "I want to testify."

But he'd hardly gotten the words out when Newt said, "I can already tell you that's not going to happen."

"Why not?" my husband asked, with a tinge of that confident rage that he always had. "It's self-defense; won't I have to testify?"

"No, there are plenty of ways around it. And I have a feeling that the prosecution is going to put you on the stand via your taped interview versus your statements."

"Is that bad?"

Newt shrugged. "It's not good. You contradicted yourself, but I'll be able to handle that."

Wyatt shook his head. "No, I want to get on that stand and tell everyone exactly what happened."

"Didn't you hear what I just said? And that's one of the reasons why I won't let you testify. You, my friend, don't do a good job of listening to other people and you certainly can't always hold in your anger. The DA will rip you apart."

"No, he—"

Newt didn't even let him finish. "That's a definite, dude. You're not testifying." And then he paused, and looked at me. "We haven't decided, but we are thinking about having Meredith take the stand."

"What?" Wyatt and I said together.

"I thought a wife couldn't testify against her husband."

Newt frowned. "Of course she wouldn't be testifying against you. She'd be one of our witnesses, part of the defense, testifying for you."

I swallowed, I shook, and I thanked God that I didn't faint right there.

"When the jurors take a look at her," Newt said as if I weren't there; and then, his eyes roamed over me as if Wyatt wasn't there, "no one is going to believe that a man married to her would kill anyone."

"Really?" Wyatt asked. "That kind of stuff works?"

"In cases like this, it's all about theatrics. Never forget Johnnie Cochran and the glove. All drama and that's what we're going to do, too."

Finally, I found my words. "But I can't testify." When both of them frowned, I said, "I'd be too nervous. And . . . I don't want to do anything to hurt Wyatt."

Newt nodded and Wyatt once again took my hand. "Don't worry about that, Meredith," Newt said. "We'll have you so prepped, you'll be fine. We haven't decided yet; I just wanted to put it out there, give you a heads-up."

"Okay," Wyatt said, and squeezed my hand as if he were speaking for me. "She'll be ready."

"I know she will be." Newt stood. "Well, if you don't have any other questions, I want to get going. There's lots of work to do before tomorrow."

Wyatt and I stood with him, though only Wyatt walked him to the door. I didn't have the strength. I had to use all the energy I had to figure out how to stay off the stand.

Why was the door open?

I took two steps down the stairs and heard Wyatt's footsteps, rushing along the marble.

And then I saw him. Running toward the door. But he slipped and dropped what he was carrying.

A bat.

Billy's baseball bat.

I frowned and wondered what was he doing with that?

Wyatt bent down, then looked up and into the glass that surrounded our door. That served as a mirror at night.

His back was still to me as he looked into that reflection.

A second passed, then another, and another.

And then he rushed out the door.

What was he doing with that bat?

I shot straight up in my bed, panting. It took a few seconds before I realized I was home, in my bedroom, in my bed, next to Wyatt.

Moving as gently as I could, I eased out of the bed, then scurried across to the bathroom. I took great care in making sure the door made no sound as I closed it, then I assumed the position.

But nothing came out. I was empty. Of everything.

I lowered the cover of the commode, sat on it, held my head in my hands, and remembered the rest of May 12. How I'd come downstairs, just in time to peek out the door. Just in time to see Wyatt trot to the end of our driveway, then watch him roll Billy's bat under a car parked in front of our home.

Then, only a couple of seconds after that, two police cars appeared with flashing lights and parked next to the car. I wanted to go outside and stand by Wyatt; I wanted to know what was going on. But I couldn't leave Billy alone.

So from the window, I watched as Wyatt spoke to the police, and watched the police help a young girl out of the car.

Then my eyes widened as Wyatt walked up our driveway with one of the officers.

"What happened?" *I asked when he was still feet away.*

"I just shot someone."

"Oh, my God, Wyatt." *I tried to get a glance out the door, but he blocked me from seeing.* "What happened?"

"I was trying to help a girl, and this thug came after me. With a baseball bat."

"A baseball bat?"

Wyatt spoke over me. "I have to go down to the police station. To give a statement." He leaned over and gave me a long, long, long kiss on the cheek. "Don't worry. It'll be fine. They just need to ask me a few questions."

The officer nodded as if what Wyatt was saying was true. Then, the two of them walked away. And as I watched the policeman escort my husband down the driveway, then open the door of the squad car, I wondered about that baseball bat. And I wondered if Wyatt knew that I'd seen him.

For weeks now, I'd been asking myself that question—did Wyatt know that I'd seen him?

I heard just the slightest creak and I looked up and gasped when Wyatt stepped into the bathroom.

"You scared me!"

"Really? I'm sorry, sweetheart." His gaze was filled with curiosity. "What's wrong with you?"

I shook my head. "Nothing."

He sighed and waited a moment before he asked, "Why don't you want to tell me?"

My heart swooped down to my feet. "Tell you what? I just wasn't feeling well, and didn't want to disturb you."

He reached for me and I was so afraid to touch him, but I did. I took his hand and he raised me up. Then, closing the gap between us, he placed his hand on my belly, and I stopped breathing.

When he leaned over and kissed my stomach, I closed my eyes. He knew!

"I hope it's a girl this time," he whispered. "That would complete our family. A girl and a boy."

VICTORIA CHRISTOPHER MURRAY

I said nothing.

"Why didn't you tell me?" he asked.

"Because with all that's going on, I didn't want this to be a burden."

His voice was soft and gentle and kind when he said, "How could a child with you, the woman I love, be a burden? I'm thrilled about this."

"I was worried . . ."

"This is perfect timing, sweetheart. We'll have to tell Newt tomorrow. So that he can expedite the trial. Because in court, everyone needs to see that you're pregnant. And then they will know that there is no way they can take a man away from his pregnant wife." He held my face between his hands and kissed me. "When they see your beautiful face and your swollen belly." He kissed me again. "I know you're scared, sweetheart, but we're going to get through this together. You won't have to worry; I'm not going to prison. This is a blessing. It's a sign that God doesn't want me in jail, that God knows my heart, that God knows what I did was right."

He leaned back and he peered into my eyes. And what I wanted to see in his was love. But that's not what I saw. His voice, his words, were the opposite of his hard stare. His warning.

I trembled.

He took two steps back and smiled. Held my hand and led me away. Back to bed.

He whispered, "It's going to be all right," over and over as he pulled back the duvet and tucked me into bed.

I wanted to run. Truly. But where would I go?

Wyatt smoothed the covers over me, and as he went to his side, I talked to the God that Wyatt said approved of what he'd done.

Seconds later, he was beside me, his body pressed against my back, and he wrapped me in a tight hug.

I trembled some more.

"Sweetheart, what's wrong?"

"Nothing," I said, though my voice shook in rhythm with my body.

"Your heart—it's racing."

I was just glad that it was still beating.

He said, "I told you, there's nothing to worry about."

"Okay." My voice sounded as high as my three-year-old's.

There was a long moment of silence before he said, "Just remember when you get on the stand, how much I love you, how much you love me." A beat. "And a wife cannot testify against her husband."

I pressed my lips together. Wyatt knew.

Wyatt totally knew.

And I was so scared. For so many reasons.

PART THREE

Janice Johnson—Meredith Spencer

I PROMISE . . .
TO TELL THE WHOLE TRUTH
AND NOTHING BUT . . .

SEPTEMBER 9, 2014

Chapter 28

Janice

Pushing the clutch onto the back of my earring, I stepped into my bedroom and stopped. Inside, I moaned. How many more times would I walk into this scene?

Tyrone sat on the edge of the bed, the remote hanging from his hand as he stared at the television screen. Long seconds passed between each blink, as if he were afraid that he would miss something.

Not even when he watched the Eagles playing on one of their losing Sundays did he stay in such a trancelike state. There was only one story that made him like this.

I walked to the bed and sat next to my husband before I reached for his hand, and the remote, but Tyrone moved both away from me. He did press pause, though, stopping the live coverage of the reporter who was already staked out at the courthouse.

Freezing the television was worse than letting the story play. Because now the screen was frozen on Clarissa Austin, holding the microphone right beneath her chin.

But I knew Tyrone wasn't looking at Clarissa. His eyes were on the upper corner—on the photo of me.

I let a couple of moments go by. Then, "I'm sorry."

Tyrone didn't turn to look at me. With his eyes still on the TV, he said, "What are you apologizing for?"

"You know."

"Well, if you're apologizing about what happened with you and Pastor Brown, you apologized already."

"I'm going to keep apologizing. Until it's enough."

He nodded like he agreed, but he didn't say that he did.

I asked, "Why do you keep watching this over and over?"

He pressed his lips together as if he wanted to keep in the first words that came to mind. Finally, "They're going to make this an issue in court," he said, not answering my question. Then came what felt like a bombshell to me. He said, "Maybe you shouldn't testify."

I was one of the fifty-six people on the prosecution's witness list. Not that I could give any kind of information about what happened between Wyatt Spencer and my son. But the DA told me that I needed to testify in order to bring Marquis alive—in a truthful manner. I needed to be on the stand to combat the thug-living, drug-dealing, juvenile-delinquent boy the defense had made Marquis out to be. I had to fight their lies with the truth that could only be told by a mother.

"I have to," I said to Tyrone. "I have to testify for Marquis."

Even though he shook his head, his eyes didn't turn away from that dang television. "No, you don't. They're never going to convict him anyway. He's white, he's rich; that cracker's never going to prison, and all of this has been nothing but a waste of time."

If I thought not testifying would provide Tyrone with relief from the pubic humiliation he felt, if I thought it would help my marriage, I would have run straight to the DA as soon as this news about my affair had come to light.

But over the last few months, I'd seen what keeping silent against the machine that worked for Wyatt Spencer had done. Silence did nothing—except give more room for lies to be told and lies to be heard. And they had told so many lies, making it seem like Tyrone and I were absent parents who'd had a child out of wedlock. They never mentioned that we'd married before Marquis turned one or that we'd been married for almost seventeen years.

They didn't mention our marriage until they broke the story about Caleb. Then, we were married. Then, they tore our marriage apart.

I couldn't figure out how Wyatt and his people got away with it. But when I'd complained, the attorney, Byron Powell, that we'd had to hire, said that there was nothing they could do about leaks when sources weren't revealed.

After all of those thoughts, I answered Tyrone, "If you thought that he wouldn't be convicted, why did you go through all of this? Why did you push? With the Guardians?" I only asked him to remind him of the reasons why he'd participated in the marches and protests and interviews. I wanted him to remember that what we'd been through was worth it, even if it was just to get our time in court.

He shrugged. "For a moment, I thought it might work. But I forgot where we lived. For a moment, I thought I was living in a country that was the land of the free. I thought I was living in a place where there was justice for all. For a moment, I forgot that I was living in America."

This was just his hurt speaking. Tyrone wanted this trial as much as I did. He prayed for a conviction as much as I prayed. But the beat down that I'd taken in the media had more than beat down Tyrone; it had broken his heart.

"I'm only testifying for our son." I repeated what he already knew. "I want the chance to tell the truth."

When he didn't say anything, I lifted my hand and moved in slow motion until I touched his. Then I held his hand. And I breathed when Tyrone didn't pull away.

That was good. That was something.

"I love you, Tyrone. I don't want to lose you."

If this were a different time and another place, Tyrone would have told me that he loved me, too. And that I would never lose him.

But he didn't say anything.

All he did was take the television off of pause.

As the reporter droned on about the trial that was beginning today, Tyrone held my hand. He hadn't said that he loved me, but he was showing it.

That was good. That was something.

From the front seat of our eight-passenger SUV, our attorney explained how the normally forty-five-minute ride would be much longer today. Between the rush-hour traffic and blocked-off streets, it would take double the time to get to the courthouse.

Over the past months, we'd done this ride so many times in the name of our son.

In May, we'd stood on the courthouse steps, shoulder to shoulder with leaders of the NAACP.

"Think about the basic tenet of the law," Tyrone had said to the crowd of thousands. "This law says that the natural order of a dispute is that first, you kill the other guy. Then, you claim self-defense. Finally, because the only other witness is dead, you walk away." He had to pause for a moment because of the jeers from the crowd. "Oh, and don't forget this . . . after you've committed murder in the name of Stand Your Ground, you get to keep your gun!"

The crowd exploded with boos before the chant began, "Enough! Enough! Enough!"

The next week, we stood with the Urban League.

"Wyatt Spencer is just another statistic," Tyrone told the audience. "Another statistic for Stand Your Ground. Because, you see, when you're white and you kill someone black, you have a much greater chance of having that murder justified if you say you were standing your ground. How can this country in good conscience continue with this law?"

Then, Tyrone led the chant, "Enough! Enough! Enough!"

We even got involved with the sororities and fraternities of the Divine Nine, reminding college students that every great civil rights movement began with young people.

"My son would have been just like you, on the campus of UPenn," Tyrone said at a gathering of undergraduate students from all the colleges in the Philadelphia area. "I don't know if Marquis would have pledged Omega, or if he would have become an Alpha or a Kappa or an Iota. But if Wyatt Spencer hadn't taken his life, I know that my son would have grown into a man who would have made a difference. Now he will never have that chance."

"Enough! Enough! Enough!" the students chanted.

I had never felt so close to my husband as when we stood together and watched our son become a national symbol of injustice while Wyatt Spencer became the face of all that was wrong with the Stand Your Ground law.

But then on June 3, Wyatt Spencer's team had been unleashed. And on June 5, everything changed.

It was supposed to be a beautiful day—our first wonderful one since we'd lost Marquis. Tyrone had arranged for me to spend six hours at Angel's Spa with Syreeta, followed by a romantic dinner with him and me.

But then, Tyrone hadn't shown up; he'd just texted me to come home. I'd rushed into our house, praying that I wouldn't be faced with another tragedy.

I found my husband in the family room, staring at the television. It had been so confusing to me, until I heard the reporter:

"According to this woman who didn't want to be identified, there has long been speculation that Marquis might not even be Tyrone Johnson's son. Mrs. Johnson is said to have been involved in a long-term affair with her pastor and many have questioned if the pastor is Marquis's father . . ."

Even now, I remembered each of the stress lines that were etched in Tyrone's face as he stared at the TV screen.

"*Oh, my God! How can they say that?*" *I shouted.*

Tyrone said, "They can say it because it's true."

"That's not true. It's all a lie!"

"Except for the part where they said you had an affair . . ."

I had to take a breath. "They said I had a long-term affair."

For the first time since I entered the room, Tyrone looked up at me. "If you had an affair that lasted longer than a moment, it was long-term to me."

"Babe." I lowered myself onto the sofa. "I'm sorry, so sorry."

He was quiet for a moment as if he was pondering my apology. Finally, "Well, now that the world knows about your affair, maybe you should tell everyone that you're sorry. Maybe that will make this all better." Then, he'd stood and walked out of the family room, leaving me to watch the newscasters talking about my affair, alone.

That night when I went to sleep with Tyrone's back to me, I'd already lost my son, and I prayed that now, I wouldn't lose my husband.

Life with my husband hadn't been the same since that day, since June 5.

Just as I had that thought, Tyrone reached across the car's seat and took my hand. I looked up, but his eyes were on the window as we sped toward the Montgomery County courthouse.

I exhaled.

There was hope.

Chapter 29

Meredith

I was trembling so much that I fumbled, not able to get the seat belt to click into place.

"Are you okay?" Wyatt asked as he stood outside on the curb, talking to Newt. "You need help with that?"

I nodded. He leaned over me, snapped the seat belt into place, kissed my cheek, patted me on the head, then closed the door before he trotted around to the other side and slid in next to me.

"Ready to go!" Wyatt shouted to Andre once Newt took his place in the front passenger seat.

"Let's hit it." Andre eased the SUV onto the street.

As we pulled off, I still trembled. The way I'd been trembling for months. I hadn't stopped since Wyatt found me in the bathroom that night, and told me that he knew what I'd seen without saying those words.

In the three months that had passed, he still hadn't told me. But I knew that he saw me and I knew that he had warned me.

Wyatt went about his life as if there were no chance that he would ever go to jail. My husband was right about that—if public sentiment was any indication. Even though we were wealthy, people who didn't have anywhere near the money we had set up all kinds of websites to collect money for Wyatt's defense. According to reports, donations to us quadrupled what had been raised for the Johnsons.

The Johnsons. Janice Johnson. I thought about her all the time.

"Are you all right, sweetheart?" Wyatt asked, taking my hand just as Andre turned onto the interstate.

I nodded and wondered if he noticed how my hand shook inside of his.

I knew why Wyatt was asking about me. Because today was not only the start of Wyatt's trial, it was my debut.

It had been planned that way, part of the strategy. I'd been kept away from the courthouse and the cameras until today. The news stations had said very little about Wyatt Spencer's wife. Because Newt wanted me to walk into court on this first day with my full and frizzy hair, and my crimson-colored lips, and . . . my baby bump.

That was supposed to take the world by surprise.

Today, Wyatt had me dressed properly for the part in a high-necked, knee-length, sleeveless navy dress that fit snugly around my five-months-pregnant belly. My pearls (no diamonds except for my wedding ring) finished the ensemble. Yes, I looked like the wife of a man who would never murder a kid on purpose.

It made me want to throw up, but thankfully my morning sickness had passed. At least I hoped it had passed.

"Look at all of this," Andre shouted, and I peered through the tinted glass.

One side of the street was completely filled with vans and cameras, and microphones and people, lots of people doing interviews and being interviewed.

My mother would have loved this. It still surprised me that my mother didn't want to come to court. Any time there was a camera,

Gloria Harris thought that was glamorous. But today, my mother had stepped up.

"I want to be home with Billy," she'd said. "No need for him to be with a sitter when he can be with his glam-mom."

That "glam-mom" was a bit over the top, but the sentiment was exactly what I needed.

A policeman waved us forward and Andre drove a few more feet then stopped. "This is where you get out," he said, as if we were all going to a party.

As Wyatt jumped out I trembled even more. But now my chest hurt, too. Because of how hard my heart was beating.

Wyatt took my hand as if I couldn't get out of the car alone; this was all part of the show. They had warned me that cameras would always be watching. So I spread my lips into that smile, and held Wyatt's hand as I slid out of the SUV.

There were shouts all around us, and Newt led us through the narrow pathway and into the courthouse, then up an elevator and down the hall to the room where my husband's future would be decided.

Inside, I paused and took it all in. I was surprised; this room looked exactly the way courtrooms did on all of those television shows. Only smaller. And older. A lot older. Like the benches were one hundred years old.

There were cameras in the corners; Wyatt had told me about that. The judge had decided that the trial would be televised so that more than the thirty-six people who would win the public seats in a daily lottery could see the proceedings.

Newt and Wyatt had already walked to the front of the room, and as I began to move to the left, I glanced to the right.

And there I saw her.

Janice Johnson.

Right away, I felt like I knew her.

When she looked up, I smiled. And when she smiled back, my smile got wider. Until I sat down behind Newt and Wyatt.

Then Janice looked from me to Newt and Wyatt, and by the time she looked back at me, her smile had gone away.

When Wyatt leaned over the rail to kiss me, Janice rolled her eyes and turned away.

Those seconds of warmth that we shared were completely over.

In the beginning, it was all so interesting. From the "all rise" to the judge hitting his gavel, it was just like on TV. I studied the jurors, the twelve and the two alternates, twelve white and two black, eight women and six men, exactly the way Wyatt had told me. Fourteen people who wouldn't get the chance to go home until this was over since the judge had decided that the jury would be sequestered.

But then, as quickly as that gavel went down, that's how fast that it went from good to bad.

It started with the opening arguments and the first words out of the prosecutor's mouth.

"Wyatt Spencer is a murderer!"

I gasped, and glanced at Janice. But her eyes were straight ahead, watching the prosecutor (who really didn't look like he was much older than sixteen) as he walked slowly back and forth in front of the jury box.

The prosecutor continued: "Wyatt Spencer fatally shot Marquis Johnson, on Monday, May twelfth, the day after Mother's Day. And he shot him for no reason other than he was angry. He was upset that this *boy* would get out of his car.

"It is not a crime to confront someone who's knocking on your car window," the prosecutor said. "Wyatt Spencer started the confrontation when he approached Marquis's car. And then, when the young man got out of his car, that grown man with a gun"—he paused and pointed to Wyatt—"finished the confrontation that he started. He finished it by taking away the promise and the hope and the future of a young man who on this day would have been a freshman at the University of Pennsylvania.

"And then, to make his crime even worse, after he shot Marquis, he planted a baseball bat at the scene. And he lied to the police and said that Marquis had attacked him with the bat."

After those words, I could barely hear anything else; I was just stunned that the prosecutor, without my help, had gotten it totally right.

That had to mean that Wyatt was going to jail. The prosecutor had just told the whole truth.

But then, when one of the attorneys who'd been working with Newt got up, he didn't make me feel much better.

Our side began, "Wyatt Spencer saw someone sitting in front of his house. The car was noisily idling on the street and Mr. Spencer did what anyone would do; he checked it out. He saw a young woman sitting in the passenger seat of the car, and from where he stood, it looked like she was crying. So now he's more than curious: Mr. Spencer is concerned.

"All Wyatt Spencer was trying to do was to provide help that he thought was needed. But before he could find out the full story of what was happening *in front of his home*, he was confronted by Marquis Johnson. And, I say 'confronted' because why else would Marquis get out of his car? Marquis jumped out because he wanted a fight. He jumped out because he was going to attack Mr. Spencer.

"And so in self-defense, Mr. Spencer stood his ground. He had a right to be there, in front of his home. And there was no way that Mr. Spencer, an upstanding family man who has worked hard all of his life, could do anything except protect himself. And his family." The attorney paused and looked at me. "His thoughts were only about his son and his *pregnant* wife."

It felt like everyone in the courtroom was looking at me—the jurors, the attorneys.

"The evidence will show that Marquis Johnson had a propensity toward violence. There are young men and women who attended school with Marquis who were very afraid of him for this reason. And violence was on his mind when he got out of his car that night."

I had no idea how I was going to do this. No idea how I would be able to sit through this tension for the eight or nine or ten days that Newt said this trial would last.

But then I looked over at Janice and my heart ached as she wiped away tears. I thought about how much she'd lost, yet here she sat. Even with tears falling from her eyes, her head was high.

If she could sit through this, then I could sit through it, too.

Chapter 30

Janice

We were almost home and I was so grateful.

I hadn't known what to expect, having never been in a court-room before, but for sure, I never expected all of the tension. The opening arguments had been tough enough, but the pressure continued when our side called Heather to the stand.

She hadn't been in the courtroom, since she was a witness, but I turned to look at her when she walked solemnly down the center aisle. She was smartly dressed, a teen with a lot of money. Her jeans, navy blazer, and white tailored shirt made her look sophisticated, older than her seventeen years.

She hadn't looked at me when she passed by. She didn't turn to look at us when she stood before the clerk and swore to tell the truth. Though I'd tried to make contact, her eyes never connected to mine.

That was a bad sign.

During one of the pretrial hearings, the defense had tried to get Heather excluded as a prosecution witness saying that since her father served on the board of Wyatt Spencer's foundation, there was a conflict of interest. When I heard that, I wasn't sure that I wanted her to testify either. Not when her parents were friends with the man who murdered my son.

The judge had ruled that that information was immaterial; Heather would testify.

By the way she walked into that courtroom, the way she wouldn't look at me, I knew that decision was not going to be in our favor.

"State your name," the prosecutor said.

"Heather Nelson."

"And, Heather, did you know Marquis Johnson?"

"Yes," she said. *"He was my boyfriend,"* she added, still not look-ing my way.

"Were you with him the night of May twelfth?"

"Yes."

"Can you tell us the circumstances."

"Marquis and I had gone to the library. And afterward, we went to get something to eat."

"Where did you go?"

"To the Cheesesteak Castle over on Mill Road. It's not too far from our school."

There was a slight mumble in the courtroom. Everyone knew that Wyatt Spencer was the founder of the Cheesesteak Castles.

"What did you do when you left the Cheesesteak Castle?"

"We decided to eat in the car and we weren't finished when we got near my house. So we parked a couple of blocks away and just sat and ate and talked."

"That's all you were doing?"

She nodded. "Yes, just talking."

"And did something happen while you were in the car?"

"Yes. Mr. Spencer knocked on my window. It scared both of us."

"Objection!" the defense attorney said.

"Sustained," the judge responded. Then the judge said, "Ms. Nelson, just speak to what you felt, what you saw."

She looked up at the judge and nodded. She still never looked at me.

Heather said, "The knock on the window scared me."

"What happened next?"

"Mr. Spencer asked if I was okay, and I said that I was. And then he asked why was I in the car with Marquis? And then Marquis told him to get away from his car and Mr. Spencer said that he wasn't going anywhere."

"Then what happened?"

Heather paused, took a deep breath, and I knew then that she'd gone to the other side.

She said, "Marquis got out of the car and went around to the back, but before he even got to the back, Mr. Spencer shot him!"

I blinked.

"So he got out of the car and that's it?"

She nodded and sniffed.

"Did he get out of the car with anything? Did he have anything in his hand?"

"No." She shook her head, and kept shaking it as if she wanted to make sure that everyone got that point. "He didn't have a bat."

"Objection!"

"Sustained. Counselor . . ."

The prosecutor nodded. "Did you see him with a bat?" he asked.

"No," Heather said. "He didn't have a bat. He didn't have anything."

"And what did you do? Did you get out of the car after Mr. Spencer shot Marquis?"

"No! I was afraid that he would shoot me, too, so I just dialed 911."

"Thank you," the prosecutor said. *"No further questions."*

The defense attorney looked like he couldn't wait to jump up. *"Ms. Nelson, how much time do you think passed between the time that Marquis got out of the car and the moment when you heard the shot?"*

She shrugged. *"I don't know."*

"Would you say five seconds, ten seconds, fifteen seconds?"

"I don't know," she repeated.

"So it could have been enough time for Marquis to open the door and pull a bat out of the back of the car?"

"I guess, but he didn't—"

The attorney interrupted her. *"I only asked if there could have been enough time . . . That's all I asked."*

She looked at the judge, then back to the attorney. *"I guess so."*

The attorney nodded, then asked, *"Why were you and Marquis sitting in the car talking? Weren't you going to see each other in school the next day?"*

"Yes, but we hadn't had a chance to hang out for a few weeks, so we wanted to spend a little extra time together before he went home."

The attorney frowned like her words came as a surprise to him. *"You hadn't had a chance to hang out? Marquis was your boyfriend; why hadn't you spent time together?"*

"Because . . . he'd been on lockdown."

"Lockdown?" Now the defense attorney wore a deep frown. *"Lockdown? Had he been in jail?"*

"Objection!" The prosecutor jumped up.

"Withdrawn," the defense attorney said. *"What do you mean by 'lockdown'?"* He rephrased his question.

"Well . . ." And with that pause, Heather looked at me for the first time. She said, *"He'd done something wrong and so his parents kinda punished him."*

"By 'something wrong,' do you mean he was suspended from school?"

I could tell she didn't want to answer that. I could tell that she was completely on our side.

She nodded.

The judge said, "You must answer the question, Ms. Nelson."

"Yes. He'd been suspended."

After that, the defense entered the school record with the reason for Marquis's suspension—possession of marijuana. And then Heather was released from the stand.

This time, when she passed by she paused, for just the tiniest of moments, and smiled. It wasn't a full smile, definitely not a happy smile. Just the kind of smile that said that she was so sorry and that she really did love my son.

If I hadn't been warned that all eyes and every camera would be watching me, I would have given her my thank-you. But all I did was nod and thank God that I'd been wrong about her. For so long and in so many ways.

We were just blocks away from our home when my cell phone rang. I clicked accept and then asked, "Hey, Ree. What are you still doing up?" knowing that it had to be approaching midnight in Germany.

"I had to check on you and see how the first day had gone. I so wish that I was there."

"I wish that, too," I said.

She'd only been gone for two weeks, having had to get back to her job. But I felt like I'd lived a lifetime without her.

"So, how did it go?" she asked.

"We're on our way home now."

"You're in the car?" Before I could answer, she said, "That means you can't really talk."

"Not yet, but in a little while."

"Okay, then, do you remember pig latin?" she asked. "Ancay ouyay oday isthay?"

I laughed.

She said, "I guess that means you've forgotten."

"Never learned. But I can talk."

"How're things with you and Tyrone?"

I glanced over at my husband, who was in the same position that he was in when we were driving to the courthouse this morning. His eyes and his heart were away from me. "The same. Hoping for better."

"Dang. Are they still going after you?"

"Yeah, it had stopped for a little while, but you know, since the trial started today."

"I can't even imagine seeing your business on TV like that. Have you heard from Caleb?"

"God no! And thank God for that," I said. If Caleb tried to contact me in any way, and if Tyrone found out about it, that would be the blade that would cut the weak thread that held us together.

"I just hope that Tyrone remembers all of that happened long ago."

I wanted to tell Syreeta that Tyrone knew that. He knew that it was long ago and long over, with no chance of it ever happening again.

But this was about the pain of public humiliation. Of our secrets coming to light on national television. Of men Tyrone knew and ones he didn't asking how could a man stay with a harlot such as me, though "harlot" was hardly the word they used.

This was peer pressure. Adult peer pressure. Stranger peer

pressure. All reminding Tyrone of how hurt he should have been. And how hurt he really was.

"Maybe you two should go back to counseling," Syreeta said.

"I thought of that," I said. "Maybe when this is over."

"It saved you before; it will save you again."

"Let us pray."

"Okay, girl. Well, I'll check on you tomorrow. When do you take the stand?"

I gazed out the window when I said, "I don't know, tomorrow. Maybe."

"I'm praying, Jan. And I love you!"

"I love you, too."

"Tell Tyrone I said hello."

"I will."

"No, tell him now, so that I can hear you."

I rolled my eyes, but did as my best friend asked. "Syreeta says hello."

Without turning my way, Tyrone only nodded.

I said, "He said hello."

Syreeta said, "And tell him to stop acting like a fool just 'cause you slept with the pastor. That was a long—"

I clicked off the phone because clearly, my friend had gone mad.

Just as I dumped my cell back into my purse, Tyrone reached for my hand. He didn't look at me, but he held me.

I wanted him to look at me, but for now, holding my hand was huge. And just like this morning, it was something.

It was hope.

Chapter 31

Meredith

We'd made it through to this last day of the first week, and even though my husband was on trial for his life, I couldn't believe how fascinating this trial was to me.

I guess I'd expected to be completely bored, just playing my role. But it wasn't like that. I was engaged with every person who took the stand.

It was easy to sit and watch since Newt kept telling us that we had nothing to worry about. According to him, it was the prosecution and the Johnsons who needed to be sweating because we were clearly winning.

"They don't have a case," Newt told us on Tuesday. "What did they give us today? I tore Heather's testimony down."

I didn't quite see it that way. To me, Heather had been clear, credible, and confident. I couldn't see how that was a win for us. But, of course, I said nothing.

On Wednesday, Newt said, "This case should never have been brought to trial. I wouldn't be surprised if the judge throws it out after the prosecution rests."

Again, I wondered what trial was Newt listening to? Two

teachers had testified. One who explained that while Marquis had been suspended, he was the tenth student that school year to have been suspended for possession of marijuana. And the other teacher was Marquis's guidance counselor, who spoke of how Marquis was not a thug—he was a young man who would have been valedictorian (save for the suspension) and he was on his way to UPenn on an academic scholarship.

But the most interesting testimony had come from the man who I still found a bit intriguing.

"State your name for the court."

"Detective Lucien Ferguson."

As the detective and the prosecutor went back and forth establishing Detective Ferguson's credentials, I was struck by his first name, Lucien. A name I'd never heard before.

"Detective, did you respond to a call on Monday, May twelfth of this year on Avon Street in Haverford?"

"Yes. I did, along with seven other officers."

"Can you tell us what you found at the scene?"

That was when I checked out because I knew what the detective had found. A dead boy. And a bat. And my husband. It wasn't until the detective began speaking about what happened at the station that I became interested again.

"During his interview, I asked Wyatt Spencer about his phone call to 911. I wanted to know why it came in three minutes after the first call."

"And what did Mr. Spencer say?"

"He said that he didn't have his phone on him. That he had to run into the house and go upstairs to get it. He said that accounted for the difference in time between his call and the first call."

"Did that make sense to you?"

"At that time, we were just taking his statement."

"Was there ever a time when you became concerned about that explanation?"

"Yes. When our detectives went back to the scene. We reenacted a man running from the front of the house, up to the bedroom, then back down again."

"And how long did that take your detective?" the prosecutor asked.

"About forty-four seconds—if he waited to call until he came back outside. If he had called from his phone when he first found it, it would have taken him about half of that time."

"Did you ever ask Mr. Spencer about the call again?"

"Yes, sir. After we'd done our test, I spoke with Wyatt Spencer again about ten days later. At that time, he said that his cell phone was downstairs, right at the front door."

"Would you consider that an inconsistent statement?"

"Yes, sir."

"Did you ask him about that inconsistency?"

"I did."

"And what was his response?"

"He never answered; he was angry."

"No further questions."

Then, the attorney on our side asked Detective Ferguson if he'd ever met an innocent man who'd given an inconsistent statement. When the detective said that he had, our attorney sat down and the detective was dismissed.

But while Newt didn't think the detective's testimony counted for anything, I thought it revealed to the jury that my husband was not only a murderer, but he was a lousy liar.

To me, between the teachers and the detectives, that day had gone well for the prosecution of my husband.

Yesterday he said, "If this does make it to the jury, they'll be out for ten minutes before they come back with 'not guilty.'"

That's when I decided the only way Newt could think that the jury would come back so quickly and decisively in Wyatt's favor was that Newt had to be sleeping through the testimonies.

It was true that the medical examiner didn't give much to either side. But what he said had to help the prosecution.

"Marquis was shot at close range, one bullet through his heart that caused catastrophic loss of blood pressure. He didn't die instantly, though. It probably took two to three minutes."

Janice had let out a gasp that made me want to cry, and there was no relief for me when the fingerprint expert took the stand.

"Mr. Henderson," the prosecutor began, *"you didn't find any prints on the bat?"*

"No."

"But does that mean that Mr. Spencer did not touch the bat?"

"No, it doesn't," the examiner said. *"The misconception is that there will be fingerprints on every surface. But just because someone touches a surface does not guarantee that a latent print will be deposited, and there are lots of reasons for this. The person's hands may be very dry, which means there is little or no sweat or oils coating the ridges. Therefore, the ridge detail won't reliably transfer to the surface. And then, of course, there is the chance that someone could be wearing gloves."*

If I had been any kind of woman, I would have stood up and given the examiner another reason for how the bat could have been wiped clean.

"So, I'll ask one more time: Just because Mr. Spencer's fingerprints weren't found on the bat doesn't mean he didn't touch it, correct?"

"Objection! The question was asked and answered."

"Sustained."

Our side didn't ask the examiner nor the fingerprint expert any questions and I was glad. I was glad because if either had stayed on the stand any longer, I may have found the courage to do the right thing.

But then my heart stopped again when the prosecutor stood and said, "The state calls Mrs. Janice Johnson."

And that was the first time that I felt my baby kick.

Everyone had to be holding their breath. That was the only way I could explain how suddenly all the air had been sucked from the room.

Janice put her hand on the Bible and swore to do what I would never do. And then she sat on the stand facing everyone.

Now that I could see her face-to-face, she was exactly how I imagined from the television images. She sat taller than anyone else had done on that stand, sitting almost like she was atop a throne.

"Mrs. Johnson, will you tell us your relationship to Marquis?"

"I am his mother," she said with an authority that I admired. "He is my son."

I noticed how she spoke of him in the present tense, even though he would never be present with her again.

The prosecutor said, "Can you tell us about your son's plans for school?"

"Well, he attended Winchester Academy. He was a high school senior and on his way to college."

"What else can you tell us about your son?"

She smiled, a mother's smile that had enough wattage to light up the city. "He was a good kid. He loved to read, loved to write poetry, he played two instruments, the piano and saxophone, and he loved to play golf."

"How were his grades?"

"He had all A's, even in his advanced classes. He was a good student, very smart."

"So, would you call your son a thug in any way?"

"No!" she said, and the smile that she'd worn was completely gone now. "I don't even know how to define a thug, but my son was a good kid. Yes, he was a teenager, and he smoked weed with his friends. We told him not to, but—"

"He was a teenager," the prosecutor finished for her, and she nodded.

I wasn't surprised that Newt and his team didn't object. In the car this morning, they had said that whenever Janice Johnson took the stand, they were going to have to play her right. They were not going to object to anything while she was being questioned by the prosecution. But on cross-examination, Wyatt had given his permission for them to go after her.

I had prayed then, and I folded my hands and started praying now.

The prosecutor continued questioning Janice, about how she had found out about Marquis being shot, about what it was like to bury her son, and what life was like now.

"There are mornings when I wake up, and once I realize that yes, my son is dead, I don't want to keep breathing. On the day that we buried him, I truly just wanted to climb into the casket with him," she said. "It is only because of God and my husband . . ." She paused and took such a long moment to look at her husband that I turned to look at him, too.

He sat stoic, like his wife, no smile on his face.

She said, "I can go on because of my husband. But it hurts every day to know that I am no longer a mother. That hole in my heart will never be filled."

The prosecutor did not say another word. He just returned to his seat, taking slow steps. He didn't even say, *No further questions.* He just allowed Mrs. Johnson to sit in that witness stand so that all of us could see the image of a grieving mother who was filled with a pain that most of us would be blessed to never experience.

Newt's associate stood up, buttoned his jacket, and said, "Mrs. Johnson, we are so sorry for your loss."

Without a beat, she said, "Thank you," which was a much kinder response than I would have given to my enemy's attorneys.

Our attorney said, "Were you always aware of what your son was doing? Always aware of where he was?"

She shrugged. "As much as I could be with a seventeen-year-old. I mean, I knew when he was at school, I knew when he was out with friends, and I knew where he was generally."

"Did you know where he was the night he was shot?"

"Yes, he was at the library and then with his girlfriend."

"You were sure of that?"

"Yes," she said, frowning, looking confused.

"But isn't it true that when the police came to your home, you thought your son was there? You didn't even know that he wasn't in the house?"

She glanced again at her husband. "Yes, but . . . I mean. No. I thought he had come home."

"But when the police got there, that was when you first found out that he wasn't there, correct?"

"Yes."

"So, often, you had no idea where your son was, or what he was doing?"

"Objection!" the prosecutor said.

"Sustained. Move on, Counselor," the judge told our side.

Our attorney said, "Mrs. Johnson, can you tell us who Caleb Brown is?"

"Objection!" The prosecutor shouted so loud this time it felt as if the walls had rattled. "Mr. Brown is not relevant to this trial."

Our side said, "This goes to the credibility of the witness. She's telling us about her son's credibility, so it's only fair that we be allowed to question hers."

The judge paused, thought, said, "I'll allow it. The witness will answer the question."

Janice lowered her head, and when she raised it up, there were tears in her eyes. Looking straight at her husband, she said, "He's . . . he was . . . my pastor."

Before she completed the last word, her husband stood and stepped over a woman before he left the room. And right after him, another man stood up—one of the men that I'd seen on TV with the Johnsons.

Her eyes were on her husband as a tear rolled down Janice's face, and I cried with her.

Our side said, "And besides him being your pastor, did you have any other kind of relationship with him?"

She nodded.

The judge said, "Mrs. Johnson, please answer the question."

She took a deep breath and said, "I had an affair. I had an affair with my pastor."

When she sobbed, I sobbed. And I did what Janice Johnson couldn't do at the moment.

I got up and walked out of the courtroom.

Chapter 32

Janice

I had another day to add to the list of the horrible days of my life. It was humiliating to sit in front of all of those people and have to confess the worst thing I'd ever done.

The only good thing was that Tyrone *had* walked out. I hadn't known that he was going to do that, but when the questions started coming, I was grateful. Because I didn't want him to hear anything about how long the affair had lasted, even though he already knew. And I certainly wouldn't have wanted him to hear my response when the attorney asked if I'd spoken to Caleb recently.

When I said, "No, I haven't spoken to Caleb," and when I didn't even mention seeing him at Marquis's funeral, my husband would have looked straight into my eyes and known that I was lying.

I didn't care if the attorneys knew or if the judge knew—they could have thrown me into jail for contempt or for perjury; it didn't matter. When I told that lie, I didn't even care that God knew—I would pray for forgiveness later.

But that was the only lie that I told. Once Tyrone left the court-room, I went toe-to-toe with the man who was defending the killer of my son. And while he probably won the battle, I made sure that everyone could see that he'd been in a fight.

By the time the judge told me to step down from the witness stand, the defense attorney was as worn-out as I was, leaning back in his chair looking like it would be hours before he would be able to get up again.

I marched past the defense table, the prosecution table, through the gallery of spectators, and out into the hall. I had done what I had to do for our son. Now I had to do what I had to do for my marriage.

Delores met me right on the other side of the courtroom doors and pulled me into a hug. "I'm so sorry about that, baby."

At least my mother-in-law had forgiven me. Maybe she could convince her son to do the same. "Where's Tyrone?"

She shrugged. "I don't know. Raj called and told me that he's with him, though."

I released a long breath. "Good."

"Raj said that the car will be waiting where you normally meet."

I hugged Delores good-bye since she'd come to court with *her* pastor, and I dashed down the stairs, hoping, praying that Tyrone would be in the car.

He wasn't. So I rode that long distance alone. Just me and the driver and enough silence for torturous thoughts to sprout like weeds in my head. Thoughts that made tears fall from my eyes, though I kept my cries as silent as I could. I cried and I prayed.

"Here we are, Ms. Johnson," the driver said, getting me home in an hour, much quicker than I expected for a Friday.

I thanked him, then jumped out as fast as I could because I had hope—our car was in the driveway.

I busted through our front door, but the moment I stepped inside, I knew Tyrone wasn't home. It was just the feeling in the house. We had found a way to warm up our home just a little since Marquis passed away. Today, though, that cold, empty sadness that had weighed us down from the day we heard the news was back.

I ignored the cold, I ignored the sadness and ran from room to room, calling Tyrone's name and checking every crevice and corner as if my husband would hide from me.

He *was* hiding, just not at home.

Once my search ended, I dialed Tyrone's cell, and even when it went straight to voice mail, I hung up and dialed once more, just to hear his voice again.

His phone was off, and he was nowhere to be found. He didn't want to talk to me, didn't want to see me.

I just prayed that he still wanted me to be his wife.

I parked myself in the living room so that Tyrone would see me as soon as he returned. Stretching out on the sofa, I didn't even take off my shoes, not caring at all about the stains that my soles might leave. I lay down because there was nothing else to do. Nothing except to wait.

So that's what I did. I cried, I prayed, and I thought about Tyrone. I cried, I prayed, and I thought about Tyrone. I cried and prayed and thought about Tyrone . . .

And then I opened my eyes. It took a moment to remember who I was, where I was—and then it came back and I remembered it all. It took another moment as I wondered if I had opened my eyes on the same day that I'd fallen asleep. But the brightness of the sun breaking through the living room's bay window told me that Friday had turned into Saturday morning.

And I didn't even have to get up to realize that my husband had not come home last night.

This was not the first time that Tyrone hadn't come home without a call, without a text, without me knowing where he was. That last time, three years ago, had led to bad things happening.

I prayed that this wasn't the worst part of my history returning for a repeat visit.

I tried my best to hold on to hope.

It was just a little before nine when I went into the shower, hoping that by the time I came out, Tyrone would be home.

It was 9:13 when I stepped from the shower into my bedroom, and still he wasn't home. I tried his cell; it went straight to voice mail.

It was 9:27 when I started getting dressed, and I hoped when I finished, Tyrone would be downstairs in the family room watching TV like my testimony never happened.

It was exactly 9:45 when I walked down the stairs and into the family room. It was empty, just like every other room in the house. Another call to his cell, and just because I wanted to hear his voice, I listened to his entire voice-mail message. Twice.

So, I sipped one cup of coffee after another, and prayed that Tyrone would come home before I got some kind of caffeine poisoning.

By 11:02, I could feel the coffee floating in my belly, and my hope was fading. I wandered back to the front of the house and sat on the bottom step.

So many times I'd heard of a family breaking up after the death of a child. But that wasn't supposed to happen to me and Tyrone. We'd been through the fire already. And since the fire hadn't killed us, weren't we supposed to be stronger?

It seemed ridiculous . . . that I was paying for a three-year-old sin. I'd repented, I'd begged God and Tyrone for forgiveness. And I'd been grateful when I received it.

I guess when it came to humans, the ransom for sins was never fully paid.

The cold, empty, sad silence of our home hummed in my ears as I stared at the door, willing it to open and for Tyrone to enter. The minutes passed, the humming got louder, and the door never opened.

It was when the silence started to scream that I jumped up, grabbed my purse from where I'd dropped it last night, and ran out the door. I revved up the engine to our car and the tires screeched as I sped out of our driveway to a destination unknown. All I knew was that I had to find my husband.

So, I made a list in my head. First stop—Raj's. It didn't take me ten minutes to pull up to my brother-in-law's row house. Before I turned off the ignition, I already knew he wasn't home, and Tyrone probably wasn't there either. Both Raj's truck and motorcycle were missing from where he usually parked them.

Still, I knocked on his door. And after I knocked for a solid five minutes, I got back in the car.

Before I pulled away, I called Delores, thinking that I might save myself a trip.

"No, baby, he's not here and he hasn't called me," she said after we got all the greetings and how-are-yous out of the way. "But I don't expect him to call me 'cause he knows I'm gonna tell him to take his butt home."

"Thank you. Thank you for forgiving me."

"Baby, our sins are forgiven before we even commit them. Forgiven and forgotten as far as the east is from the west. And

Tyrone's gonna remember that. Just give him a minute, and he'll remember that he ain't no saint either."

I told her good-bye, and then drove to Tyrone's auto shop. There was no way I was going to go inside looking for Tyrone. No way I was going to let people know our business like that. Enough of our life was already on display.

But even from where I sat, I could see a good many of the guys in the shop. And there was no sign of Tyrone. I eased the car around to the back, just in case he'd parked Raj's truck or motorcycle (I didn't know which he'd taken) back there.

No sign of my husband.

If Tyrone wasn't at Raj's, Delores's, or his shop, I had no idea where to go next. Tyrone had never been a hanging-out-with-the-fellas kind of guy; he always said that with his wife as his best friend, who else did he need?

With nowhere else to look, I just drove through the streets. Making lefts and making rights. I wandered through just about every street in West Philly, then made my way up to Germantown before I hooked back around through North Philly, Center City, and then home to my neighborhood again. I just drove, stopping nowhere, seeing nothing.

I was about two hours into my drive when I started to cry. And pray. As time passed, my tears thickened, really blurring my vision. At a red light, I rested my head on the steering wheel, needing just a moment. A moment to control my tears, a moment to figure this all out.

When the car behind me honked, I jumped, looked up, and right there on the corner was Sweet Carolina's! Tyrone's favorite restaurant.

That had to be a sign, and I made a quick, sharp turn, lined up my car into a parking space, wiped my eyes, then ran inside. I had such a good feeling because there were no coincidences in life.

"May I help you?" the hostess asked.

"Uh . . . I'm looking . . . for a friend. I was supposed to meet him here."

She looked behind her. "There are only a few people here; you can look around." She moved to help a couple who'd walked in behind me and I rushed through the informal restaurant that raved about having the best soul food north of the Carolinas.

I checked every table, every booth, not caring about the question I saw in everybody's eyes as they stared back at me.

When I didn't see Tyrone, I checked every table, every booth again. Just in case he'd been hiding during my first go-round and I could catch him as I doubled back.

But there was no sign of my husband. And that meant riding past Sweet Carolina's hadn't been a sign at all.

As I walked back toward the door, I was filled with a dread that made my heart sink to my feet. Maybe this time, it had been too much for Tyrone. Maybe between Marquis's death and the resurrection of my infidelity, it was all too much and Tyrone couldn't take it anymore. Maybe this time, he wasn't coming back.

I tried to hold my feelings in until I got to my car. Really, I did. But I didn't. And I cried. I mean, I really cried as I stumbled through the restaurant's doors, bumping into someone on my way out as they came in.

"Janice?"

I could hardly see him. But I knew his voice.

"Janice . . ." Caleb called my name again. "What's wrong?"

My tears not only blinded me, they choked me. And I couldn't get a word out.

Caleb took my hand and led me away—just like he did three

years ago. And I followed him because, like before, I didn't know what else to do.

He led me to a car—a Lexus, the same car he'd had when we were lovers.

I slid into the passenger seat, and I cried. He slid in on the other side, and I cried. I cried and Caleb just sat there, as if crying was just something I had to do and he was patient enough to wait until I finished.

There came the time when I finally stopped. And found my voice. And said, "I'm sorry."

"For what?'

"For . . . this. For this . . . again."

I looked up at him and could tell that he remembered, too. That day, three years ago, when he'd found me in the church's parking lot, a crying mess, just like this.

Tyrone had been so angry when Raj called him from the police station, telling him he'd been arrested and needed an attorney and bail.

"I can't believe you did that, Janice!" Tyrone screamed. "I can't believe you turned my brother in."

"What was I supposed to do?" I shouted back. "Just let him keep beating on Syreeta? Your brother has a problem, and now maybe it will stop."

"You should've let them handle it."

"Well, Syreeta didn't want to handle it." Then I thought of another approach, another way to get him to see what I was trying to say. "If someone were beating on Marquis, you would want it reported."

"Marquis is a boy, Syreeta is a woman. You should've let grown folks handle their own business."

Tyrone stomped out of our house pissed, but I was as angry as he was. I didn't care. I wasn't going to stand by and let my friend be beaten no matter who was doing the beating.

Tyrone didn't come home that night and I was really pissed. But when he didn't come home the next night, I was frantic. By the third night, I was truly scared.

Had Tyrone really left me? He was willing to break up over his brother?

I called his cell, every hour on the hour, and every fifteen minutes in between. But he never answered. And though Delores did answer her phone, she didn't say too many words to me, and the ones she did utter gave me no information about where I could find my husband.

I did my best to hide my distress from Marquis, telling our fourteen-year-old that his dad had an emergency business trip, though I wasn't sure he believed that since Tyrone, an auto mechanic, had never gone out of town on business before.

But that's all I had to give him, and now I needed someone to give something to me, someone to give me hope. It couldn't be Syreeta; she was part of the problem and felt bad enough about what was happening with me and Tyrone.

So my pastor was my only choice, but the best choice because he would do more than talk to me . . . he would pray, too.

On the fourth day, once Marquis had left for school, I ditched work and went off to church, crying all the way, and asking God not to let my marriage end just because I was trying to do the right thing.

By the time I got to the church, my tears had blinded me, weakened me. I couldn't even get out of the car.

Then a tap on my window made me look up.

"Janice?"

"Pastor . . ." That was all I could get out.

He opened the door, took my hand, and led me away. Not into the church, but into the parsonage next door, where he lived.

His voice brought me back from my memories. "You don't have anything to apologize for," Caleb said. "No one ever has to apologize for being hurt, for being upset."

I looked at him for a quick moment, then turned away. "You know what's going on?"

He nodded. "I think so . . . the trial? And you? And me? Last night, every station recapped everything about yesterday. And you. And me."

"Oh." I prayed that wherever Tyrone was, he hadn't seen any of those reports.

"And then," Caleb continued, "my phone started ringing. Members of the church started calling."

"Oh," I said again. I hadn't thought about that. I hadn't thought about what this news that was destroying me and Tyrone was doing to Caleb. Again I said, "I'm sorry."

He shrugged. "It's been going on all summer. Since all of this first broke back in June. It's been tough, but it looks like the congregation is willing to stand by me."

"I'm sorry."

He chuckled just a little bit. "You can't think of anything else to say, can you?"

I shook my head.

He said, "I really should be the one apologizing to you. If I hadn't let it get out of hand . . ."

"You were grieving, too," I reminded him. "We were both at fault, and then neither of us was at fault. It was just the time, and circumstances, and—"

"Two people who needed to be comforted," he finished for me.

I nodded, thinking about his words. Thinking about how I had really needed to be comforted then.

Caleb said, "So is that why you're upset? About what happened at the trial?"

"I can handle what happened in court. But Tyrone can't. He's gone . . . again. Just like last time."

"Wow," Caleb said, making the word sound like it had five syllables. "I thought you guys had worked it out. I thought that's why you didn't come to church anymore." He held up his hand. "Which I understand."

"I thought we had worked it out, too. But I guess we really hadn't, because at the first sign of trouble—" I stopped because I could feel the tears and I tried my best to send them back to wherever they were coming from. I just didn't want to cry anymore.

He reached for my hand. "I want to pray with you."

I looked down to where he touched me. And once again I thought about his words.

Two people who needed to be comforted.

Again I thought about all the comfort that I'd really needed then. And I thought about all the comfort that I could really use now.

As gently as I could, I slipped my hand from his. There was only one man who could give me what I needed.

I looked up at Caleb so that I could explain to him what I knew now that I didn't know then. But the tap on the window made me turn the other way.

"Janice!"

"Oh, my God!" I screamed as if I'd seen a ghost. And in a way, that's exactly what I was seeing.

The car door opened. "Get out."

For a second, I stayed right where I sat. Because I was hoping and praying that this wasn't real. How could it be? Lightning didn't strike twice in the same place.

"Get out of the car, Jan," Raj repeated.

It was only because I was so scared that I did what my brother-in-law told me.

Caleb leaned over from his seat. "Raj, it's not what you think. We were just—"

Raj slammed the door on the rest of Caleb's words. Then, with a gentle hold on my arm, he led me to his truck, parked right next to the Lexus.

There were a gaggle of thoughts going through my mind. And at first, I wasn't able to capture a single one. But then, when I stood on the passenger side of Raj's truck, one thought became clear— Tyrone was inside!

I trembled as Raj opened the door, almost wanting to close my eyes. There was no way I would be able to stand if I had to see the hurt on my husband's face.

But then Raj said, "Get in," and I breathed. Because that meant we were alone.

Then Raj got in on the other side. He gave me one glance and those dang tears rushed back. Yeah, I was tired of crying, but crying was all I could do. Because if I hadn't been sure that my marriage was over before, it was over now.

Tyrone would never understand. Especially not after he heard this story from Raj, which is exactly the way this had all gone down before.

What happened with Caleb had only happened three times.

Just three times.

The first time, Caleb had taken me into the parsonage instead of the church, so that no one else would see my tears. So that my pain could stay private.

He had been so shocked to find me and so caring when I told him how I was losing my husband.

And then Caleb reminded me that he completely understood that pain because he'd just lost his wife.

It wasn't like I'd really forgotten that his wife had died six months before, from cancer that was already stage four by the time Caleb had discovered the lump on his twenty-nine-year-old wife's breast. It was more like I had just been focused on myself until he made me remember.

And for a while, we just sat there and cried together, and held each other, and ended up in bed.

It had really been that quick, that simple, though I knew that if anyone heard about it they would've said that either Caleb or I had preconceived motives.

But only a person who had walked in a pair of sorrow's shoes would ever understand how it could go down like that. I was sure that even God would have understood—if it had been just that once.

But there was no way to explain why I'd gone back two days later when Tyrone still had not come home. Nor to justify the third time, when two days after that, Caleb called and said that he needed me. And Tyrone still had not come home . . .

It was after that third time, when Raj just happened to be driving by the Walmart on Christopher Columbus Boulevard, where I parked my car because Caleb and I were being so careful in our duplicity . . .

Though I never believed it was one of those just-happen-to-be moments. Those things just didn't happen. And from that moment three years ago until now, I would have bet all kinds of money that Raj had somehow followed me.

But not today. Raj wouldn't have followed me today. So how did I end up here?

Like Caleb had done a few minutes before, Raj just sat in his truck, with the engine running, and waited for my tears to pass.

He just didn't know that I never planned to stop crying.

It was only physiology that made my tears finally end. A human couldn't cry forever, I suppose.

"So, you just happened to be passing by again?" I sniffed, accusing him with my tone more than my words.

He shook his head. "You didn't know that the Guardians have been following you since the trial began?"

I twisted in my seat. "What?" I wouldn't have to worry about tears now. I was too pissed to cry. "Following me?" I knew it! Just like before. "Why? Why would you have someone following me?"

"Not just you; Ty, too. I thought Tyrone told you. Threats had come in."

"What?" I said, blinking, trying to figure out what he was talking about.

"Threats to you and Tyrone."

"Why would anyone threaten me and Tyrone? We're the ones who lost our son."

"We live in America. This is how Americans handle people they don't know and they don't like."

"Wow."

"I'm sure they've had a lot of threats on their side, too." Before I could say anything, he added, "Not from our people, but from all over."

I shook my head.

He said, "So we had you covered. For protection. Not that we think anything's gonna happen. No one wants to go up against us. The Guardians are better than the Secret Service."

I blew out a long breath knowing there wasn't any way that I could be mad at this. Still, I said, "Someone should have told me."

"I thought you knew." He looked over at Caleb's car. "I guess you didn't."

"Raj," I said, and then I paused. What was the use? Like last time, he was going to run to his brother. Tell Tyrone. And then what I'd been trying to save would be over.

But in the next second I decided that my marriage was worth fighting for, no matter what I had to say.

"I know you won't believe me."

He waited a couple of moments. "Try me."

So I did. "Nothing was going on with me and Caleb. I'd been driving around all morning, looking for Tyrone, and I came here and he just happened to be walking in as I was walking out and . . ." I had to pause. "He took me to his car and we were talking. That's it. Just talking."

Raj nodded, but when he didn't say a word, I knew it was time to beg.

"Please, don't say anything to Tyrone. He's so upset already, and if he finds out . . ."

Raj shifted his truck into park. He said, "One of the Guardians will come back for your car. I'm taking you home."

What I wanted to do was jump out of this car and stomp back to my own. But I didn't because I was tired, just so tired. So my silence was my agreement.

We'd driven for only a few minutes, when Raj said, "You and

Tyrone both need to stop running. You both run; at the first sign of trouble, you run."

"I wasn't running," I said. "I told you, Caleb and I were there together, by accident."

"I believe that. But what would've happened if I hadn't knocked on that window? Would you have turned to him like last time?"

"No!"

"That's good." And then he spoke words that sounded like more than just music; they were a whole symphony. "I believe you; I'm not going to say anything to Tyrone."

Gratitude made me want to cry again, but pride kept my tears inside. "Thank you," I said.

I felt like I needed to give him something for what he was giving to me. Maybe I needed to tell him that I was sorry for turning him in to the police and for the months that he'd spent in jail.

But the thing was, I wasn't sorry about that. So I had to think of something else. Maybe I could tell him that I was sorry for the way I'd been treating him. I mean, I was a little bit sorry about it, especially with the way he was coming through for me now.

"Raj."

Before I could say more, he held up his hand. "You don't need to say anything, Jan." He spoke as if he'd read my thoughts. "Let's just start over from here 'cause like I've been trying to tell you, I've changed, you changed, and everyone deserves a second chance."

I nodded, feeling even more gratitude now.

When he stopped his truck in front of my house, I gave him the key to my car. Then I did something that I hadn't done with Raj in years.

I gave him a hug.

Chapter 33

Janice

I had a dozen messages on my cell phone, but none of them were from Tyrone. All were from Syreeta, and I knew she was probably a mess by now, wondering what was going on.

It was just that I didn't want to talk to anyone, except Tyrone. And I figured Syreeta would call Raj eventually, and he would fill her in.

I just wanted to keep all of my attention on Tyrone. And that's why I was on my knees at the side of my bed, praying, when I heard the first sound.

A car door slamming. Then, a few seconds later, the key in the door.

I leaped up and dashed to the stairs. I was halfway down when the door opened and Tyrone walked in.

He looked up; I looked down. I was afraid to say a word and he said nothing either. All he did was open his arms and I ran down the rest of the steps.

"I'm sorry!" we said together.

He took my hand and led me into the living room. When we sat down, I still held his hand, deciding right then that I would never let him go.

"I spoke to Raj," he said.

At first, I blinked and my heart called Raj a traitor. After what he promised! But then I blinked again. If Raj had told Tyrone where he found me, my husband wouldn't be sitting here.

"My brother and I had a long talk. He told me to stop running," Tyrone said. "My little brother told me to man up and handle the situation." He chuckled. "My little brother ain't so little anymore if he's telling me what to do."

"I know. He kinda talked to me a little bit today, too," I said, hoping Tyrone wouldn't ask for specifics.

"He told me." Tyrone looked at me sideways. "He said if the two of you could make up, then what was my problem?" He paused. "Look, Jan, this has been a lot for me to handle."

"I know and—"

He squeezed my hand. "Let me finish. It's just . . . it's just that it's so hard to imagine you with another man, with . . . him, when I love you so much."

"I know and I will never be able to say that I'm sorry enough."

"That's not true. You've already said you're sorry enough. And, I think, I know, that I'm ready to accept that. Finally. Because the bottom line is I love you."

"And I love you, too. It wasn't about love with Caleb. You have to believe me."

"I know that. Still . . . it's a man thing."

I nodded.

"But you know what? It's a man thing to save his family, too. It's a man thing to live up to the for-better-or-for-worse. If I'm strong enough for the better, I'd better be man enough for the worse."

"I'm—"

He pressed his fingertips to my lips before I could apologize again. "Love means never having to say that you're sorry."

For a moment, I stared at him. "You know that's the corniest line ever!"

"I know, it just kinda came out."

And then he repeated it. And I smiled, and the smile turned into a giggle. And he chuckled, too. And his chuckles made me laugh. And he laughed, too.

And we laughed. And laughed. And laughed.

We laughed until Tyrone rolled off the sofa and pulled me down with him. I tumbled and fell on top of him, still laughing as if I would never stop. But then I looked down into his eyes. And I stopped. And he stopped, too.

The way we gazed at each other, it was probably as corny as his line. But it was real to me. Because this was the man that I loved. Really loved. And the only man that I had loved. Ever loved.

And right then, I made a silent vow, to do all that I could to make up for the hurt that I'd caused.

I had a feeling that Tyrone made a vow like that, too, because he cupped my head in his hand and pulled me close.

And when his lips touched mine, I felt like I was being kissed by an angel.

This was love. With all of its ups, and all of its downs, this was what love was meant to be.

Chapter 34

Meredith

I was embarrassed.

Truly, I was embarrassed to be married to Wyatt Spencer. It had been bad enough watching what he allowed, what he encouraged the attorneys to do to Janice Johnson on the witness stand.

But the embarrassing part came in the way that Wyatt and the attorneys had celebrated what they called a victory over the questioning of Janice.

"She has no credibility anymore," Newt had said on the drive home. "If a woman would cheat on her husband, she would do anything, including lie for her son. And the female jurors know that."

I hoped that they didn't; I hoped that the women on the jury were smarter than that. I prayed that they knew that we all made mistakes and what Janice Johnson did in her personal life had nothing to do with the trial.

But as bad as it had been on Friday, I dreaded what today would bring. I'd found it all out last night when Newt had come by for yet another strategy meeting. This time, even my mother had sat in with us.

"So how long do you think it will take to present our case?" Wyatt asked as we all once again sat in his office.

"Really, I'm thinking we'll just need tomorrow."

"And then it'll be over, and all of this nonsense will go away?" my mother asked.

Newt chuckled. "We hope so. We've decided that we only need three witnesses. Two who will negate that perfect picture that his mother and his teachers tried to portray. The first is a kid who had a fight with Marquis. He said Marquis pulled out a knife on him."

Wyatt let out a long whistle, my mother gasped, but all I did was frown. Because if there was one thing that I'd learned, it was that with Newt, what started as a fact ended in a lie.

"A knife," Wyatt said. "That's good."

"Yeah." Newt nodded. "It was really a box cutter, but the kid is gonna call it a knife."

That revelation didn't bother my husband or my mother. Because she laughed and Wyatt just said, "Okay, good. And who's next?"

"The next one is a great one. A girl. A white girl. From their school."

Wyatt's frown was as deep as mine. "How's that gonna help? We already know that he liked white girls. That didn't seem to bother anyone."

"Well, this girl is gonna say that she was afraid of Marquis."

When he stopped, Wyatt said what I was thinking in my head. "And?"

"She was afraid," Newt said, putting extra emphasis on the last word. "Afraid, like she thought he was gonna rape her."

Even Wyatt's eyes got big with that one.

"He raped somebody?" my mother asked.

"No, but she's going to say that she was afraid that it might have come to that one time when they were at a party. And that's all that has to happen. We don't need an actual rape; we just need to put it in the jurors' mind—a strong black boy, a frightened white girl, and rape.

That's the white woman's greatest fear, and let's be honest . . . white men think black men eat white virgins for lunch."

My mother laughed again. While these men were talking about destroying a young man's reputation with innuendos, my mother was behaving like she was at a comedy show.

Newt said, "We'll have all of those white jurors shaking. You'll never be convicted."

Wyatt nodded slowly, and when he said nothing, I knew he approved.

I wanted to throw up.

"You said three," Wyatt reminded Newt. "Who's the third?"

That's when Newt turned to look at me. Then Wyatt and my mother did, too.

I shook my head. "No."

And I watched my mother take a deep breath. There was nothing funny to her about this.

Newt said, "We're thinking that after the girl testifies, we need you to get on the stand, Meredith, and say what a wonderful man, what a wonderful husband, Wyatt is."

"No," I said, speaking in a voice that I never had used before with Wyatt. Even though I wasn't talking directly to him, my response was for him.

Wyatt frowned at me, but didn't say a word.

Newt continued as if I hadn't spoken. "Plus, it will give the jurors a chance to see you a little bit closer. Everyone knows that you're pregnant, but I want them to see you pregnant."

Newt may not have been paying attention, but for once, Wyatt was. He hadn't taken his eyes off of me and I hadn't turned my eyes away from him.

There was no doubt about it; I was still afraid of my husband. But after what they'd done and what they planned to do tomorrow, this was the only way that I could fight back. I may not have had the guts to stand up and tell the truth, but I could stop them from using me.

So I said, "No," again.

And there must have been something in my voice. Or maybe it was in the way I sat. With my shoulders high and my chin up. And my eyes clear.

I sat, I spoke, the way Janice Johnson did.

It must have been all of that because with his eyes still on me, Wyatt said, "No. I don't want Meredith to testify." He said it as if it were his idea. Turning to Newt, he added, "This has been a lot on Meredith. And I'm concerned about her."

I didn't believe that.

"I'm concerned about the baby," he added.

I did believe that.

"Let's just go with the two witnesses," Wyatt said as if that would be the final word. "From what you said, that will be enough."

Newt had agreed, and now we were on our way to court; the routine was the same. We pulled up to the courthouse, Wyatt played the overly attentive husband, holding me, guiding me with every step, and we rushed past the people who flanked the narrow pathway—those on the right were holding signs and cheering for us. And on the left were the Marquis supporters with their signs and with their chant, "Enough! Enough! Enough!"

And we made our way into the courtroom.

I was already sitting when Janice and her husband and the other people there to support them entered. And once again, she and I made eye contact, but only because of me, and only for a moment. Because like always, she never gave me the privilege of more than a couple of seconds.

Not even ten minutes later, we were on our feet after the bailiff commanded, "All rise."

As the judge came in and sat behind the bench, I was already a couple of degrees past queasy. My stomach was rumbling and tumbling and the first witness hadn't even been called.

I prayed to God that I would somehow be able to handle it without spilling my emotions all over this courtroom.

The first witness had been bad enough. The boy was only seventeen, and though I knew that Newt didn't believe in witness tampering, I would have sworn that kid had been paid. It was the way that he spewed off his story, sounding just like a mini-Newt. I knew they prepared the witnesses, but his testimony sounded like more than preparation, it sounded like a performance.

But then the girl got on the stand. And she was crying before anyone said a word to her.

My stomach rumbled.

"State your name."

"Winona Rumsfeld." She sniffed.

My stomach grumbled.

"Ms. Rumsfeld, did you know Marquis Johnson?"

She nodded and a tear fell from her eye.

My stomach tumbled.

"He was my classmate and he . . . he . . ."

I jumped up and rushed from the courtroom. I already knew where the bathroom was—just a few steps to the right. I tore in there knowing that I just had seconds as I pushed my way past the women, noticing none, focusing only on finding the first empty stall.

I didn't even have time to close the door, just time to assume the position—seat up, head down. And I gagged, and gagged and gagged.

While I was still on my knees, a woman behind me asked, "Are you all right?"

I nodded, though I wasn't sure she could see me with the way my head was halfway down the toilet bowl. It took a few more moments, but I was finally able to gather strength. And when I had enough energy, I mumbled, "I'm fine, I'm pregnant." Pushing myself up, I steadied myself before I turned around.

And faced her—Janice Johnson.

She gave me a long moment's stare, then turned away. I wanted to yell for her to come back because there was something I wanted to say.

But I got another chance when she didn't walk out of the restroom. Instead, she pulled a few paper towels from the dispenser, dampened them, then returned and handed them to me.

"Here," she said, giving me half of what she held in her hand. "Wipe your mouth."

I did as she told me, patting my face with the damp paper. But I kept my eyes on her. Before, I'd admired the way she carried herself, but now I loved her voice. It was the way she spoke. Even in the middle of this, she was so calm, so caring. A nurturing voice.

A mother's voice.

I had to say something. Tell her everything that I'd been thinking about her. Maybe even tell her the truth, the whole truth.

"I'm so . . . I've been praying for you" was what came out. "Every day."

Her eyes narrowed, and I felt like I was under a microscope until she took one of the towels and pressed it against my forehead.

It was just three taps, gentle taps, kind taps, and then she handed the paper towels to me.

Without saying a single word, she turned away, and this time, she did move toward the door.

She had never responded to the revelation of my prayers, but I hoped that she would accept my next words.

I took a few steps forward. "I'm so sorry," I said right as she put her hand on the doorknob.

She paused—a beat—turned—another beat—and looked me in my eye. In the seconds that passed, I put myself in her place and thought of all the things that I would've said to the wife of the man who'd taken away my Billy.

She said, "Thank you," before she walked out of the door.

I stood there and let myself smile. Those were the two best words I'd heard in a long, long time.

Chapter 35

Janice

The defense had rested. And the closing arguments had been given. The closings were just like the openings.

"Wyatt Spencer is nothing more than a cold-blooded murderer," the prosecution said. "Don't let this killer claim self-defense. Don't allow him to hide his crime behind Stand Your Ground."

The defense responded, "What would you do if you came face-to-face with a bat-carrying thug in the middle of the night? Wyatt Spencer was defending himself. Wyatt Spencer was standing his ground."

The cold-blooded murderer.

The bat-carrying thug.

Who was the jury going to believe?

After the closings, the judge gave the jury the instructions. He'd spoken for about twenty minutes when he added, "Self-defense means that Mr. Wyatt had a right to stand his ground with no duty to retreat." When the judge said that, he sounded an awful lot like the defense attorneys and I wondered, whose side was the judge on? Was he going to add anything about my son's rights?

When he didn't, when the judge only spoke up for the defense, I stopped listening and my eyes wandered to the other side of the well. To where Meredith sat behind her husband.

She was a beautiful woman, at least in the way that Americans described beautiful. But it was more than the way she looked. It was her eyes. I could see it in her eyes . . . She was kind. But she was also sad.

I wondered where that came from? I guess if my husband was on trial for murder, I'd be sad, too. But what I saw felt like it was . . . deeply embedded. Like it was a sadness she'd been carrying for a long time.

Whatever it was, I wondered how she felt being married to a murderer, though she probably didn't see him that way. She probably saw him as a loving, wonderful husband who showered her with attention and expensive clothes and jewelry.

Oh, and with children. I knew that she had one son and another child on the way.

He'd given her a new life right about the time that he'd taken away mine.

I wondered if she could live with that.

My attention came back to where it was supposed to be when the judge pounded his gavel for a final time, and we all stood until His Honor exited the courtroom.

Then I breathed. I mean, really breathed for the first time in weeks. Maybe even months. Maybe for the first time since May 12.

Tyrone pulled me into his arms and held me, letting me know, without a single word spoken, that we had made it. One hundred and twenty-eight days after our son was murdered, his murderer was now faced with the possibility of spending 128 days times 50, times 60, times 70 and beyond in prison. That was my hope; that was my prayer.

Tyrone shook the prosecutor's hand. "How long do you think it will take?" he asked the man who had fought for our son.

The baby-faced prosecutor shrugged. "I've done this for more than twenty years," he said, though that was hard for me to believe. "It's like reading tea leaves. There's just no way to know."

"But the fact that the jury is sequestered, doesn't that normally mean they'll come back faster?" I asked. Of course, it was the OJ trial that was on my mind. I didn't remember a lot about that since I was only thirteen at the time. But I did remember the uproar with how fast the jury had come back with a verdict.

"That's what many believe," the prosecutor said. "But it's not necessarily true. Again, there is just no way to tell."

"Well, thank you," Tyrone said, giving him another handshake before I reached over and hugged him.

"We'll be in touch. Stand by," he told us before we left the courtroom.

Right outside, Delores and Pastor Davis stood, and after we exchanged more hugs, she said, "Come over to my house. I ordered some food and we can have a little celebration."

"Celebration?" Tyrone said. "Isn't it a little too early for that?" Then he chuckled. "Unless the Man Upstairs has told you something that He hasn't told us."

I took my husband's hand and said, "We'll be there," because I understood exactly what Delores meant.

We did have a reason to celebrate. So many of these cases never even made it to court. But we'd pushed, we'd crossed that hurdle, and we'd put a man and a law on trial. It was already a victory that many parents in our situation didn't get the chance to experience.

So after the driver dropped us home, we changed clothes, then jumped into our car for the ride to Delores's.

I was never quite sure how my mother-in-law did it, but at times like these, she made a few calls and always packed the house.

We'd been out of court for less than two hours, yet there was standing room only in her home by the time Tyrone and I arrived.

But once we arrived, it was like we were the guests of honor and I felt so different today than I had during those days right after Marquis had been murdered.

Today, I was grateful for their hugs, and I thanked them for their support. Today, I ate with them and drank with them and chatted with them about so much more than the trial. Last time, we'd only talked about death. But today, we talked about life.

I had settled in, chatting with women from Delores's church, when Raj showed up along with five other Brown Guardians. I was the first person they saw when they walked through the door.

They looked down at me and nodded. I looked up at them, laid my plate down on the side table, stood, and hugged each of them.

I'm sure it was a bit surprising since I'd never hidden my feelings about the Guardians. The whole time, I remained wary of the group that I still saw as little more than a motorcycle gang.

But how could I hate when they had abided by *my* wishes, and had not caused any kind of trouble for Wyatt Spencer and his family? And how could I hate now that I knew that they had protected me and Tyrone when I didn't even know that I needed protection?

I thanked them for all of that.

Raj spoke as the others stood behind him like soldiers. "We got what you wanted, Janice. We got our day in court for Marquis, so whatever happens from here, we're good."

"Thank you," I said again. "Thank you for understanding how I wanted it done, and thank you for making sure that it was done that way."

Behind Raj, one of the Guardians spoke up. "We control these streets, Mrs. Johnson. You didn't want any trouble, so we made sure of that."

I'd known that they controlled the streets, and before, that disgusted me. But with the way they had handled all of this, maybe there was a place for this kind of group. Maybe our neighborhoods needed them.

We didn't leave Delores's until almost midnight, and when Tyrone and I got home and climbed into bed, we were both asleep before we could even say good night.

It was probably the most restful night that we had shared, but the night ended early because we were both up before dawn, ready for day one of the verdict watch.

We knew that the jury didn't begin deliberations until nine. But I was thinking that we needed to be tuned in early, just in case they'd met in the middle of the night, taken a vote, and at 9:02 this morning, they'd announce that they had a verdict.

But though I stayed pasted to my Twitter account and we had every television in our home turned to a news station, there was nothing about a verdict. Just dozens of talking heads pontificating much about nothing.

The day passed, and even when the clock rolled past six, which was when the deliberations were supposed to end, we kept the televisions on, watching, waiting, hoping that there would be a surprise and this would be over.

But day one ended with Tyrone and me posted up in the family room with me stretched out and my head resting on his lap. And that's where we stayed, that's where we slept all night.

When we woke up on Thursday, I knew there was no way that I could stand a repeat of yesterday.

But when I said to Tyrone, "Let's go out," he wasn't feeling that idea.

"Suppose we miss something?"

"How?" I held up my cell. "We have this new invention. It's a telephone that has no cord and rings anywhere."

He twisted his lips like he thought my joke was only kind of funny.

"Look," I said. "We have our phones, and the news comes fastest across Twitter. We will be in touch. Let's just go out and pretend that we're tourists. And do things that we would never do rather than sitting here and watching every second of the clock go by."

He acquiesced, I guess because the thought of sitting at home was torturous. There was only one problem: I hadn't considered that our images had been everywhere—on television, in the newspaper, on the Internet.

So when we got to Love Park, which was a place I enjoyed going to since it was where I met Delores, it was surprising when people started snapping our photos. And then we were asked for our autographs. Just a couple of minutes after that, three Brown Guardians stepped to us, and escorted us out of the park and brought us home.

We were back in front of the television and the clock in less than an hour from when we left.

We didn't even try to leave the house on day three. We just watched TV and paced. Checked social media and paced. Responded to e-mails and paced.

And it wasn't until I woke up on day four that I realized (with a little bit of horror) that it was Saturday.

"Do they deliberate on Saturdays?" I asked Tyrone. The thought of nothing going on for the next two days already had me shaking.

But Tyrone didn't know. "I think I heard of a couple of cases where the verdicts came back on a Saturday, but I don't know about this one."

Still we spent Saturday the way we'd been spending every day. Just watching. Just waiting. Feeling now like we were the ones being sequestered.

The only thing that was different was when Delores came by.

"Y'all need to go with me to church tomorrow," she said. "Because if you don't find a way to have some peace, neither one of you is going to make it through another day."

So on day five, Tyrone and I rolled out of bed, actually a little excited about having someplace to go. This was our first time attending church in three years—not counting, of course, the day that we said good-bye to Marquis.

And attending the service was the best thing that we could have done. Because love was poured all over us from the moment we walked into that church. Neither Tyrone nor I saw ourselves as heroes—I would have given anything to have Marquis back and have no one ever know our names.

But I was glad that we had stood up because maybe we could prevent just one child from being murdered.

We sat in the fourth row with Delores through the praise and worship and the opening of the services.

Then Pastor Davis stood at the altar and said, "It is an honor to have with us today the parents of Marquis Johnson."

That was all he had to say. The congregation stood on their feet and applauded like we were special. And we stood with them because that's not how we felt at all.

When everyone had settled down again, the pastor continued: "These young people, and yes, they are young compared to me."

He paused through the laughter. "These young people have been through what no parent can ever imagine. And I just want them to come up and share with us." He looked directly at me and Tyrone. "Nothing too long." More laughter. "Just tell us a little bit about your journey and what you've learned."

There was more applause as Tyrone took my hand and led me to the altar. We didn't know the pastor was going to ask us to do this, but Tyrone had spoken at so many places since this all began that I knew he could handle it.

I stood by his side as he said, "My wife and I want to thank you for everything. This has been a hard road, one that so many times I asked myself, why me, Lord? Why did You allow my son to be taken? But then right after that, I had to ask myself, why *not* me?"

"Preach," someone from the congregation shouted, and I wanted to shout the same thing.

Tyrone continued, "God never said that this walk was gonna be easy, but He said He would take the walk with us. That He would never forsake us. And that's what He's done. I'm telling you. When I thought that I wasn't gonna breathe again."

"That's right!"

"When I felt like I wanted to go out and kill somebody myself!"

"Tell it!"

"God was with me. He helped me to focus on His way so that I would do the right thing. Because you know what? I didn't want to always do this the right way. When my son was murdered, I wanted to murder somebody. But if it wasn't for the Lord"—he paused and took my hand—"and my wife . . ." He stopped, shook his head, and people stood to their feet shouting and clapping. "All I can do is say thank you, Lord. And thank you to all of you for taking this walk with us and holding us up."

Everyone clapped again and then he handed the microphone to me.

Nuh-uh! I wanted to say. First of all, I wasn't a public speaker. And if I were, how was I supposed to follow what Tyrone had just said?

But with a nudge, Tyrone encouraged me, and I did owe a thank-you not only to everyone here, but to God as well.

So I took the microphone, cleared my throat, and spoke with a little softer voice, and a little more tentative tone, than Tyrone.

"Like my husband, I want to thank all of you for your support, your prayers, and all of that good food that you brought to our house."

When everyone laughed, I relaxed.

I continued: "It's been a long walk, but like my husband said, we're making it . . . because of God. And Pastor Davis, you asked what we had learned from all of this. I think one of the biggest things I've learned is that sometimes we say things that we really don't mean and we need to be careful with our words.

"Specifically, I'm talking about a woman who came up to me during one of the many rallies we attended. And she said, 'Mrs. Johnson, just know that this was God's will.'

"I didn't say anything to the woman because I knew she meant well, but I wanted to tell her that this wasn't God's will. God's will wasn't for my son to be shot down in the street for no reason. God's will is not for white men to hunt black boys like they're target practice. None of that is God's will and we have to stop blaming our human mess on God. My son is not dead because of God. My son is dead because Wyatt Spencer murdered him!"

"That's right!"

"Now God allowed it to happen for reasons that I don't

understand right now. But I know that wasn't *His will*. Because I know that God cried right along with me and Tyrone and Delores and Raj."

"You betta preach, little girl!"

I busted out laughing at that one, and I was glad to have that little reprieve. Because I needed that moment. I continued with, "So, if there is anything that I would love for us to get out of this, it's that we really need to start praying *for* God's will. Because that's the only way that men like Wyatt Spencer will pay for their crimes, and that's the only way we can get Stand Your Ground repealed. Tyrone and I will fight. And we hope you will fight with us."

The congregation was back on their feet, and when I faced my husband to give him the microphone, there were tears in his eyes. The sanctuary was rocking from all of the applause, and the stomping, and the cheers.

Tyrone held me and kissed me. And it wasn't some little peck on the lips. It was one of those *I love you with all of my heart* kisses. Right there on the altar.

In front of God and His people, it was just me and my husband. United.

If I didn't know anything else, I knew in that moment that no matter the outcome, no matter what happened with this trial, everything was truly going to be all right.

Because where I'd come from and where I was now with Tyrone standing by my side—this was God's will.

Truly, His will.

Chapter 36

Meredith

We'd been called back into court, and after ten days, Newt didn't know what this meant.

"The jury must want more instructions or something serious."

"Could it be a verdict?" Wyatt asked.

"Nah," Newt said. "They would have told us that. They just said that we needed to be back in court."

For the first time since this all began, my husband's friend and lawyer sounded weary. Gone was the arrogance and the surety that I was so used to hearing in his voice.

Maybe it was because ten days had passed already, and when we'd left court on that final day, Newt had been convinced that it was going to be a quick, not-guilty verdict.

But the days had passed. One had turned into two, which turned into a week, and we were coming up on another week. And now we had this mysterious call back to court.

No one in this car was sure of what to expect when the eleven-o'clock court session started.

And I wasn't sure either. Every day my opinion changed. In the beginning, I thought what Newt thought—that in days, my husband would be home, having completely gotten away with murder.

But then as the days went by, I imagined the jury getting this right.

And it was only now that we had been called in that I really considered the possibility of what it could mean. What would happen if Wyatt went to jail for a murder that he *had* committed?

Is that what I wanted? I kept asking myself that question. To me, it would be the fairest thing, it would be justice.

But at the same time, I had to admit that it would be the easiest way for me. Because there was the other side . . . What if Wyatt got off? What if he walked away, completely free? I couldn't imagine what that would do to my husband's mind.

He would turn from just being cocky to believing himself invincible. An invincible Wyatt Spencer would be a dangerous man.

There had always been a crowd when we stopped in front of the courthouse. But today there was an electrical spark flowing from the people. A kind of excitement was the only way to describe it. Like a cliffhanger that people had been waiting to see resolved— waiting to see how the story would end.

Like always, Wyatt helped me from the car before we rushed into the courthouse. By the time we got upstairs, it was just minutes before eleven and it looked like we were the last ones there. The well was already full, every seat taken. And the Johnsons were in their seats on the left side of the room.

Wyatt hugged me in a long and tight kind of way before he took his place next to Newt and the other attorneys.

We rose when the judge came in, and then again for the jury.

I held one hand against my belly and the other in the middle of my chest, trying to will my heart to calm.

"Counselors, please approach," the judge said.

And I wanted to run up there with them when the two attorneys for Wyatt along with the prosecutors stepped up to the judge.

There was a lot of nodding and whispering, though we heard nothing since the judge kept his hand over the microphone.

When the attorneys turned around, I searched their faces for some indication of what was going on. They were stoic, but I was sure I saw something, a little twitch in one of the lawyers.

Oh, my God!

Then the judge said, "Ladies and gentlemen of the jury, we understand that you cannot reach a verdict."

I was sure that every single person in the room gasped.

The foreperson, who I would have bet was the oldest white male, said, "No, Your Honor."

"And I understand that you don't believe that more time will help you reach a unanimous decision?"

"No, Your Honor. We're hopelessly deadlocked."

"Well then, I declare this case is a mistrial. The defendant will remain free on bond until a decision is made by the prosecution. Ladies and gentlemen of the jury, thank you for your service, and you are excused." With a final look out to all of us in the well, the judge said, "Court is adjourned."

The judge's gavel hit the bench and the moment the judge was gone, there were pats on the back and shared congratulations between Newt and his attorneys.

Then Wyatt turned to me. I gave him that smile that he was used to seeing. But as he held me, I trembled.

I knew that with a mistrial, the prosecution would decide whether or not to retry my husband.

But I knew Wyatt. He was already feeling invincible.

When I stepped away from his embrace, I said, "Congratulations." My voice sounded as if it were shaking as much as my body.

"Thank you, sweetheart. We're going out to celebrate." Then he rested his hand on my belly and said, "We're all going out to celebrate."

He turned back to his attorneys and I couldn't help it: I looked to where the Johnsons sat, and were still sitting. Janice was in her husband's arms, they were holding each other up as a woman and her husband's brother stood over them.

They were a couple in love, surrounded by nothing but love.

My eyes were still on her, when she opened her eyes and looked up at me.

Like so many other times, our eyes locked, but this time, Janice didn't look away. This time, I got to study her and I tried to figure out what was in her eyes . . . What was that? Pity?

Still she kept her gaze on me.

In that moment, we weren't friends. But we *were* something.

We were two women. Two mothers. One with a son and one without. We were two people whose lives were forever linked and forever changed.

We were Janice Johnson and Meredith Spencer.

Forever hopelessly connected.

PART FOUR

Wyatt Spencer

THE TRUTH...

OCTOBER 24, 2014

Chapter 37

I kissed my wife, then stepped back just a little. My hands were still on her shoulders, and that's why I could feel it; I could feel her trembling. The way she always trembled, at least for the past few months.

How could this woman be afraid of me? Why didn't my wife realize that she had nothing to fear? I loved her, really loved her.

Especially after the way she'd stood by me.

I pulled her into my arms again, and this time kissed her forehead, hoping that somehow she would feel the energy and understand my love.

"I won't be too late," I said.

All she did was nod.

"I love you."

This time, she gave me two words. "I know."

Stepping outside, I stopped for a moment and looked back at the door. Maybe I needed to finally talk to Meredith. Maybe we needed to sit down and discuss what she saw . . . or what she thought she saw.

Yeah, she saw me with the bat, and yeah, she deduced that I planted it on that thug. But what she didn't know was that I'd only done that to protect her. Because if there hadn't been a bat, I would've been on my way to prison. And who would take care of her, and Billy, and our soon-to-be-born child if I were locked up for no reason?

That boy deserved everything that I gave him and more. The way he jumped out of his Jeep, disrespecting me, raising his voice. Next, he would've raised his fist and attacked me. I was not going to be beaten in front of my own home; I had to get him before he got me.

I was just going to have to figure out a way to make Meredith understand that and believe that. So that she would stop trembling. That's all I wanted—for my wife to stop trembling.

Once I hopped into the SUV at the bottom of my driveway, though, all thoughts of my wife were gone, to be dealt with at a later time.

"What's up, buddy?" I asked Andre, and slapped him on the back.

He gave me a grin that showed all of his teeth before he pulled away from the curb.

I was so grateful that Andre was still with me. He'd hung in there from the beginning. I never asked him if he'd had any idea what he was walking into when Newt hired him, along with the three other guards from that security firm, but whatever he thought, he'd stayed, and now, out of the four that started, only Andre was left.

I kept him because first, he was bigger and broader than the others and I knew he'd be able to handle himself in any kind of altercation. But I also kept him on my team because he was one of the brothers. Keeping him was like having a firewall around me. When black people saw Andre with me, they'd have to ask, How bad could I be if I had a brother working for me?

So I kept him on for the rest of the year and I was paying him well to be my driver and the brawn that I needed to move around the city.

Not that I really needed this kind of protection. The Brown Guardians had kept their word. They said there would be no violence as long as the DA got me into court. Well, they'd won that battle, and I'd won the war. I was still mad that I'd had to spend all of that money for my defense. Nobody had that kind of millions to spare.

But having millions kept me out of jail, and now it kept the peace.

Andre said, "Another honor tonight, huh?" as he maneuvered onto the Interstate.

"Yup!" I said, hoping that I didn't sound too excited.

Even though this had been going on now for the four weeks since the mistrial, I was still as juiced up as when I got that first call. This was the third event where I was being honored, but in between those, I'd been on a couple of TV shows, dozens of radio stations, and I couldn't even count the number of newspaper and blog interviews that I'd done.

And then I'd been offered a new job! My favorite TV news station wanted to hire me as a contributor, focusing on race relations.

"Have you ever heard of this group where we're going tonight?" I asked Andre. "The Defenders?" Before he could answer, I said, "They're a group of retired cops."

"Nah," Andre said, his eyes still on the road. "It's not like I'd be affiliated with a group like that, especially not one out in Shrewsbury."

Yeah, I guess he was right about that. Shrewsbury was nearly two hours away, out in York County. And I bet that while I was out there tonight, Andre's would be the only black face that I'd see.

"Well, having a couple of beers with a bunch of cops sounds great to me."

This was different from the other two honors. The Conservative Mothers of America had hosted a Sunday brunch where they honored me and Meredith for being a couple who stood strong and with grace while under all of this fire. And then Americans United had honored me at a black-tie event last Saturday night with lots of caviar and champagne and kudos for all that I'd done. Both of those were classy, jazzy events.

But this one tonight was something I was really looking forward to. Dressing down and having a few beers with law enforcers was exactly the way I wanted to spend this Friday night.

There were a couple of minutes of silence before Andre asked, "You feeling good about the next trial?"

"I don't think they're gonna retry me," I said right away. "Everybody already got what they wanted out of this. The Johnsons and the Brown Guardians got their day in court, and a jury of my peers said I was innocent. We're all even."

His eyes were on the road, but he still kinda looked at me sideways like. "They didn't say you were innocent. It was a mistrial."

"Same thing. It was eight to four—in my favor. And if this hadn't been turned into a race thing, it would have been unanimous for me. I know how the jury voted—the blacks voted that I was guilty and I understand that 'cause blacks always stick together. And then the two young gals. You know how young people are these days. They're for all kinds of diversity and everything."

"But the DA knows that the next time, she might not even get any blacks on the jury." I paused. "Plus, I'm thinking about finding a way to make a large campaign contribution to her since she'll be running again. She's more of a Democrat, but I'm sure a few dollars from me would not only help her run, but also help her to make the right decision about a new trial."

Andre said, "You better run that by Newt first."

"Trust me, I will. Without Newt, who knows which way this trial would have gone."

Andre nodded. "Newt was hard-core. He tried to tear everybody down and I can't see the Johnsons wanting to go through this again."

"Well, a mistrial works for everyone. The Johnsons can claim a win because I didn't get off completely, and I won because I'm not sitting in some prison somewhere in western Pennsylvania. But it really needs to end here because as long as there's one white person on my jury, I will never be found guilty."

Andre waited a couple of seconds before he said, "That's a sad commentary on America, don't you think?"

Now I was the one who gave him a sideways look. Was Andre getting radical on me?

But then he chuckled and I realized he was just kidding.

We steered the conversation away from the trial, and for the rest of the drive, we chatted about everything else: my foundation, my business, and how I was really looking forward to becoming a father for the second time.

"I never thought I'd be fathering children at this age, but I got a young one for a wife, so it works."

Andre laughed. "I see the way you are with Billy. Age ain't nothing but a number."

"You're right about that."

It took just about two hours until we exited I-83 and were in Shrewsbury. I never ventured this way much, never ventured too far out of the Philadelphia area since my business was primarily for city folks. But as we drove down North Main Street, I wondered how a Cheesesteak Castle would do out here. I might have to alter the menu just a bit, include something that might appeal more to the folks who called this place home. Like instead of cheesesteaks, I could have chicken-fried steaks. Yeah, a Chicken-Fried Steak Castle!

That made me chuckle just as Andre turned the SUV off the road. The tires crunched over the gravel of the packed parking lot and I wondered if all these people were here for me. Every space was taken with F-150s, Silverados, and Denalis.

I grinned. Oh, yeah, these were my kind of people. There would be no black ties in here tonight.

At the front of Big Red's, Andre stopped. "You go in; I'll find a parking space in the back. I'll be right behind you."

"All right." I jumped out of the SUV, thinking how much I loved this door-to-door treatment. I might have to rethink Andre's contract. He might need to become one of my permanent employees.

Even from the outside of Big Red's, I could hear the sounds of celebration. Nothing but music and laughter, and when I opened the door that was painted to look like it belonged on a saloon, the sounds wrapped around me. I took two steps inside, and a couple of guys standing at the bar looked up, then turned and started clapping.

That caught the attention of everyone else, and within seconds the place exploded with applause, cheers, and whistles.

I stood there, soaking it all in. No one had even come up to me and asked if I was Wyatt Spencer. They just recognized me—and I loved it.

"Welcome, Wyatt." One of the men who saw me first stepped

up to me. He was a burly guy, almost a cliché with his cutout denim vest that put his biceps on display even in the forty-degree temperature. And then there was the navy bandanna tied around his head. "My name is Buck."

"Hey, Buck," I said, thinking that he must've been undercover during his policing days.

We shook hands as the others surrounded me. They had names like Clint and Cash and Dallas. And they said things like "Atta boy," and "We're proud of you, cowboy," and "Thanks for standing up for all of us."

Like all of the events that recognized my bravery, I felt proud.

Buck raised his hand toward the bartender. "Get this guy a beer and let the party begin."

The place filled with laughter and then music filled the air. I didn't have much time to look around, but when I did, this place really did look like an old-time saloon, with its wood-planked floor, red-and-white-checkered tablecloths, and dartboards on three walls.

"So, Wyatt," Buck began as he slid me a beer. "How does it feel to be a national hero?"

"I don't see myself that way. I was just doing what was right."

"Well, you're a hero to us," Cash said.

Dallas nodded and added, "You're a hero to all of America. You put SYG on trial again."

The guys around us nodded and I did, too. I was glad that I knew what they meant by SYG. The first time I'd heard it at the Conservative Mothers of America brunch, I didn't know what the emcee was talking about. Thank God Newt was there with me to explain it. I guess in some parts, Stand Your Ground was so familiar, its acronym stood in for its full name.

Buck spoke up. "I don't know how many times we're gonna

have to defend it, but SYG is the American way. There is not a state in the union that is going to take that law down. So these niggers better understand, that is our right as Americans. They come over here, trying to change everything about this country. This is our land!"

There was a chorus of "yeahs" all around.

"We've got to protect ourselves against these thugs!" someone shouted.

"Yeah," Buck said. "Anybody coming at me with a baseball bat is gonna find themselves up close and personal with my Beretta and their gut."

"I'm going for the balls," one of the other guys said, and that caused more laughter. "Castrate 'em!"

Then, "I'm aiming for the brain." More laughter. "That's if I can find a thug who has one of those."

I chuckled along, but I can't say that I really found any of this funny. They were talking as if they wanted to use people as target practice.

"Well, all I know," Buck said, "is that every time I see a black boy from now on, I'm gonna be thinking about you, that boy, and that baseball bat. And I'm telling you, if he even looks at me the wrong way . . ."

Buck left his threat right there, and while it brought on another round of loud laughter, this time I didn't even pretend to join in. Was this dude talking about every black boy? He couldn't be.

Lots of black boys worked for me and I worked with lots of black boys through my foundation. All of them were polite and respectful—none would deserve to have happen to them what happened to Marquis Johnson.

And what about someone like Andre? That guy was a good

dude. Were Buck and these guys talking about gunning down someone like Andre?

Just as I had that thought, the bar became silent. Like really silent. Like all talking, all moving, all breathing stopped. All that was left was the chorus of "Cleanin' This Gun," by Rodney Atkins over the speakers.

I turned my focus to what had everyone's attention.

The front door.

And Andre.

Buck took a step toward him. "Buddy, I think you're in the wrong place."

"No!" I jumped to Andre's side as the words they'd just spoken played through my mind. More than one of these guys were strapped, I was sure of that. And I had to make sure no one pulled out anything. "This is my friend Andre."

Every face twisted into a scowl.

For his sake and mine, I added, "He's my driver."

"Oh," they all exhaled together.

Then Buck said, "You wanna beer, Andre?"

And Andre did exactly what I would've done if I were wearing his shoes. He looked around, took in all the faces, studied the scene, and said, "Nah. I just came in to tell you"—he turned to me—"that I gotta make a couple of calls. So I'll be out in front when you're ready to go."

"Okay, okay. Right. Right."

"You take your time," he said. He looked around once again. "I've got plenty of calls to make."

"No problem."

The group was still staring Andre down when he gave them all a final look-over. "Nice meeting you, fellas."

Not a good-bye was given or another word was spoken until Andre walked out and left us to our business.

Buck said, "You had me worried for a moment."

"Why?"

"You said he was your friend," Cash said as if he knew what Buck had been thinking.

I guess he did. Because Buck nodded. And all of the rest of them did, too. And then they all laughed again.

I wasn't going to say anything, but I did consider Andre a friend. A friend was someone who was by your side when you needed them, and that's what Andre had been for me since May. He was as important to me as anybody else on my team.

But there was no reason to tell these guys that. In fact, there was no reason for me to hang out here much longer. I'd only been at Big Red's a few minutes, but this was not what I thought it would be. I'd come here expecting to maybe find a couple of guys to hang out with. But while on the outside I looked like I had a lot in common with these guys, I guess I really didn't. I mean, I didn't think *every* black person in America was bad. I just didn't like thugs. But it felt like this crowd thought every black person was a thug.

Still I stood there for a while, put in my time. They were honoring me, so I had to at least make it look good. My second round of beer brought a new group of friends. Guys kept coming by, patting me on the back, telling me how proud I'd made them, saying there needed to be more men like me.

"What's up?" someone said as he gave me another slap on my back.

Turning to face him, at first, I thought the guy was white. But then, after a quick scan of the olive tone of his skin, I figured he was Hispanic.

"My name is Carlos," he said, holding out his hand.

"What's up?" I responded, giving him a handshake. Everyone else had come up to me in groups of two and three. But Carlos came alone. "So, you're part of—I paused for a second to look around—"the Defenders?"

"Yeah. I retired from the force two years ago."

"Oh," I said, hoping my surprise wasn't in my voice or showing on my face. It's just that this guy didn't seem to fit in with this all-American, all-white gathering. But I guess every group had to have a token.

"So, you've had quite a time, haven't you?"

I shrugged. "I really wish it had never come to this. Wish there had never been a trial. But there was such social pressure; the DA was just trying to be politically correct."

He agreed with a nod. "But like everybody said, the law was put on trial once again and you won."

"No," I said. "We won."

He chuckled. "No, I think it was *you*." Then he took a long swig of his beer. "You showed the blacks; you and your lawyers set the example, showed everyone that if they try to bust that law, there will be a price to pay. I bet you Marquis Johnson's parents got that message. Especially his mama." He didn't wait for me to respond. He just laughed out loud and walked away, leaving me standing there alone.

Out of all the guys, that dude made me the most uneasy. It was time for me to get the hell out of Dodge.

I grabbed a third beer and texted Andre:

I'm ready. Where are you?

Two seconds later, his text came back:

Meet me out back. Crowded up front.

I replied:

Great. Really ready to go home.

Then:

Car running, I'm waiting.

I began my round of good-byes, starting with Buck.

"You're not leaving already," he said. "We're just getting started. We haven't even done our tribute to you."

"This was tribute enough. And you know, my wife, she's pregnant, any minute. Gotta get home," I lied, figuring none of these dudes had paid enough attention to know that Meredith's due date was still three months away.

"Oh, yeah." Buck slapped me on the back and I almost keeled over. "Maybe you'll bring another boy into our world."

I didn't know what he meant by "our world," but I knew that I didn't want Billy growing up and being like the guys I'd met tonight. I mean, yeah, I agreed with their views—America was our country and there was too much changing. But I wasn't trying to put anyone else down or out. I just believed that as white Americans, we should be lifted up.

I kept my sentiments to myself, though, as I hugged my way out of there. They all embraced me as if they'd known me for a long time. Everyone called me brother, extended their good wishes, and invitations for me to join them again soon.

"Yeah, maybe once the baby is born," Buck said.

I glanced around, checking for Carlos, wanting to say good-bye to everyone. But when I didn't see him, I shrugged it off. I wasn't going to wait around for him to come out of the bathroom.

With a final general good-bye to everyone, I made my way to the back, found the exit, and stepped outside into the day that had become night.

I inhaled, then exhaled, feeling relief. Feeling like I'd just left a place where I never should have been.

I'd only taken a single step, I was sure of that.

Just one step.

And then, one blow.

One blow to my head. Made me dizzy, made me stumble, made me fall to my knees, then collapse all the way to the ground.

I didn't even know what hit me. I wanted to scream, but all of the pain kept me silent. If I could just reach for my head, and hold it, then maybe . . .

A foot. No, a boot—in my mouth. A boot in my mouth that filled my mouth with blood. I swallowed, I gagged, I swallowed what felt like small stones.

But right after that, I had no more thoughts. At least not thoughts of what was happening. All I could think about was the pain. From the fists and feet. Everywhere. Jabs and jolts. All over me.

It was blow after blow after blow.

Strike after strike after strike.

From the front. The back. The side. And the other side.

I writhed on the ground, struggling to get away, but there was nowhere to go. Because everywhere I moved, there was another fist. Another foot. Another blow waiting for me.

Maybe if I'd been able to see, I'd've been able to fight. But I could see nothing through my swollen eyes. Saw nothing but the blackness of night. And the blur that came from my tears.

I was crying, though that wasn't my intent. The tears just came. Just came with the pain.

Then the pain was almost gone. I could hardly feel it anymore. The fists were still beating. The feet were still stomping. But it had gotten to where hurt didn't hurt anymore.

That was when my senses shifted. To sound.

I heard nothing. Except cracking and crackling.

What was that?

Crack.

Crackle.

My bones?

My bones!

There was nothing I could do but lie there and swallow stones that were seasoned with my blood. And listen to the cracking and the crackling.

I heard death coming.

I needed to do something. Something to dodge death. So I concentrated. Breathe in. Breathe out. In. Out. Breathe. Breathe.

But that was getting harder and harder to do.

And then it stopped. The fists, the feet, it all stopped.

Then, faint sounds of steps. How many steps? How many men? Or was it the clicking sound of a woman's heels that I heard?

I tried to figure it out. Needed to know so that I could tell the police . . . or God—whoever came first.

Now there was nothing but quiet.

Except . . .

The sound of something falling. And rolling toward me.

Through the slits in my eyes, I saw a little bit of light. And then felt a hand, maybe two, roll me onto my side. Now I could see.

It was rolling toward me.

A bat.

Someone knelt down beside me.

A man. Or a woman. Maybe one. Maybe two.

With a towel, he/she/they wiped the bat clean.

And then, he/she/they leaned over me. "Enough" was whispered into my ear.

I struggled to keep my eyes open, but I couldn't anymore.

It became black. And I lay there, waiting for the white light to come. Like the stories that had been told before, my life flashed. In just seconds, I saw every scene, every moment that was important to me. My father, my mother, my brother. And then Meredith, Billy, and my child to come.

Thoughts of all of that love. All of that wasted.

But my last thought, my final thought, the thought that took me to the other side . . .

Enough!

And then my world ended.

Epilogue

The district attorney announced today that the case of the *State v. Wyatt Spencer* is officially closed. Of course, that was just a formality since Wyatt Spencer was found fatally beaten on October twenty-fourth, three weeks ago. There are still no leads on what happened to Spencer when he left Big Red's on that Friday night. His driver was waiting for him in the front of the club and there are several witnesses who saw his driver out there. It was the club owner and Spencer's driver who discovered Spencer beaten behind the club.

"The police have no idea why Spencer was in the back of the club, nor have they ruled out that this may have been a random assault and robbery since Spencer's wallet and cell phone were missing. But there is still that question of the baseball bat that was found near his body. As you know, a baseball bat played a major role in Spencer's trial, in which he was accused of shooting seventeen-year-old Marquis Johnson. The district attorney has always claimed that the bat was planted by Spencer, and so it was a curious piece of evidence at Big Red's that just might be a coincidence.

"Meanwhile, in related news, Spencer's widow sent out a formal thank-you to all of the employees of the Cheesesteak Castles. She thanked them for their support, assured them that the business will continue, and gave them all a bit of good news. We all found out at the beginning of the trial that Spencer's wife, Meredith, was pregnant. Well, she told the employees that she's pregnant with twin boys. So though she is still in mourning, the widow does have those new lives to look forward to.

"This is Clarissa Austin reporting. Back to you in the studio . . ."

Acknowledgments

Stand Your Ground is so different to me. And while I will always be thankful and grateful for the support of my family (especially my mom and my sisters), friends, and all the professional people who take care of me with every book that I write, this time I want to acknowledge the people who specifically helped me put these words onto the page for *Stand Your Ground*.

So major, major, major thank-yous to:

LaJill Hunt: You said, "Victoria, you need to write this book." And because of those words, I did.

Lauren Spiegel: Before the first word was written, you really challenged me to make this a full story. I hadn't considered showing both sides. I'm so glad you talked this through with me.

Sally Kim: I was shocked when I first heard your suggestion of this title! So obvious, so perfect!

Nakea Murray: Whew! Without the Philly hookups, this story wouldn't have been right! Thanks for reminding me that in Philly, cheesesteaks are way more important than hamburgers!

Manny Brown: Without apology, you looked me straight in my eyes and told me what the ending had to be. I was really scared to write it. But because of you, I wrote the right ending, not the "girlie" one.

Deon Browning of the Browning Legal Group: I will always be so grateful for the time that you spent with me discussing the legal ramifications and the legal proceedings. Thank you for not getting too technical—just helping me enough to tell the legal part of this story well. I don't think you will ever know how important your conversation and contributions were.

ReShonda Tate Billingsley: Only a dear friend can say "Take that crap out!" And only a dear friend can receive those words. I needed to hear that when I wrote one of those angry scenes. You helped me to step down from my Angry Black Woman pedestal and tell a truer story. Thank you for caring enough to tell me the truth.

Liza Dawson: You were the first person to read this from beginning to end. And your words of how much you enjoyed this story allowed me to (after months and months and months) finally exhale.

Miya Kumangai: Your patience is amazing. Thank you for going through this book with me word for word so that we could get it right!

Cheryl Y. Powell, Rhonda McKnight, King Brooks, Tiffany Tyler, Princess F. L. Gooden, Michelle Lindo-Rice, and Candy Jackson: You were the first to read *Stand Your Ground* when the galleys became available. I have never been so afraid to let people read a book I've written. (I know, duh—I write so people can read, right?) But I just didn't know . . . and you all helped me TO KNOW! Thank you for your enthusiasm for this story. It means so much to me.

Yolanda Rodgers Howsie: My Soror who said, "This book is important. We need to get the buzz going now!" Thank you for all of the great ideas—including those videos!

My Sorors of Delta Sigma Theta: I told you the premise of the story, and you said, "We're ready! Let's roll!" Your support always brings tears to my eyes. Truly! Because of God and Delta Sigma Theta, I'm able to continue my pursuit of my passion. Thank you for believing in me—always!

And finally, the most important thank-you goes to the readers. All of you who picked up this book. Whether it was because you've read my work before, or you just wanted to read this title, I thank you for trusting me enough to spend your money on this gift that God has given to me.

Now, I have to get started on my next book. After writing *Stand Your Ground*, though, I think my writing will never be the same . . .

Stand Your Ground

For Discussion

1. Tyrone's mother responds to Janice's hesitation about allying with the Brown Guardians with, "Well, sometimes violence is what you need. Sometimes violence is the only language that white folks understand." Discuss Janice's feelings about the vigilante group versus Tyrone's opinion. What are the reasons for their respective views? Who would you side with?

2. In the aftermath of Marquis's death, Tyrone begins spending nights with his brother, Raj, away from Janice. Discuss how their physical separation mirrors their growing emotional distance.

3. When Janice sees Wyatt Spencer's brother, Wally, on television defending Wyatt's actions in the name of Stand Your Ground, she dons mourning clothes and heads to the courthouse, saying she "[wants] America to see [her] in [her] black." Why is this a major turning point for Janice? How does it affect Janice and Tyrone's relationship?

4. Discuss Meredith Spencer's internal conflict, which pits her loyalty to her husband against the truth she witnessed that night and the deep knowledge she has about her husband's character. How do her feelings evolve and shift throughout the trial, especially when she meets Janice Johnson?

5. Despite coming from vastly different backgrounds, Meredith and Janice are both women of faith. How does their relationship with God differ? Consider Janice's affair with her pastor and Meredith telling Janice that she is in her prayers.

6. Raj discovers Janice with Caleb after the case is announced to be a mistrial. Why does he decide not to tell Tyrone about her perceived infidelity? How has Raj changed in Janice's eyes?

7. In chapter 32, Janice says, "When it came to humans, the ransom for sins was never fully paid." What does she mean by this? Is she referencing Wyatt Spencer, speaking of her own circumstances, or both?

8. Janice undergoes another transformation as she lets her voice be heard in front of the congregation in chapter 35. Why does she begin by saying that the shooting was not God's will? The chapter concludes with Janice observing that, "Where I'd come from and where I was now with Tyrone standing by my side—this was God's will." What is "this"? What is the differentiation she is trying to make?

9. Go around the room and share your reactions to the last chapter. Did you find yourself sympathizing with Wyatt as you

became privy to his perspective? How did you feel about his fate?

10. *Stand Your Ground* is extremely relevant to the state of our country at this time. How do you feel about the way Marquis's trial unfolded compared to the way real-life Stand Your Ground trials have been portrayed in American media?

11. How do you think Marquis Johnson will live on, not only in his hometown of Philadelphia, but in the hearts of his family and that of Meredith Spencer?

12. Victoria Christopher Murray weaves together the perspectives of Janice Johnson, Meredith Spencer, and Wyatt Spencer. If you could hear the internal narrative of another central character in *Stand Your Ground,* who would you choose and why?

Enhance Your Book Club

1. Janice mentions that Twitter is her main source of news in the aftermath of Marquis's shooting. Search for mentions of Trayvon Martin, Michael Brown, Eric Garner, and Tamir Rice on Twitter. How are reactions to their stories rippling in our collective consciousness?

2. Take some time at the beginning or at the end of your book club meeting to check in with your fellow readers. Has anyone in your group ever feared for their child the way that Janice and Tyrone did? What emotions did you experience after reading the traumatic events described in the book?

3. Visit Change.org and sign the petition "2 Million Want Justice for Trayvon," or donate to the Trayvon Martin Foundation at trayvonmartinfoundation.org. Discuss how your voice can effect change in our world.

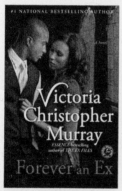
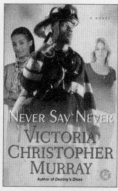
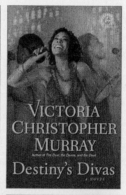
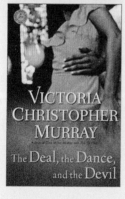
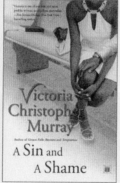